HOOKED

EMMA SHELFORD

This is a work of fiction. Names, characters, places, and incidents either are the product of the author's imagination or are used factitiously, and any resemblance to any persons, living or dead, business establishments, events, or locales is entirely coincidental.

HOOKED

Kinglet Books
Victoria BC, Canada

ISBN: 978-1989677407 (print)
ISBN: 978-1989677377 (ebook)

www.emmashelford.com

First edition: November 2021

DEDICATION

To Clare the mermaid,
for swimming with me through so many pages

CORRIE

Corrie put down her pipette with a sigh and stripped off her latex gloves. Three o'clock had rolled around like a stone down a mountain: fast, furious, and with no regard for what it disturbed. Her experiments cried for her attention, but she had an appointment she couldn't miss.

After her latest cruise with her friend Zeballos Artino, during which she'd been shot at by spearguns and witnessed a murder by one of the pale sea people, she'd had little scientific data to show for her efforts. She'd explained away her lack of samples to her supervisor as a diving accident, but he hadn't been convinced. She had plenty of other samples to analyze, but she didn't know if any were of interest. Time would tell. Time, and plenty of hours in the lab.

Corrie shoved her samples in the lab fridge and strode down the hall. The woman she was due to see worked in a building across the university campus, and Corrie hustled to make up time.

A few minutes later, she entered a building and knocked on the correct doorway inside. She entered when a cheery "hello" filtered through the closed door.

"You must be Corrie Duval." The woman leaped up from her desk with energy and strode to Corrie with her hand outstretched. Gray streaked throughout the woman's frizzy auburn hair, but she moved with the energy of a much younger woman. Loose linen pants clung to narrow hips under a tunic-style shirt in a geometric pattern of bold colors.

Corrie extended her own hand, and the woman shook it vigorously.

"I'm Dr. Penelope Stroud," the woman continued, finally releasing Corrie's hand and gesturing her toward a wooden chair beside a desk piled with papers and sample jars. "But please, call me Penelope. I've been wanting to speak with you ever since I looked at your samples. Ever since I spoke to our mutual friend Adrianna, in fact. Her request to analyze the samples from Patient X set my curiosity radar beeping. You're a researcher, you understand."

"I do." Corrie smiled, thinking of the creatures she and Zeb—Patient X—had discovered on their scientific cruises. At the time, she had barely contained her excitement. Even now, she squeezed in analysis whenever she could in between her regular, less legendary, work. "It's hard to avoid diving into a subject when there's so much to explore."

"Indeed. I started work on obscure genetic disorders, and here I am, twenty years later, still amazed by the discoveries we unfurl every week. Being a scientist is to unleash a whole new world of understanding, clue by clue. I can't imagine doing anything else."

Corrie smiled in agreement. She was impressed by Penelope's passion for her subject, not least because Corrie felt the same to a degree. If Penelope analyzed Zeb's samples with similar vigor and interest, then she might have answers about the origins of Zeb's differences. Corrie's veterinarian roommate Adrianna and Penelope had worked together on some high-profile animal rights lobbying a year ago, and Adrianna held her in high regard. Corrie hoped Adrianna's belief in Penelope would deliver.

"Adrianna said you had some interesting results to share."

"I do, I do." Penelope rubbed her hands together with vigor. She turned to her desk and rummaged through a pile. "I had the printout here just yesterday. Give me a moment."

Corrie's eyes wandered around the office while Penelope searched. The bookcases were lined with medical textbooks, although a picture of a much younger Penelope holding a laughing girl of five with her husband's arms wrapped around them both. It was a sweet photo, but Corrie wondered why there were no more recent ones.

"Ah ha." Penelope waved a folded sheet of paper in the air.

"Here it is. Based on your request, I looked at a few common genetic markers to look for detrimental mutations, but nothing came up. Then I examined the cells, and again, nothing. The patient's white cell count is depressed, certainly, which indicates that whatever is affecting them is not a pathogen. You were right to come to me."

Corrie's shoulders slumped. Penelope hadn't found anything useful yet. What was wrong with Zeb?

"But you didn't find anything," she said.

Penelope fixed Corrie with a piercing stare. "You know, I could find out so much more if I knew who Patient X was. Pieces of the puzzle that I can't even imagine yet would likely fall into place. With the patient's permission, I could run further tests and take different samples to find out even more. Sequencing the patient's genome would get us much farther than the markers I used. I could even roll him into my next grant to fund the sequencing. Assuming the patient is still alive, that is."

"Yes, he's alive."

As soon as Corrie blurted out the words, she wished she hadn't. Now Penelope knew that Zeb was alive and male. That wasn't much to go on, but she'd promised Zeb that his samples would be completely anonymous. She knew how nervous he was about being studied.

To her credit, the gleam in Penelope's eye didn't translate to more pressure on Corrie.

"That's up to you and the patient, of course," she said. "But know that we could find out even more with a visual inspection. I'm happy to sign whatever nondisclosure agreements you feel are necessary."

"I'll discuss it with Patient X," Corrie said in what she hoped was a noncommittal tone. It was hard, since she wanted to know more about Zeb's genetic make-up as much as Penelope did. What if Zeb's genome was key to discovering the genetic history of the pale folk, and, by extension, the legendary animals that came with them? Corrie desperately wanted to know how they existed, evolutionarily speaking. Was Zeb sitting on a goldmine of information?

Could she convince him to join forces with Penelope? So far, the researcher had given them no reason to mistrust her. She'd even generously analyzed Zeb's tissue samples using her own grant money. Corrie thought wistfully of her own anemone samples that awaited analysis because she was too busy earning her way teaching laboratory classes instead of working on her own project.

"It's interesting," Penelope said in a delicate tone that didn't suit her previous passion. "But I recognized a protein sequence from Patient X. I couldn't remember where from until I dug into my early records."

Corrie tensed. Had Penelope found a sample from another creature, or even a pale person, in the past? Corrie's breath came faster, but she tried to control her face to appear politely interested. This visit taxed her nerves. Corrie usually resorted to chatting indiscriminately when she was nervous—or tired, or happy, or anytime, really—and holding herself in to avoid giving away Zeb's secrets was nearly killing her.

"Something similar?" she said in a detached tone.

"Yes." Penelope pulled out another piece of paper, which she spread on a bare patch of desk. Corrie leaned forward to examine the lines of letters. "Notice here, and here? The sequence is identical. Considering no other human genome yet sequenced has that protein coding, I don't know what to make of it. I ran the sequence against every database I could find, and the closest match was for an anemone sample from the West Coast. Strange, right?"

"Hmm." Corrie nodded without speaking further. Her tongue felt atrophied from her lack of speech in this office.

"There is one possibility," Penelope said, her eyes on Corrie's face. "Did you know Clicker Artino?"

Corrie couldn't stop her eyes from widening. Clicker

Artino was Zeb's mother who died when he was eight. How did Penelope know that name?

"I've never met anyone by that name," Corrie said carefully, but it was too late. Penelope sat back with a twitch of her mouth, although she didn't mention Corrie's reaction.

"A pity. I took samples from an unusual woman at her husband's request, and the match between her and Patient X is extraordinary." Penelope sat up and dusted off her hands. "A strange coincidence. Never mind. Patient X is more than welcome to come in for a follow-up series of tests—I'm happy to work after hours to maintain his anonymity to the university—but until that point, there isn't much more I can do with the samples you gave me."

"I appreciate your work," Corrie said by rote, her mind churning over Penelope's revelation. "And your discretion. I'll let you know if Patient X changes his mind."

Corrie left Penelope's office without noticing where her feet took her. Penelope had known Zeb's parents. How? What had she found out about Clicker? Corrie wrung her hands. What she wouldn't give for more answers. Could Zeb have a key to discovering more about the world of the not-so-mythical sea creatures they had uncovered? If Penelope examined him, what would she find? Clicker had died eighteen years ago, and technology had exploded since then. What new information could Penelope find today?

Corrie's heart sank when she thought of Zeb's fear of discovery. There was no way she would convince him to reveal his identity to Penelope. Should she even tell him that Penelope knew his parents? There was nothing he could do about it, and it might distress him to imagine that his secrets could be uncovered. No, she would leave that information until she knew what to do with it.

Or until she couldn't keep it in any longer. She was terrible at keeping secrets.

ZEBALLOS

Sweat dripped down Zeballos Artino's forehead in rivulets, tracing his jawline and dripping onto the tarpaper below his feet. It was the closest he'd been to saltwater since his swim this morning, and his body felt the strain. His skin itched under his sweat, and his limbs trembled with unusual frailty. He gripped his nail gun more tightly and gritted his teeth. He could push through this.

"Almost done that side?" Tony, the roofing foreman, called out.

Tony had been a friend of his father George, and when Zeb had been looking for work a few weeks ago, Tony had delivered. Roofing was dirty work, and stinking hot even on cool days, but it paid his rent. And every dollar he could squirrel away on top of expenses was earmarked for fuel for his boat the *Clicker* so he could resume his search for his mother's people.

"Getting there," he shouted back, and Tony waved at him before turning toward his pickup truck. Zeb slung another asphalt shingle into place and positioned his nail gun.

His phone rang and nearly startled him off the roof. Who was calling him? His list of phone correspondents was short. Jules never called, only texted, and Corrie was a rare voice since their chaotic cruise a few weeks ago. His sister Krista sometimes called, but not at this hour.

He pulled out his phone and frowned at the unknown number.

"Hello?"

"Is this Zeballos Artino?" a low female voice answered.

"Speaking."

The line clicked. Silence followed. Zeb looked at his phone which showed that the call had ended.

That was strange. Zeb shrugged and wiped his forehead

with his sleeve, too hot to ponder a mystery. Maybe it was his bank, and they were accidentally disconnected. If the woman wanted to talk, she'd call back.

The next half hour passed in a blur of heat and snapping nail guns. Zeb's itching intensified, and his stomach growled constantly. He shoved a piece of dried jellyfish in his eager mouth—he carried a bag with him everywhere he went these days—but the chewy morsel barely made a dent in the insatiable hunger that consumed him.

The black shingles under his gaze grew blurry and fluttered like eelgrass in waves. Zeb blinked furiously, but his vision didn't clear. His hands shook so hard that he dropped his nail gun, which fell to the roof with a distant thud. His vision tunneled. The last thing he saw was clear blue sky above.

"Zeb. Wake up, buddy."

A rough hand slapped his cheek gently. Zeb groaned and blinked his eyes open. Tony's face swam between Zeb and the sky. Greenery surrounded Zeb in a cloud of prickles and pokes. Was he lying in a bush?

"There you are." Tony hauled at Zeb's arm, and Zeb slowly rose, his head swimming. "You passed out and fell off the roof. You were lucky and landed on this hedge. It's squashed, but I'll deal with the homeowners on that one."

Tony dusted off Zeb's back with hearty swipes. Zeb pressed a hand to his head.

"Sorry about that," he muttered.

Tony stared at him for a long moment while Zeb tried not to hurl on his boss' feet. His stomach cramped almost unbearably.

"Something's wrong," Tony said finally. "With you, I mean. This fall isn't the first time you've been off. I don't know if you're hitting the booze too hard, or what, but I can't have guys falling off the roof. You were damn lucky this time, but what about next time?"

"It's not booze," Zeb said. He wiped his clammy forehead again with his sleeve. "It's a genetic disorder. But I'm fine, I swear."

Tony's face softened from hard-edged suspicion to understanding.

"Good to hear. I'd hate to think of old George's kid turning to the bottle. But if this is going to happen again, you got to find yourself another job, Zeb. You need to be on the ball for roofing. I don't want you crippled, and that on my conscience. Go home, get some rest. I'll pay you for the rest of the week, for George's sake, but then you're done here, okay?"

Tony patted his shoulder in a paternal fashion, and Zeb swallowed the angry words born of desperation that he wanted to fling at Tony. Zeb needed the money, but he knew Tony was trying to help. Besides, even the thought of confronting Tony with a raised voice nearly made him pass out again. He didn't have the energy for that.

"Yeah, okay." Zeb scrubbed his face and wondered who else was hiring in this town. The weight of his illness and his empty bank account pressed on his shoulders until he wanted to sink into the ground. Without money, he couldn't buy fuel. Without fuel and time, he couldn't search for answers, and his illness would remain unsolved and uncured. He swallowed past his tight throat. "See you around, Tony."

JULES

Jules turned the corner on his rusty Ruckus scooter and roared toward his place. Man, it was hot today. Sweat ran down Jules' neck despite the breeze on his face. He drove faster, hoping to cool off. He'd cut three separate lawns today, and the scent of grass clippings clung to him like grease from a deep fryer. But the money he'd earned today and the lawn-cutting cash from the previous week would pay his rent this month. Tomorrow's money would start filling his cupboards. Jules had a longing for Cajun gumbo after finding an intriguing recipe online.

It wasn't until he pulled up next to his trailer that he noticed an unfamiliar SUV parked on the dirt road. Jules eyed it with interest. He didn't have many visitors as a rule, and Zeb drove his dad's old pick-up. Maybe it wasn't for him. It was a pricey vehicle for his neighbor's visitors, though.

Jules shut off the engine and climbed off the scooter. In the shade of Jules' ripped awning, a man sat on a plastic lawn chair. He looked cool and collected in Bermuda shorts and a straw hat. His unkempt graying hair was long and wild, but his shirt printed with a jazzy seashell motif was neatly pressed. Jules sauntered toward the visitor who stood and held out his hand.

"Jules Elliot, I presume?"

Jules inwardly shrugged and hitched an easy smile on his face. He was curious and returned the handshake.

"That's me."

"My name is Briscoe Carlisle. I'm an instructor at the Culinary School of the West. I'm here for an impromptu interview."

Jules' body flushed hot then cold. An interview was a good thing, right? They hadn't thrown his application in the trash as he'd feared they would. But right now, when he was sweaty and tired and hadn't thought about his application for weeks? What would Briscoe ask him?

"Okay." Jules tried to inject some false confidence in his voice. "An interview. Great. Can I get you something to drink? A beer?"

Jules winced. Was a beer the wrong thing to offer? Maybe he should have offered something more serious. But what? His fridge wasn't exactly well-stocked.

Briscoe's face broke into a genuine smile.

"A beer would be great."

After Jules cracked open a cold can and brought it out to the older man, he slid into another lawn chair and waited for his questions. Briscoe chuckled.

"This won't be your typical interview." He pointed at two grocery bags beside the trailer that Jules hadn't noticed before. "I want to see what you can whip up for me. Cook me a three-course dinner using the ingredients from those grocery bags."

Jules stared at the bags. A lemon and a cluster of prawns peeked out of the top. Immediately, his brain raced through possibilities. He didn't know how to answer questions. But cooking? That, he could do.

"I would apologize for the surprise," Briscoe continued. "But thinking on your feet and working under pressure are both important qualities in a chef. You have," he checked his watch. "One hour. Go."

Jules stared at the older man for another moment, but when Briscoe raised his eyebrows, Jules leaped to his feet and grabbed the bags. He heaved them onto a folding table beside his trailer and examined the contents.

The first bag contained a variety of spices, fresh herbs, butter, slabs of chocolate, cream, and bottles of Worcestershire sauce and vinegars. The second held the prawns and lemon, as well as a bag of flour, fresh vegetables, a head of lettuce, and other goodies. Jules spread the ingredients on the rickety table and surveyed them. He was intensely aware of time ticking away, but there was no point in cooking at random without a solid plan in place. He allowed his brain to flip through ideas without rushing it.

After three minutes of pondering, during which he stared in silence at the table of food, Jules clapped his hands.

"As long as there's propane left in my barbecue tank, I'm set."

Briscoe smiled.

"I already checked. There is."

Jules disappeared into his trailer and reemerged clutching a cutting board and his chef's knife. Its handle was worn and strapped together with metal clamps, but its blade was as sharp as Jules could make it with his whetstone.

He measured flour, diced herbs, and whisked melting chocolate over the warming barbecue. Once, he ducked into his dark trailer to grab salt and another can of beer, but most of the food prep happened on the outdoor folding table. He preferred to work outside—especially in this heat—and it seemed churlish to leave his guest alone. While he worked, he chatted with Briscoe, although his answers to Briscoe's questions were necessarily absentminded. He had a lot of proverbial and literal pans in the fire.

"What got you interested in cooking?" Briscoe asked.

Jules poured batter into his smaller cast iron pan and slid it onto the top rack of the lit barbecue.

"Mum worked on a coast guard ship when I was growing up, so she'd be away for weeks at a time. Dad's a terrible cook and will happily eat takeout Chinese every day, so I taught myself out of desperation. Don't get me wrong, I love chow mein as much as the next guy, but variety is the spice of life." He grabbed his salt grinder and seasoned the prawns. "When she left us, my cooking skills came in handy."

Briscoe left a pause of silence, which Jules was grateful for. He needed to decide the correct ratio of Worcestershire sauce to beer. After he whisked the two together, Briscoe spoke again.

"What made you apply to culinary school?"

Jules held up the sauce to the light to check for color and consistency, then he set it aside and poured olive oil on his cut vegetables.

"I was tired of doing nothing with my life." He poked a fork into the cooking batter and shook his head. Not cooked enough. "But I was never good at anything. A new friend suggested cooking school, so I looked it up. Cooking is the only thing I really like. People say they like my food," he added, trying to sound modest. People raved, but he didn't want to set expectations too high with Briscoe.

The older man nodded and sipped his beer with a thoughtful expression, and Jules returned to his meal. When the cake was finally cooked and Jules was laying prawns on the grill to sizzle, a battered old truck lurched to a stop in front of Briscoe's SUV. Zeb slid out of the driver's seat and slammed his door, looking morose. He stopped when he noticed Briscoe.

"Sorry, Jules, I didn't know you had company." He looked at Jules with a raised eyebrow. "I can come by later."

"No, join us." Jules waved his best friend closer. "There's a ton of food here, and I'm almost done. I mean, if that's okay with you," he said to Briscoe. Maybe he should have asked first.

To his relief, Briscoe chuckled and rose to shake Zeb's hand.

"Food is meant to be shared. Never forget that, Jules. Sometimes people make it out to be more rarified, but breaking bread with friends is the first and best value of a meal." To Zeb he said, "I'm Briscoe Carlisle from the Culinary School of the West. Jules is giving me a demonstration of his skills."

Zeb looked taken aback, but he shook Briscoe's hand then disappeared into Jules' trailer, returning after a moment with a can of beer for himself.

"Push the table over, will you?" Jules said to Zeb. "We'll

eat out here. Find some knives and forks while you're at it."

Once the others were seated, Jules slid plates of prawns in front of them.

"New Orleans style barbecue prawns. I added lemongrass for a Thai twist," he said, his shoulders tense.

Briscoe took a bite of his meal and chewed slowly, his expression blank. Jules dropped into a chair but didn't touch his own plate. Was this meal good enough? Maybe he should have gone with sweet chili prawns instead. Yes, that would have been perfect, with the mint that he hadn't even used in this meal. Damn it, would that count against him?

"Delicious," Briscoe finally said. Jules nearly wilted in relief. "The spices you chose enhance the delicate prawn flavor instead of masking it. The lemongrass gives a nice zip, too. Could have used a touch more actual lemon, though. Eat up, Jules, you're missing out."

Zeb caught his eye and gave him an encouraging look. Jules sighed happily and tucked into his meal. Briscoe was right, it needed more lemon. All in all, though, it was decent.

The grilled vegetable salad was well received, as was the chocolate barbecue cake garnished with raspberries and thyme sprigs. Briscoe praised his ability to evenly cook a cake over the barbecue. Zeb was even quieter than usual, but he praised the food, and Jules was grateful for his support.

Finally, the meal was complete, and Briscoe sat back in his chair with a contented sigh.

"I want to be brutally honest with you, Jules," he said. Jules tensed. "Your application caused quite a stir when it arrived. Laughter and derision, mainly. Some of your answers were simplistic to the point of childish, and most of the admissions team was in favor of tossing your application in the reject pile."

Jules' stomach shriveled in on itself like a black hole of shame. It was as he'd always suspected. He was good for nothing except to be a laughingstock. A part of him wasn't surprised by Briscoe's news. What other reaction had he expected?

Zeb's face darkened on his behalf, and Jules looked away. He wished Zeb hadn't heard his disgrace. He wanted to bury it so deep that no one would ever suspect he'd had the gall to apply to culinary school. He should have known better than to reach so high. What had he been thinking? Stupid. So stupid, just like usual.

"But I couldn't laugh," Briscoe continued. "Not when I could have written that application myself, at your age. It hit too close to home. And if I hadn't met my own teacher at a food truck on the Sunshine Coast, if he hadn't taken me under his wing and nurtured my fledgling interest, I would never be where I am today."

"What are you saying?" Jules croaked. Briscoe wasn't laughing at him, but what was he doing? Jules wished he would leave, him and Zeb both, and Jules could crawl into his trailer and never leave it again.

"Student interviews like this aren't typical," Briscoe said. He smoothed his shorts over his thighs in an absentminded gesture. "But I wanted to meet you and see if you have what it takes."

"And?" Zeb said in an aggressive tone. "What do you think?"

"Every teacher," Briscoe said in a measured voice, not rising to Zeb's confrontational posture. "Is allowed to choose a protégé from the pool of applicants. Tonight, you showed your ability to work under pressure, to think on your feet, to adapt to difficult scenarios, and—of course—to cook a delicious meal. If you promise to work hard and make me proud, I would like to select you for September enrollment."

Jules stopped breathing as he took in Briscoe's words. Briscoe wanted to mentor him. Briscoe thought he had what it took. Jules was accepted into culinary school.

Jules' eyes flicked to Zeb. Zeb looked as flabbergasted as Jules felt, but when their eyes met, he gave Jules a quick nod.

That was all the encouragement Jules needed.

"Of course I'll work hard. I—thank you."

Briscoe grinned.

"And thank you for dinner. I'll remember to add lemongrass to my next prawn dish."

CORRIE

Waves rocked the powerboat under Corrie's bottom. Alistair sneered at her, but behind him the pale woman lurked with a long bone knife. Her dispassionate face melted into an expression of manic glee, and she plunged her knife into Alistair's back. His mouth opened in a gush of green blood which sprayed over Corrie. She screamed, and the pale woman crawled over Alistair's collapsed body. Closer and closer to Corrie she scuttled, her mouth filled with sharp teeth dripping green blood, her eyes boring into Corrie's with a crazed light…

"Corrie." A hand shook her shoulder, and she gasped herself awake. She blinked at her roommate Sophie Trip, whose dark eyes in her fine-boned face gazed down at her in concern.

"Trip." Corrie struggled to sit up. "I guess I fell asleep. Thanks for waking me. I was having a nightmare."

"I could tell." Trip sat next to her on the couch and put her feet up on the coffee table. Corrie rubbed her arms, trying to smooth away the dream that clung to her with sticky tendrils of fear and loathing.

The nightmare was a recurring one. Ever since she had witnessed the scientist Alistair Stone's murder by one of the pale sea folk earlier in the summer, the dream had plagued her with regular visits. Part of her shuddered at her dream, but her scientific side marveled at the fabricated details that her brain included. Green blood? The pale woman's teeth had been as square as her own, and she had never deviated from her expression of calm detachment.

Corrie wanted the dreams to stop. She'd tried everything she could think of—chamomile tea before bed, meditation, even a sleeping pill once—but nothing worked. She'd even considered visiting a therapist, but she didn't know how to hide the secrets while baring her soul, and she was a terrible liar.

Three minutes with a therapist, and the whole of Zeb's strange world would come gushing out, she was sure. Then Corrie would either be prescribed strong drugs, or the hidden world would be exposed to scrutiny. Either way wasn't a good outcome.

Trip was still gazing at her with searching eyes, so Corrie hitched a smile on her face. It wasn't her brightest attempt, but it seemed to pacify Trip.

"You probably fell asleep because you've been working too hard." Trip said. "Didn't you come in at midnight last night? And I know you weren't at the bar because you would have invited me."

Trip threw her a stern look, and Corrie chuckled.

"No secret partying here. Yeah, I was at the lab. I have so many samples, and now more teaching duties on top of that. My supervisor is riding me hard after not applying for that award. Plus, he's still suspicious of why I didn't sample in the northern inlets, and I can't exactly explain about the creatures we were protecting."

"True. But still, you need a break." Trip snapped her fingers and sat upright. "I know what. Let's go camping this weekend."

Corrie wavered, but the sun outside caught her eye. Escaping the lab for a weekend sounded heavenly. Her dreams might follow her, but she couldn't help that.

"Where?"

"I was looking online, and there's a nice hike-in campsite up island. By hike-in, I mean twenty minutes. I'm no masochist." She glanced at Corrie sidelong. "It's right near Campbell River. We could ask Jules and Zeb to join us. I want to see Jules again, but it will only happen if I make it happen. Typical, right?"

Various organs in Corrie's chest thumped and jolted at Trip's idea. She had deliberately avoided reaching out to Zeb in the aftermath of the murder she'd witnessed. It was unfair, she knew, but the nightmares had been so strong and so vivid in the weeks after the incident, that she'd wanted to divorce herself from Zeb's world for a while to gain perspective.

She'd still analyzed her creature samples, because test tubes of DNA were easier to be objective about. She hadn't yet looked at the data for conclusions, but the numbers were sitting on her computer, waiting for her.

The pull in her chest at the thought of Zeb was finally stronger than the aversion to his world. Maybe she was ready to dip her toes into those waters once more. The pale woman's face flashed through her mind, but Corrie pushed it away firmly. It was time to get over her fears.

"Let's do it," she said firmly. "I'll call Zeb."

ZEBALLOS

Zeb drummed his fingers on the steering wheel. He'd parked in the shade at the grocery store, but the breeze flowing through his open window was still hot. Even his hair had dried in minutes after his swim a half hour ago.

Where was Jules? He'd said he only had a few items to pick up. Zeb wanted to get to the campsite and see Corrie. His stomach tightened uncomfortably at the thought of her. Or was it a need for jellyfish? Zeb wasn't sure.

Regardless, he was looking forward to seeing Corrie. It had been almost two months since he'd dropped her off at the dock in Victoria and she'd clutched him in a soft embrace. The memory could still force his eyes closed and send a shiver of longing rippling through his body.

They hadn't spoken for weeks—Zeb wanted to hear her voice, but every time he picked up the phone, he didn't know what he would say—then Corrie had called him out of the blue with an invitation to go camping. Zeb had agreed without checking with Jules, without checking anything. It wasn't like he had a job to work around or any other obligations. He was free to do what he wanted, when he wanted, as long as it didn't cost much. The thought twisted his mouth in a grimace.

The passenger door opened, and Jules dropped into his seat and twisted to shove two bags of groceries in the back. Zeb raised an eyebrow.

"It's a night of camping, not a week."

"You'll thank me after dinner." Jules buckled his seatbelt then pointed to the parking lot's exit. "Onward! The girls await."

They shared a grin, and Zeb backed out of the parking spot with a pleasurable jolt in his stomach.

When they arrived at the parking lot of the campsite, most spots were filled. Zeb loaded Jules with supplies from the truck bed before hefting the rest in his arms. They funneled into a path strewn with fir needles that wound between towering Douglas firs and down toward the beachside campsite.

"Wait." Jules stopped in his tracks and stared at Zeb in horror. "I forgot booze."

"You do food, I do drinks." Zeb patted the heavy duffel bag slung across his chest that slammed against him with every step. "I got your back."

Jules sighed in relief, and they continued to walk. "I know you do."

"If we don't look out for each other, who's going to do it?"

"Yeah." Jules huffed a laugh. "That's the truth. Hey, are you going to be good when I go?"

Zeb shrugged. He was dreading the day that Jules disappeared to Vancouver and left him alone, but Jules didn't need to hear that. He could hardly remember a time when his best friend wasn't in the same town.

"I'll be fine." Zeb glanced at his friend, whose shoulders were unusually tight. "But you're kind of tense. Looking forward to seeing Trip?"

Jules heaved a heartfelt sigh.

"Yeah."

Zeb nodded. He understood, mainly because he felt the same way about Corrie. They continued to stride over roots in silence, both lost in their own thoughts.

Crashing waves finally interrupted Zeb's musings, and he looked up. The sea beckoned its siren call, and Zeb almost dropped his bags right there to dash into the waves. He restrained himself, but the effort took him a moment. His eyes closed and he swallowed several times.

"You good?" Jules stopped beside him. "I thought camping by the water would be easier."

"It is," Zeb assured him. "It's good. I just feel like a swim right now, that's all. I'll get over it in a minute."

A few deep breaths later, and the feeling subsided enough

to put one foot in front of the other. Jules followed, concern in his eyes, but Zeb ignored him. He would be fine. And tonight, under cover of darkness to avoid the prying eyes of fellow campers, he would go for a swim. He didn't have to hide from Corrie, and the relief at not having to keep secrets swamped his longing for the sea.

Campsites dotted the hightide line, but they were far enough apart and the waves loud enough that privacy was assured. Halfway along the beach, Jules pointed.

"There they are."

Zeb's heart leaped at Corrie's petite form as she clipped in the last poles of her tent. She brushed a lock of brown hair from her face, then her eyes spotted Zeb. They widened, then a brilliant smile lit her face like a lightbulb. She pointed at them, and her friend Trip waved.

Jules picked up his pace, and Zeb followed eagerly. Jules greeted Corrie then made a beeline straight to Trip. Zeb stopped in front of Corrie.

"Hi," he said, feeling foolish. Never more than now did he resent his inability to think of the right thing to say.

Luckily for him, Corrie needed little help.

"Zeb!" She flung her arms around him and gave him a brief squeeze. Zeb barely had time to regret the bags impeding the press of her body against his when she stepped back. Her cheeks were pink, and she fidgeted with her fingers while words poured out of her mouth. "It's so good to see you. Looks like you guys brought everything but the kitchen sink. Luckily, it wasn't a far walk. We've already set up our tent here, but there's a flat spot right beside it. It's busy today, isn't it? The good weather brought everyone out. Trip and I got here an hour ago, and lucky we did."

Zeb blinked at the barrage of words and grasped at something to say. He felt like a gasping fish overwhelmed by air.

"I'm sorry you had to wait. Jules wanted to go grocery

shopping."

"Not a big deal. It's so beautiful here. And I would never get in the way of Jules' cooking. Whatever he needs."

She laughed lightly, and despite the manic tinge to her voice, the sound was a balm to wounds Zeb didn't know he'd been carrying. He dropped his bags and yanked the duffle bag strap off his shoulder. Corrie's eyes followed the movement of his arms and chest, and Zeb had an insane urge to rip off his shirt and give her a better view. He inwardly snorted at the idea.

"It's really good to see you." He wanted to say he'd missed her, but the words didn't come out. "It's been a while."

The smile she gave him was apologetic.

"It has. I—" She swallowed and looked out to sea. She scuffed her foot in the sand then turned back to Zeb. "It's been hard getting over Alistair's—well, you know. I needed some space."

Zeb nodded like he understood, but his heart shriveled. Space from him? Was he too tied up with the pale people in Corrie's mind that she lumped him together with them? Zeb ran his hand through his short white hair and sighed. He couldn't blame her. He was one of them, at least in part. Whatever they were.

Corrie narrowed her eyes at him, her uncertainty apparently overridden by concern.

"Are you okay? You don't look well. Is it that medical issue you mentioned?"

Was it that obvious? The face Zeb saw in the mirror changed so little day-to-day that he didn't notice, but his jeans hung looser on his hips than they used to, and the dark circles under his eyes were hard to ignore. But now was not the time to delve into his illness, so he simply shrugged.

"I'm okay."

Corrie looked at him for another moment then nodded.

"Good. Hey, do you want to go for a swim once you set up

your tent?"

Zeb's eyes flicked to the ocean. "Yes," he said with fervent longing. "Yes."

JULES

Jules stretched out his legs in front of the fire and raised his beer can.

"To friends," he said.

"To good food," Corrie replied with her beer in the air.

"To Jules getting into culinary school," Trip said. She tapped her can against his, and Jules grinned at her.

"To Jules," Zeb said, and he took a swig of his beer.

Jules had been too busy paying attention to Trip to notice Zeb much, but even he saw the despondency that fell over Zeb at Trip's toast. Zeb was happy for him, Jules knew, but it was still a wrench leaving Campbell River. Jules hadn't lived anywhere else since he was eleven. He didn't know anyone in Vancouver—well, he knew Zeb's sister Krista, but she thought Jules was an idiot and would never roll out the welcome wagon for her younger brother's friend—and when Jules left their hometown, he knew Zeb would be on his own. Jules wished Zeb could figure out something for himself like Jules had figured out culinary school, but he didn't even know what to suggest.

Zeb would manage. He always did. Jules' self-assurances did little to ease his guilt.

"I saw a side path off the main trail that supposedly leads to a great viewpoint," Trip said to Corrie. "I'm far too full, but why don't you and Zeb go check it out? Then you can tell us if it's worth visiting in the morning."

The two women traded intense looks, far more poignant than Trip's words warranted.

"Good idea," Corrie said. "I'll bring my flashlight since it's almost dark. Who knows how long we'll be out there? Maybe we can see the stars come out."

Zeb, seemingly oblivious to the odd exchange, stood with a stretch.

"I could use a walk after that meal," he said. "See you in a bit."

The two departed. Once they were three campsites away, Trip scooted closer to Jules. She draped her hand casually on Jules' thigh, and his breath caught. She looked into his eyes with a knowing expression.

"I'm glad you came camping with us," she said in a low voice that teased Jules' ears. "I've been wanting to get to know you better." She rubbed her hand in circles on his leg.

"Have you?" he croaked then cleared his throat. "I mean, I'm moving to Vancouver soon. Is that a problem?"

His body didn't care at all, but the move to the city was such a huge part of his life right now that he couldn't imagine that it wouldn't upend everything he knew. It seemed worthy of mentioning, even as his torso leaned closer to Trip. He caught a waft of vanilla, and his eyes half-closed as he breathed in the heady scent.

"I don't mind long-distance," she whispered. "I like visiting Vancouver, and now I'll have a bed to sleep in."

Jules' breath caught at Trip's suggestion. His body roared its approval and finally shut down the final stirrings of his thoughts. He pressed his lips against Trip's waiting mouth.

CORRIE

Corrie strolled along the beach, breathing in the salty scent of the ocean and enjoying the crash of waves on the sand. Zeb walked beside her, hands in his pockets and looking out to sea as if he couldn't keep his eyes away. She wished he would look at her like that.

Where had that thought come from? It had been easy to forget about her attraction to Zeb when they hadn't been in the same town, but now that he was in front of her, solid and undeniably *there*, her thoughts inevitably drifted to places she wasn't sure she wanted them to go. Secrets were his life, and although he had recently confided in her, Corrie was certain he hid more. It was nothing she could pin her finger on, but the certainty of more secrets gnawed at her and fought against her attraction.

And his connection to the pale folk… Corrie shivered. Zeb glanced at her.

"I didn't think to bring sweaters. Do you want to head back?"

Corrie pushed her gloomy thoughts away and chuckled.

"Trip wouldn't thank me for that. We're supposed to be giving her and Jules some alone-time."

"Oh." Zeb digested that. "Huh. How long are we supposed to stay away?"

"I guess that depends on Jules."

Zeb snorted, and Corrie burst into laughter.

"I have no idea," Zeb said. "And I don't want to know. But if you're cold, do you want to go back to my apartment? Get a drink, escape the mosquitoes."

Corrie was instantly consumed with curiosity of what Zeb's place looked like.

"Sure. I could use a hot drink if you're offering."

Zeb's place was a three-level apartment block in need of a paint job on its stucco walls. It did, however, boast a location only two blocks from the ocean, and Corrie imagined Zeb walking the stretch from his front door to the shore, his flippers dangling from a loosely clenched fist.

Zeb led the way up a dimly lit staircase to his door on the second floor. Corrie entered his apartment and was struck by the sparseness of the space. Sure, there was an empty pizza box on the table and a pair of socks that Zeb kicked into a closet while he thought she wasn't looking, but furniture was constrained to the essentials, and few personal touches graced the walls. The only unusual appliance was an old dehydrator from his father's storage locker. It was set up on the kitchen counter, and translucent white blobs sat in rows on its racks.

What Zeb did have were shells. They lined the windowsills, clustered on the table, and teetered in piles beside the TV stand. Corrie walked forward and grabbed a huge abalone shell that balanced on the nearest stack. Its interior shimmered with iridescent mother-of-pearl.

"These are gorgeous," Corrie said. "Did you collect them?"

"When I'm out diving." Zeb shifted and gazed at her with an uncertain expression. "I like them. They remind me of being underwater when I'm on land."

Corrie's eyes swept over the copious shells, and her heart squeezed. They represented so many dives. Zeb was so strange, so different, but she did understand the pull of being underwater, at least in part. She'd experienced a slice of that life for herself when she'd licked the unicorn fish. The freedom of not worrying about cold, and the power in her limbs as she swam, had been intoxicating. How much more must it draw Zeb, whose connection to the sea ran in his very blood?

She jumped when Zeb's finger touched the abalone. He was so close to her that she could smell the warmth of his body and a lingering brine of saltwater. Her skin tingled.

"I found this one off Hornby Island," he said quietly. "The visibility was terrible that day. A seal kept me company for a while."

"Do you remember how you found all of these?" Corrie found herself whispering. Zeb was so close that her breath came short in her lungs.

"This abalone is hard to forget."

He glanced at her, and his pale gray irises were only rims around his black pupils, grown large in the dim light. His warmth radiated over Corrie, and her breath hitched. She leaned closer, unable to resist his lure.

His hand wandered to her forearm and rested there for a moment before it swept up her arm and drifted across her back. She closed her eyes and allowed a shiver to travel across her skin. She wanted Zeb, wanted his firm body pressed against hers, wanted to clutch his pale hair in her fingers, wanted to taste him.

His game of touching was suddenly unbearably slow. She didn't want to wait any longer. With swift movements, she blindly placed the abalone on a nearby table, then coiled her arms around his neck and drew his head down to hers.

His lips tasted better than Corrie had hoped—sweet chocolate and salty waves—and she welcomed his questing tongue when it parted her lips. She pushed against his mouth harder, needing him to show her he wanted her in the way she wanted him: urgently.

As if her action were a trigger, he responded. He groaned against her mouth then walked forward with his hot hands guiding her hips. Corrie hit the wall, and then Zeb's hands and body and lips were everywhere on her, touching every part of her. She moaned in anticipation, her breath coming hard and fast. She wrapped one leg around his, needing to get closer to Zeb.

He slid his large hands under her thighs and lifted her in

one smooth motion. He pressed her hard against the wall, rocking his body against hers until she moaned again. Her moan was cut short by his hungry mouth on hers once more.

Zeb's hands on her thighs dropped, and she slithered to her feet. She barely had time to feel indignant when Zeb's eyes rolled back in his head.

He collapsed to the carpet like a boneless eel.

Corrie dropped to her knees, her heart hammering.

"Zeb," she cried. She patted his cheek then shook his shoulder when he didn't respond. "Zeb, wake up."

She felt helpless in the face of Zeb's distress. What was this mystery illness that he suffered from? She knew he hadn't looked well today—far worse than the last time she'd seen him—but she hadn't wanted to pry into his personal affairs. Well, now she was involved, and she didn't know how to help him. What good were his secrets now?

Zeb finally groaned, but with far less ardor than his previous utterances. His eyes flickered open, then he curled around his stomach with a grimace of pain.

"Zeb. What can I do to help? Is there anything you need? Water, medicine, what?"

"Jellyfish," he croaked. "Kitchen. And cream in bedroom."

Corrie leaped up and raced to the kitchen. In a flash, she realized what was in the dehydrator, and grabbed a few of the dried white blobs. She made a face—she'd tasted them before and found them chewy and bland—then she ran to the bedroom. She inwardly thanked the sparseness of Zeb's apartment, because there was nothing on the night table except a lamp and a jar of cream that Corrie recognized from the boat.

She ran back to the living room, where Zeb still curled in the fetal position on the floor. She slid to her knees and shoved the items toward Zeb.

"Here, I got them." She shoved a jellyfish blob between Zeb's lips. He opened his mouth and eagerly chewed. Corrie opened the cream and stuck her finger into the whitish-green goo.

"Where do you want it?" she said.

"Anywhere," he whispered. "It doesn't matter."

Corrie took his arm and twisted it until she exposed the soft skin of his inner wrist. Blood vessels were close to the skin here. If he were to absorb a substance from the cream, it would enter his bloodstream rapidly. She rubbed a small amount of cream onto his skin and wiped the rest back into its container.

A scant thirty seconds elapsed, then Zeb's tense body melted into lines of relief. Corrie was forcibly reminded of her druggie ex-boyfriend Dylan near the end of their relationship. She shuddered. Was this cream a recreational drug?

Zeb was alert enough to unbend himself and shuffle to the couch, although the relaxed planes of his face spoke to his blissed-out state. He smiled happily, and his head rolled against the backrest.

Corrie gingerly sat next to him.

"Are you okay now?" she asked softly.

He rolled his head toward her and gazed with his too-pale eyes.

"I'm dying," he said in a conversational tone. "My mother went the same way. The need to swim, the jellyfish obsession, the itching skin. It's all the same. If I don't figure out what's wrong with me soon, I'll be done for."

He held up his hand and examined the fingers with playful detachment, clearly still under the influence of the cream. Corrie barely breathed in her shock. Her heart pounded until she worried it would escape her ribs completely. She suppressed a ridiculous urge to laugh hysterically at the image: paramedics stumbling upon a blissed-out Zeb and her with her chest burst open and her heart jumping around the room like a hyperactive rabbit.

Zeb's news hit her properly, and she pushed a fist into her stomach. Zeb dying seemed ludicrous, impossible. He was too strong, too present, too important to her to die. Everything could be fixed. She just had to figure out how.

"Dr. Penelope Stroud," she said aloud. "She told me she knew your mother. She was researching how to help her. If anyone has answers, she will. You have to visit her."

"She didn't save my mum."

Zeb finished his examination of his knuckles and flipped his hand over to its fascinating palm. Corrie clenched her fists. Zeb was infuriatingly calm. She knew it was a mix of the cream and the fact that his news wasn't news to him, but she wanted to scream at his serenity.

"Maybe she didn't have enough time. But, with you, she has another chance. And technology has improved in leaps and bounds since you were eight. Just imagine what's possible now that they couldn't have dreamed of twenty years ago. If anyone can find answers, Penelope can."

"I don't know."

A crease appeared between Zeb's eyebrows. Was the cream finally wearing off? Corrie pressed her advantage.

"In fact, why don't you come stay in Victoria for a bit? You're between jobs, right? You can find one down there while you visit Penelope and she studies your illness. I expect she'll need to take samples and examine you more closely."

Corrie warmed up to her subject. Having Zeb in town would allow her to keep closer tabs on him. She didn't like the direction of his cream use. He probably needed some oversight, especially since he didn't have anyone left in Campbell River that she knew about. Jules wouldn't be around much longer.

And she couldn't bear leaving him up here, alone, friendless and dying. Her heart squeezed painfully.

"Maybe." Zeb didn't sound convinced. He looked around his apartment, as if imagining leaving it.

"Why don't you live on the *Clicker*? Moorage must be cheaper than renting a place. Then you can get a job, Penelope can figure out what's wrong, and everything will be fine."

Zeb's gray eyes met hers. In them, fear and uncertainty flickered. He didn't want to be alone in this town any more than she wanted him to be.

"I'll think about it," he said finally.

Corrie squeezed his hand hard and tried to push the thought of Zeb dying to the very back of her mind so it wouldn't expand and take over her entire brain with screaming fear.

JULES

Jules didn't have much to pack. He glanced around his trailer, and then at the three duffel bags and a cardboard box that sat near the door. One had clothes and towels, another his cookware and dishes, and the rest held sheets and his few electronics. He'd thought his life would amount to more.

Jules straightened his shoulders. This move was the first step toward making something more. He was going to school to learn to be a chef. The notion still thrilled and terrified him. What if he couldn't make it? He wasn't smart like Trip nor strong like Zeb. Did he have the chops to do this?

He sat on a bench and gripped his hair with his hands. This was ridiculous. He should call the school and tell them he wasn't coming. They didn't want him, anyway. He was a laughingstock to them.

Briscoe's face swam in his inner vision. He hadn't laughed. He'd seen something in Jules that Jules only saw in his more optimistic moments. What would Briscoe say if he heard that Jules wasn't coming to orientation tomorrow?

Jules heaved a sigh and stood to open a drawer that he'd forgot to check. It was full of odds and ends—dead batteries, twist ties, some frayed rope—and he shut it with a bang. The next occupant could deal with it. There was no way he was getting his damage deposit back, anyway. The landlord had made that clear when she'd spotted a water stain in the bathroom on her last inspection. Jules didn't mind since it gave him an excuse to leave behind whatever he didn't want to carry with him. She could haul it away in garbage bags herself.

An engine roared outside then silenced. Zeb was here to give him a ride to the ferry since Jules had already sold his scooter. Trip had assured him that public transit was good in the city, and Jules needed all the cash he could muster.

Zeb's arrival stirred guilt in Jules' chest. He wouldn't miss anything in this town except for Zeb's easy companionship. They'd only had each other since Jules had arrived as a scrawny eleven-year-old and, on the first day of school, had promptly shot his mouth off at Kiefer, the class bully. Bruised and frightened, he'd slunk to a corner of the schoolyard to nurse his injuries and wounded pride. Everyone had avoided the new kid—already marked by Kiefer's displeasure—except for the strange boy with white hair and transparent eyes, who had sat next to Jules in the dirt while he tried to hide his snuffles.

"Hi," the strange boy had said eventually. "I'm Zeb."

"Jules," Jules had replied after a curious glance at Zeb. "That's a funny name."

Zeb had waved dismissively.

"Parents." He said the word with the disdain of youth, and Jules nodded fervently. "Long story. Keep your head down with Kiefer. He'll move on soon. No memory—sponge for brains."

Jules had snorted in mirth, then he'd sobered.

"If I last that long."

"I'll stick around," Zeb had said, glancing at Jules with his pale eyes. "Kiefer doesn't bother me. Everyone thinks I'm a weirdo, though, so I get it if you don't want me to."

Zeb had stared into the distance like he hadn't cared what Jules thought, but his jaw had been tight. Jules had bumped Zeb's shoulder with his own, pleased beyond expression to have found an ally.

"I've seen weirder."

The adult Zeb swung open the trailer door and grinned at Jules. The circles under his eyes spoke of his illness, and Jules felt another stab of guilt at leaving. Not that he could do anything to help, but if he weren't there for Zeb, who would be? Zeb was the closest thing to a brother that Jules had, and he was deserting him in his hour of need.

"All packed up?" Zeb eyed the duffel bags. "How are you

planning to carry those on the bus?"

"I'll manage. I always do."

"At least lose the box. Come on, I bet we can squeeze stuff into the duffels."

Jules unzipped the nearest bag, and they shoved and squeezed until his bedside clock, pillowcases, and plates were nestled snugly in the duffel bag. Jules stood and sighed as he gazed around his trailer for the last time.

"Going to miss it?" Zeb asked.

"This old dump? Hardly."

"Where are you going to stay in Vancouver, anyway?"

"I'm crashing in the basement of my mum's friend until I find a place. Dad loaned me enough cash for a few months' rent, then I need a job. I'll figure it out."

Zeb nodded and heaved a duffel bag over his shoulder with a grunt of discomfort. Jules frowned. The duffel wasn't that heavy, not for muscular Zeb.

"You going to be okay?" Jules waved his hand vaguely at Zeb. "Your sickness and all that."

Zeb shrugged tightly then gave a strained grin.

"I'll manage. I always do."

Jules huffed a laugh at his words repeated back to him.

"Fine," he said. "Come visit when I get a place, though. You look like you could use a night out, and Vancouver has a whole world of new pubs to explore."

"I'll do that."

ZEBALLOS

Zeb left Jules at the ferry terminal, looking ridiculous with his three stuffed duffel bags dangling from his shoulders like some misshapen camel. The drive back to Campbell River was long and too quiet, even with the radio shouting top forty hits from his crackling speakers.

When Zeb crested a hill, the ocean sparkled below him, bright and inviting. Zeb itched his arm. Maybe he should stop for a swim on his way home. It wasn't like he had anything better to do. His halfhearted job hunt hadn't turned up any prospects yet, and now that Jules was gone, there was nothing to occupy his time.

Zeb banged his head against the backrest, unreasonably angry. At what, he wasn't sure. Jules, for leaving? Tony, for taking away his only source of cash? His mother, for passing him whatever genetic disease now ate at his body and his sanity? The pale people for refusing to show themselves?

There was nothing in Campbell River for him anymore. But was there anything elsewhere? Zeb's mind drifted to thoughts of Corrie. Before they'd returned to the campsite that night, she'd suggested he move down to Victoria on the *Clicker*. He'd brushed off her idea when she'd brought it up, but now that Jules was gone, it didn't seem so absurd.

His arm itched again, and he flicked on his turn signal and took an exit to the sea near Campbell River. A swim would help him think.

But that was the problem, wasn't it? A swim would help, but it was no real remedy. The cream wouldn't last forever, and Zeb's mouth dried with fear at the thought of running out. It was time to face the truth, deep in his heart: Zeb was dying, and there was no cure.

Involving Dr. Penelope Stroud was a huge risk, and one that Zeb wouldn't have considered a few months ago. But what was the risk of exposure compared to the certainty of death? If he wanted to survive, then he had to join forces with the researcher. He wasn't getting anywhere on his own.

Zeb pulled onto the shoulder of the road. The sea winked at him invitingly, the water his balm and his bane. He would jump in for a quick swim, then it was time to pack the *Clicker* for a new phase of his life.

However long it would be.

The sea soothed Zeb, as it always did. The turmoil in his mind melted away. Life was simpler down here, and not for the first time, he wished he could always stay below the waves. Too bad he couldn't breathe water. He recalled the pale woman spitting up seawater. One day, he wanted to try it. Not here, not alone, where he would drown if his experiment didn't go to plan. But one day he would muster his courage.

He floated over a cluster of fluffy white plumose anemones, looking like huge marshmallows with frilly tops. He brushed one with a gentle hand, and it retracted into itself.

His senses warned him of the topography ahead, and he recognized the seafloor rise. He approached the headland where he'd scattered his parents' ashes after their deaths.

His chest felt tight, and he aimed his body toward the rocky point. When he surfaced, the shore was empty of people, so he carefully climbed the jagged rocks and found a semi-flat stone to sit on. His body dripped saltwater into cracks in the rock, but his gaze fell inward, to the other times he'd stood at this spot.

The first time, his emotions had vacillated between raw terror at his mother's absence and numb disbelief. His father George had carried the container of ashes with eight-year-old Zeb trailing behind. When George had finally stopped with Zeb beside him, he'd cleared his throat and glanced at his small son.

"She would have wanted to be here," he'd said, his gruff tone barely masking the pain in his voice. "No burial for your mum. The ocean is where she belongs."

Zeb couldn't disagree. He'd been silent as George had upended the container above the water's edge. The pale dust had blown away in a cloud and settled on the surface of the sea.

The two were silent for a long while. Zeb had desperately wanted his father to reach an arm out and cover his small shoulders with a comforting weight—it wouldn't nearly replace his mother's embrace, but he would have accepted anything at that point—but George had remained still.

"I guess it's just us now, kid," he'd said eventually. Zeb had stared into the waves, wishing he could follow his mother.

The second time, he and Krista had been together. Zeb hadn't wanted any company except his anger, but he could hardly refuse his half-sister.

"Why here?" she'd asked. "Not that I care—Dad's gone, and where we put his ashes doesn't matter to me—but this place seems important to you."

"We put my mum here," he'd muttered. "I'm doing it for her. She loved the old bastard, for some reason. And no way am I going to pay for burying an urn somewhere."

Zeb scrunched up his face at the memories. Krista had been right—his parents were gone, and where their ashes lay didn't matter. Still, this headland would remain in his heart as their final resting place. And he was leaving it behind.

"Goodbye," he whispered out loud.

CORRIE

Corrie slipped her hand into the crook of Zeb's arm and tucked herself close to him as they walked down the university boulevard. He glanced at her in surprise but didn't move away. She wanted to reassure him—or maybe herself—that going to see Penelope was the right thing to do. That they were in this together. That she was correct to push him into this leap of faith.

Because it was the right thing. She didn't know how to fix Zeb's terminal diagnosis, but Penelope might. Zeb might think he could manage on his own, but sometimes people needed to be pushed in the right direction for their own good.

"This is a good step," she said aloud. "Penelope seems like a great woman. Adrianna trusts her, especially after their work together with the animal rights protests. Adrianna said that once Penelope gets behind a cause, she worries it between her teeth like a bulldog until she gets her way. If anyone can figure out your illness, she can."

Zeb's mouth twisted.

"I know she didn't help your mother." Corrie squeezed his arm. "But that was years ago. Think of how much she knows now, not to mention the equipment and advances in scientific techniques. Plus, she's not starting from scratch. She has all your mother's data, so she can leap off that. This is a great step forward, you'll see."

Zeb nodded tightly. He wasn't convinced, Corrie knew, but he was walking from the parking lot toward Penelope's building anyway. That was all she could ask for.

Corrie pulled Zeb up a wide set of stairs in Penelope's university building. Glass and metal dominated the modern space.

"This department must have got funding recently," Corrie muttered. "This building is gorgeous. Mine smells like mold when it rains. We're supposed to be moving next year, but I'm not holding my breath. Oh, here we are." She pointed at Penelope's door. Her stomach flopped with nerves. "Ready?"

Zeb took a deep breath, his eyes on Penelope's nameplate. "Yeah." He breathed out. "Let's do this."

Corrie rapped on the door and let go of Zeb's arm.

"Come in," a muffled voice called through the door. Corrie reached for the doorhandle and pushed it open.

"Corrie," Penelope said with warmth. She leaped up and strode with brisk steps across the small space. "So good to see you again." She turned to Zeb and thrust out her hand. "I'm Dr. Penelope Stroud. But please, call me Penelope."

Zeb held out his own hand with reluctance. Penelope grasped it with a hearty handshake.

"I'm Zeballos Artino. Zeb." He glanced at Corrie then back at Penelope. "You know me as Patient X."

Penelope didn't give any indication of surprise but merely nodded her head.

"I did suspect. I even looked you up and tried calling you once, but the line disconnected. Then I thought better of it— your privacy was more important than my curiosity." She had the grace to look sheepish. "But your resemblance to your father is remarkable. Although your mother had a hand, too, I can see." She grimaced. "And not simply hair color, as your tissue samples indicate. Please, sit down. We have much to discuss."

Penelope whirled around in a flutter of peasant shirt and a wave of lavender-scented wind then perched on her desk. The energy emanating from her was clearly too intense for a mere chair to contain.

Corrie lowered herself onto a wooden chair before the desk and watched Zeb do the same. His eyes looked so tired, and her heart wrenched with sympathy. She straightened her shoulders. That was why they were here, to fix Zeb. It was time to get some answers.

"You mentioned last time we spoke that you studied Zeb's mother Clicker during her final illness," Corrie said. "Zeb is suffering from the same symptoms. Can you help us figure out what's wrong with him? He's getting worse, and we're concerned that—" Corrie stopped and swallowed. "I was hoping that you could help us find answers. Your work with genetic disorders is unparalleled, and you have a head start after studying Clicker."

"Yes, yes." Penelope rubbed her hands together with a dry rasping sound. "I still have all my notes and data from my work with Clicker, but there was only so much I could do with the samples she gave me. Besides which, they've degraded over the years, despite being stored cryogenically. Now that equipment is so much better, technological advances in protein assays and genetic testing have improved drastically, I can really dive in to studying what makes Zeb different."

"To find out what's wrong with him, you mean," Corrie corrected her.

"Of course," Penelope said. "But to do that, we need a basic understanding of his genetic background. I'm certain the key to our conundrum lies there." Penelope clacked her fingernails on the desk, then she leaned forward to gaze at Zeb. "You might be interested to know—it might help—your father George contacted me a few years ago. He wanted help finding your mother's people, wanted to tell them the news about Clicker's passing. I thought it was odd at the time—it had been years since she'd died—but grief can manifest in different ways and at different times. I was the only one who had an inkling of Clicker's unique heritage, so George confided in me."

Zeb sat back, looking winded. Corrie blinked, and her heart pounded. Penelope knew about the pale folk? She and Zeb had only just discovered them.

"My father knew, and he didn't tell me?" Zeb's anger simmered under the surface of his words. He breathed heavily and clenched and released his fists in an unsteady rhythm. Corrie gently placed her hand on his shoulder. Why hadn't George told his son about his heritage?

"I don't know why he didn't tell you," Penelope said with a shrug of her shoulders. "But he was a secretive man. He didn't even breathe a word of your existence to me."

"Have you ever told anyone else about Clicker's people?" Corrie said. Zeb didn't seem to be thinking straight, and they needed to know where Penelope stood.

"No, no." Penelope waved her hand in dismissal. "For one, I don't have any evidence. We followed directions and clues that George pieced together from Clicker's stories. What would I tell others?" Her eyes flicked between Corrie and Zeb. "I've tried seeking them out on my own—scientific curiosity—but without George's clues, I couldn't get far. He did leave me with some pieces of information and some devices of his own making, but without the rest, it's useless."

"What kind of information?" Zeb said. He leaned forward, his intensity matching Penelope's. She gave him an appraising look.

"I have it safe. If you'd like to work together, we can pool our resources."

"Why do you want to find them?" Zeb crossed his arms.

Corrie agreed with his suspicion. Penelope's mention of "scientific curiosity" didn't bode well for the pale folk. She understood that motivation all too well and had fought her own battles against exposing Zeb's legendary world to the greater scientific community. What would stop Penelope from doing the same?

"This is your best chance to find a cure." Penelope's bald words thrust a spear of pain into Corrie's heart. "I can certainly take blood and tissue samples from you and analyze what I can, but there is an excellent chance that your answers lie with your mother's people."

"I know." Zeb's jaw tightened, and he glanced out the

window with a hard look. "I've been trying to find them, but they won't talk to me."

A flash of sympathy crossed Penelope's face. She reached out and patted Zeb's shoulder in a motherly way.

"If they won't come to you, then we will go to them."

"Why do you want to help me?" Zeb faced Penelope once more. She leaned back and sighed deeply.

"Your mother was a lovely woman," she said finally. "I grew to like her very much. Her death caused me much grief. Nothing to yours, I know, but still, I mourned her loss. Honestly, I feel that I failed her. If I can help her son avoid the same fate, maybe that will balance the karmic scales a little in my favor."

Zeb stared at her for a moment longer, then he turned to Corrie. His eyes were filled with desperation and uncertainty.

Corrie was nervous, too, but she didn't see another way. Penelope was already in too deep, and they needed her. What clues did she have, what devices did she own, that might aid them in their search for answers? Zeb didn't have time to waffle. In the months since they'd last traveled on the *Clicker* together, he already looked worse for wear. How long did he have left?

Corrie gave a firm nod and a reassuring glance. Zeb nodded slowly then turned back to Penelope, who watched their exchange with interest.

"Okay," he said. "Let's find them. Together."

"Excellent." Penelope rubbed her hands together again with undisguised glee. "Wonderful. Where do we start—what progress have you made so far?"

Zeb looked too overwhelmed to talk, so Corrie pitched in.

"We have George's notebook, filled with stories that Clicker told him. It's all in Greek, but we're having it translated." Corrie glanced at Zeb, but he didn't look appalled at her admissions, so she plunged on. "We also have a few devices. Some we don't know what they do. One acts as a communicator with sea creatures."

"And my cream," Zeb said.

He pulled out a small tub from his pocket. Corrie supposed he'd decanted a portion of the larger jar for carrying around. The cream caused a shiver of unease to crawl over her skin.

Penelope's eyes gleamed, and she held out her hand.

"May I?"

Zeb dropped the tub into Penelope's hand with clear reluctance. She unscrewed the lid and peered at the contents.

"Yes," she said. "It's just the same as Clicker used. I don't know how she made it, but it was the only thing that brought her a measure of relief. Fascinating." She handed it back to Zeb then clapped her hands. "Now, you must be wondering what I know. First, let's talk about you."

"Me?" Zeb said.

"Yes, your samples that I took a gander at. The bloodwork came back disappointingly normal—slightly elevated sodium levels, but that's all—but your genome sequencing was intriguing. I ran them against the databases, and certain sequences are not found in any human except for your mother—I managed to scrape together enough of her old samples to sequence her genome for comparison's sake. However, those odd sections have hits to three unidentified marine fish, but the fish were only labeled with a number and weren't identified to genera or species." Penelope shrugged. "I'm not sure what to take from that, except that you and Clicker are unique."

"Can you tell what protein that gene codes for?" Corrie asked. She leaned forward, intrigued. Her work with anemones didn't generally delve into genetics, instead focusing on protein analysis.

"Sure, we have the list of peptides, but that doesn't tell us much." Penelope spread her hands in defeat. "We can make guesses, based on similarities to other proteins, but that's all."

"Now what?" Zeb gripped his knees with his hands.

"Where do we go from here?"

"I could use a sample of hair. That might give me a history of your diet, although your hair is pretty short." Penelope scrutinized Zeb's hair, then she climbed onto her desk with surprising agility. She reached to a shelf near the ceiling and extracted a yellowed file folder. With a happy sigh, she flopped back onto the desk and flicked through the pages with rapid excitement.

"Here it is." She slapped a piece of paper on the desk. Corrie leaned closer. It was a hand-drawn map of Vancouver Island with dots and stars liberally sprinkled along the western edge. "George's clues. These are the places we looked based on what he knew. There was a long list of instructions leading to the home base of Clicker's people. In her story that George shared with me, she called it the Seamount."

Corrie traded an excited glance with Zeb.

"Do you have the rest of the instructions?" she said. "Does that mean we can just follow them to reach the Seamount?"

"If only it were that easy." Penelope grimaced and smoothed the map with her hand. "Some of the instructions didn't make sense from the vantage of a boat. Also, George didn't give all the instructions to me. We'll have to fill in the blanks. Of course, if you have that notebook of his, more of the answers might be in there."

"We'll get it translated as soon as we can," Corrie promised.

"Good. Let me scan these files and send them to you. Then we'll both have copies to comb through for clues. And, Zeb, let's get those hair samples from you before you leave, and I'll see if I can find evidence of diet changes."

Zeb nodded and stood to follow Penelope out of the office. Corrie took a deep breath and exhaled in relief. Penelope really seemed on board. She was willing to share everything she had with them. With that, and Adrianna's unswerving trust in the researcher, Corrie felt that they were in safe hands.

And, with a large dose of luck, they would find a cure for Zeb before it was too late.

ZEBALLOS

Zeb stood on the dock of his new marina and took a deep breath of the blissfully salty air. It coated his lungs with a delicious brine that he missed whenever he was inland. A seagull yowled from a piling nearby, and Zeb smiled at the familiar sound.

He walked down the gently shifting wooden dock toward the *Clicker*. This marina was small and its docks shabbier than most—a few boards looked like they might give way with enough weight on them—but it was cheap and only minutes from Corrie's house, so it was worth every splinter. Besides, the *Clicker* fit right in. Its peeling blue paint matched the faded varnish of the sailboat next door and the battered aluminum hull of the dinghy across the dock. He'd driven the boat down here yesterday. Two of Tony's roofing guys had been planning to come down to Victoria anyway, so he'd asked them to take his truck and drop it off in town. Now, there was nothing in Campbell River to return for.

Zeb climbed aboard and ignored the creak in his joints. Some days he felt seventy-six, not twenty-six. The water was a welcome relief to the pressures of gravity. Now that he lived on the *Clicker*, a swim was never far away.

This living arrangement was the best option of his otherwise grim prospects. His body was failing him. He'd left his hometown for strange surrounds. His best friend lived hours away. He had no job and no idea of how to get one to pay for moorage and electricity to prepare dried jellyfish, not to mention regular food.

But he now lived on the ocean and within walking distance of Corrie. His stomach tensed with pleasure as he traced her curves in his memory. If only he hadn't passed out at his apartment just as things were getting interesting.

Zeb swung into the wheelhouse and sank onto the captain's

chair with a groan of contentment. He stretched his legs across the dashboard and leaned back, his phone in his hand. Maybe he shouldn't lead her on. Dead men had no futures to offer.

Zeb shook his head. He'd never promised her a future, and she'd never asked for one. She was a grown woman who knew the facts. She could make up her own mind. He didn't think he had the willpower to resist her advances, anyway.

And he couldn't start thinking of his death as a foregone conclusion. Without hope, what was the point of anything? He might as well throw himself in the sea right now and never rise again. Penelope thought that there was hope, so he had to believe the same.

His sister Krista had emailed him. Zeb idly clicked on the message, then he sat up straight. His heart hammered. Krista had sent him an audio file accompanied by a message.

Here's your next installment of the adventures of Dad. Here's hoping you can make sense of this gibberish.

Zeb clicked on the file twice before his overeager finger contacted the button. Krista's familiar voice filled the wheelhouse with her strident tones, speaking entirely in Greek. Zeb listened for a moment, entranced by the beginning of a story. Then he paused the audio and scrambled for a pen and paper to transcribe the words into English.

A knock on the *Clicker*'s hull broke Zeb's trance as he stared at the words on the page.

"I came as soon as I got your text," Corrie said when she entered the galley.

She squeezed onto the bench that surrounded the tiny dining table, and Zeb caught a waft of her floral scent which, along with the bouncing of her chest as she settled into her seat, momentarily distracted him from the page. When his brain caught up, he waved the paper at her.

"Krista sent another story from my father's notebook. Do you want to hear it?"

"Obviously." Corrie's face gleamed. She bounced again in her excitement, and Zeb quickly looked at the paper.

"Okay, here it is," he said.

"Chaos reigned where the land met the sea. In storms, Ramu's people suffered the wrath of the ocean, and their tender bodies dashed against the cruel rocks.

"'Help us!' they cried out to her. 'Where is our true home?'

"Ramu heard their cries and her heart bled for her precious people. She roamed the ocean, but there was nowhere for her people to rest that was shallow enough for their needs. Above a rise in the plains of the ocean's depths, she swept her mighty form through the water, around and around in a gyre so strong that the seafloor rose in a spire almost to the surface.

"Ramu gathered the sacred Grace flowers and planted them on her creation, then she led her people across the waves to their new home. The other Grace-animals followed where the Grace flowers grew. When Ramu's people beheld their new home, they danced for joy.

"'This is where we will live, on the Seamount of Ramu's making.'

"A few were saddened at leaving the coast, as inhospitable as it was. Ramu's pale folk sang to them until they grew content.

"What do you think?" Zeb looked at Corrie. She stared at him, her gaze far away.

"The Seamount," she murmured. "Just like what Penelope said. It makes total sense. Remember when we thought your mother's people were island dwellers, but then we wondered how they hadn't been discovered yet? What if their 'island' didn't poke out from the surface of the ocean?"

"They live their whole lives underwater," Zeb whispered. His stomach cramped at the notion. What a state of bliss that would be. The pale woman from their summer encounter had breathed water, not air. It all fit.

Had his mother come from an underwater city of pale folk? Had she lived fully underwater until she came to land? Zeb could hardly draw breath for the revelations. Did that mean he could breathe underwater, too? Did he have enough of her blood in his veins to allow it?

"Amazing," Corrie said. She grabbed the page with the story, and her eyes flitted over Zeb's hasty scrawl. "What's this about the pale folk singing people happy?"

"I don't know. I can calm fish down. Maybe it's something like that?"

"Could be." Corrie scanned the story again, then she slapped it on the table. "This is incredible. Write Krista and tell her to send more audio files. We need every clue we can get. Let's go see Penelope soon with this story. She might have some more ideas of what it means. This is invaluable, along with Penelope's files that she sent along. Have you had a chance to look at them yet? I tried last night after I got home from the lab, but I fell asleep, it was so late."

She looked apologetic. Zeb wanted to reach out and smooth the frown lines on her forehead. She suited happy, and he didn't like it when she worried about him. He didn't want to be the cause of her concern. He wanted to make her smile, instead.

"Yeah, some of it. Penelope's notes are a description of my mother's journey from her home to the village of Zeballos. Penelope's right, though. The clues are cryptic and out of order." He pulled a piece of scrap paper from a sleeve beside the table and wrote with the stub of pencil that he'd transcribed the story with. "*When the moon's pull was as strong as its silver light, I followed the current that flows against the earth's tug.* That's the clue Penelope mentioned. She figured it meant a current that went from north to south, during a full moon. They placed it a little below Zeballos itself. Then this one: *Stay down-current of where the taste of sulfur fills the mouth.* What do you think that means?"

"Sulfur," Corrie whispered. "Sulfur in the ocean. Do you think they meant underwater hydrothermal vents? How sensitive is your taste underwater?"

"I don't know." Zeb frowned. He rarely opened his mouth underwater since he held his breath. How much had he been missing by not immersing fully under the sea? He had the mad urge to jump overboard and breathe deeply. Would he drown, or would he experience a whole world of new sensations?

"Okay, if the story refers to vents, it's a good clue. I can find a map of vents that we can use to narrow down locations. Any other clues?"

"The story Krista sent mentioned a rise in the seafloor. We could get topographical maps of the North Pacific."

"Good, good." Corrie bounced again in her seat. Zeb tightened his lips to avoid smiling. "But are we sure the Seamount is in the North Pacific?"

"Penelope had another clue." Zeb wrote as he spoke the memorized words from his mother's stories, transcribed by George. *"I stayed far from the waters of heat and clarity."*

"That sounds like tropical waters, for sure. I went scuba diving in southern Mexico once. The visibility there puts our waters to shame, although it's only because the lack of nutrients means that hardly any phytoplankton grow. Our waters are far more productive." Corrie tilted her head. "Have you ever swum in tropical waters?"

Zeb shook his head. He'd seen pictures and wondered what it would be like.

"We'll go one day." Corrie put her hand on Zeb's wrist above his pencil. "I'll bottle some strolia slime, and we can frolic in the warm waters."

Zeb's mouth twitched as he imagined her "frolicking". Her words were filled with a confidence that he didn't share, a confidence that they would find a cure to Zeb's mysterious illness. He hoped her faith had basis in reality. He met her hopeful gaze.

"I'd like that."

JULES

When the teacher's back turned, Jules hissed at his fellow student next to him.

"Did she say one hundred and fifty degrees, or one hundred and fifteen?"

"Fifteen," she hissed back. Her eyes rolled but she couldn't stop her mouth from quirking upward. "Honestly, Jules. Clean your ears."

"Thanks, Nousha."

Jules flashed her a grin. She shook her head and stirred the pot in front of her. Jules turned to his own double boiler, where liquid chocolate oozed over his spatula. If he were in his own kitchen, he would dip a finger in to test the temperature. Here, hygiene was strictly enforced, so he dipped a thermometer instead and watched the line rise.

Classes were stressful, but he never felt more alive than when three pots were bubbling and something waited in the oven. So far, culinary school had met and surpassed his wildest dreams. High school had been a years-long snore fest that he hadn't attended with any regularity. These classes were exactly what he wanted to learn. He soaked up information like the sponge of a kitchen sink. His new friends laughed at him in a good-natured way, but Jules didn't mind.

He'd never had a problem fitting into social situations on a superficial level, but he'd found something more here. The friends he'd made, although it was early days yet, understood him and his interests far more than anyone else. His friendship with Zeb had been built from long history, and although they were very different, the trust and friendship they'd built were on a different level. Zeb had given him fierce and tangible loyalty that had always contrasted sharply with his parents' benign neglect. But with his new friends Nousha, Triston, and Isaac, he slotted in like a hot knife in butter.

It was enlightening and freeing to discover others with the same passion for food that he had fostered alone for years. Restaurant meals were lively as they critiqued every dish, and each weekend usually involved at least one trip to an out-of-the-way delicatessen. Triston had dared him to try a century egg from Chinatown, and Jules had earned laughter and admiration when he'd swallowed it without hesitation.

He stirred his chocolate and watched the temperature rise to one hundred and five. Some of the students were as snobbish as he'd feared, but it didn't bother him when he had the others at his back. It was easy to ignore slights with the support of friends.

"Don't forget to have your seeding chocolate ready," a female voice murmured behind him. Jules' back stiffened. He'd forgotten to chop some chocolate into small pieces, and he scrambled to grab his knife.

"Thanks, Byssa," he said with a quick glance at the teaching assistant. Byssa Sweetcurrent was the same age as him, which wasn't surprising, since he was the oldest in the class. Jules got on well with her. She responded to his easy jokes with a solemn mouth but dancing eyes, and the occasional dainty blush that rose on her pale cheeks encouraged Jules to joke more often. Her deep brown eyes, the same color as the chocolate he stirred, gazed at him now under her fringe of obsidian-black hair.

"I'd hate to see my prize pupil forget such a basic step. It would be a shame to waste such glorious chocolate on a silly mistake."

Jules flushed and finished chopping the chocolate block. She was right. Chocolate was expensive, and working with it was new to him because he'd rarely justified the expense of playing with it at home. It was easier to try new dinner recipes, since he had to eat anyhow.

"Thanks for the catch," he said. His chocolate was up to temperature, and he added his chopped pieces. "Messing up chocolate would be sacrilege. I'd hate to have that on my record."

"You're doing fine," Byssa said earnestly, clearly afraid she'd worried Jules. "It might be early days, but so far you're near the top of the class."

Jules was surprised to hear that. Nousha's souffle had been far taller than his yesterday, and Triston's bread had a much more delicate crumb. If it were true, then he wished he could see the astonished faces of the administration who had nearly thrown out his application. Better still, he hoped that Briscoe had noticed. Jules never wanted Briscoe to regret his decision to mentor Jules.

"In fact," Byssa continued. "I wanted to ask if you're looking for work. The best way to learn how a commercial kitchen works is to jump right in. Many students find jobs as prep chefs while they're in school here to give them a leg up."

Jules hadn't thought about that. He was still looking for a part-time job for when his father's rent-money loan ran out, but nothing had come up. He'd been looking for odd jobs, but he hadn't even considered restaurants.

"They hire people without a certificate?"

Byssa pointed at his chocolate.

"Don't forget to keep an eye on your temperature." Byssa smiled while Jules scrambled to stick in his thermometer. "Sorry for distracting you. Yes, they sure do. It's nothing fancy—grunt work, often—but it's great experience. I only ask because there's an opening at the Japanese restaurant I work at, and the hours would fit with your classes. If you like, I can put in a word with the manager."

Jules forgot about his chocolate and stared at her. She looked back, waiting for his answer.

"You really think I can do the job?" It was almost beyond belief that she would single him out for this. He really wasn't any better than anyone else in the class. Probably worse than most, and some skills that were obvious to the others had been revelations to him. How to hold a knife properly, for example.

Byssa chuckled. "I have no doubt. Come by the Crispy Prawn at four this afternoon. I'll introduce you, and you can decide if you want the job. And don't forget to watch your chocolate."

Byssa walked away, and Jules took his pan off the stove without looking. His mind swirled with the opportunity Byssa had dropped in his lap. Then his eyes fixed on the back of Byssa's head. At the crown of her shiny black hair, pale roots showed. Jules frowned. Was Byssa naturally platinum blond? That seemed like an odd color to dye over. Many women tried for that shade. He imagined Byssa with blond bangs instead of black, but she suited the darker shade. It complemented her pale skin well.

"Jules!" Nousha said. "Wake up. Your chocolate is seizing."

CORRIE

Corrie checked her phone again. Zeb strode silently beside her in the suburban neighborhood, his face calm and his gait steady.

"It should be around here somewhere," she said. "Penelope said her house was behind a big Douglas fir. Number six hundred and forty-seven."

"There it is." Zeb pointed at a tidy rancher behind the towering trunk of a fir. A large garage squatted beside the house, but a car sat outside. The garage must be used for storage, or maybe a workshop. Did Penelope do woodworking? Corrie could imagine it. Penelope seemed like the type to throw herself into passion projects with abandon. If she took up woodworking, she would outfit her garage with every tool needed and start churning out exquisite furniture, Corrie had no doubt.

"It feels weird to visit her at home," Corrie said. "But I guess our mission has nothing to do with the university, except for analyzing your samples. We could have waited until tomorrow, but she was so insistent on chatting about the story tonight. It's great that she's on board with the urgency we need."

Corrie glanced at Zeb, guilty for reminding him of his illness. He caught her gaze and the corners of his eyes creased.

"I'm not a delicate flower," he said. "I know what's happening to me. I've had a while to come to grips with it. You don't have to dance around the truth."

On a whim, Corrie slipped her hand into his large palm. It fit so well she wondered why she hadn't held hands with him before. He squeezed his fingers as if glad for the contact.

She had to let go when they entered Penelope's narrow walkway to her front door. When Corrie pressed the doorbell, the resulting sound triggered a frenzy of barking from within.

A door slammed, and the barking dropped in volume. A moment later, Penelope answered the door wearing an embroidered kaftan.

"Come in, come in." She waved them forward with a flapping hand and chivvied them through a hallway and into a kitchen with a long island.

Corrie hopped onto a bar stool and let her short legs dangle. She tried not to glance with envy as Zeb slipped onto his own stool and tucked his knees up to rest his feet on the stool's crossbar. Penelope flung open the fridge with dramatic flair and snatched at three cans of flavored soda water. She slid two across the island, cracked open her own, then looked expectantly at the others.

"Well?" she demanded. "Let's have the story."

Corrie tugged a sheaf of papers out of her pocket and passed them to Penelope.

"I photocopied the stories we've translated so far, so you can keep these."

Penelope's eyes skimmed over the lines of text so fast that Corrie felt dizzy on the older woman's behalf. She and Zeb sat quietly while Penelope read. They didn't have many stories yet, so it didn't take her long. When she finished, she took a long drink from her can.

"Fascinating," she murmured. "And so full of clues if we have the wit to decipher them. Did you notice the northern shoveler duck story, how it mentioned their migration path?"

Corrie glanced at Zeb with mounting excitement. He gripped the edge of the counter with whitened knuckles. She shoved her hand in her pocket once more and spread out a map that she'd printed and a pencil.

"What do we have so far?" Corrie brought her pencil to paper and drew lines as she spoke. "The Seamount is in the North Pacific, we're pretty sure. 'Don't cross the hot, clear water.'"

"Northern Shoveler migrations follow this line." Penelope

traced a swath of ocean with her finger, and Corrie followed with her pencil.

"Are these patches where the seafloor is higher?" Zeb pointed at darker gray areas on the topographical map. Corrie nodded and circled the patches that fell in their zone of interest.

"The vents are marked in red pen," Corrie said. "I drew those in earlier." She sat back and examined the map with a pounding heart. The area they had narrowed down was a huge region of open ocean, but it wasn't the entire Pacific anymore.

"It's a start," Penelope said. She circled the region with her finger. "We need more clues. This area is far too big to search on our own. A more fine-grained map would show us the locations of seamounts in the region, but I guarantee there are too many of them to search. We need to keep following your mother's path, Zeb. She'll lead us right back to the Seamount, if we let her."

"I think this is the next clue," Corrie said. She thrust her finger at a page on the counter. "Look. It says, 'pass over the eelgrass that surrounds a holed stone.'" She pursed her lips in thought. "I guess we'll know it when we see it?"

"We know it's more southerly than Tofino, because that was the location of the last clue that George and I deciphered." Penelope glanced at Zeb. "This is a job for a better swimmer than me."

"We can figure out the most likely places for eelgrass beds." Corrie smoothed the paper in front of her. Their task was monumental, but with enough research and logic, they could solve this mystery.

"Good." Penelope sat back. "Keep translating that notebook. Any clues that lead us in the right direction from shore would be helpful. They might tell us how far away the Seamount is from land. The area we've narrowed it down to is still a large area."

"But still," Corrie said. "We're closer."

"Damn straight." Penelope tossed back the rest of her soda

water and threw the empty can in the sink across the kitchen. "We're going to crack this nut, Zeb. I can feel it in my bones."

Zeb was silent, but the hope in his eyes as he stared at the map was almost too much for Corrie to bear. She ran her hand along his forearm until she reached his hand under the table and gave it a squeeze.

They left Penelope a few minutes later. The gleam in her eyes promised results, and Corrie couldn't help the hope bubbling in her chest. She held onto Zeb's forearm and leaned into him as they sauntered down the walkway.

"We're going to do this, Zeb. Do you feel it? In here?"

She touched his chest, partly to emphasize her words, and partly because she couldn't stop herself touching him. That night at his apartment hung between them, heavy with poignancy. She wanted him, very much. His eyelids flickered.

The setting sun flashed in his white hair, and she drew back her hand with a jolt in her chest. Blood splatter on the cheek of the pale woman flashed through Corrie's mind. Her hair had been the same colorless shade of Zeb's.

Damn it. How could she separate the two in her mind? It was beyond aggravating that reminders of that traumatic event kept pushing to the forefront of her mind when she saw Zeb. It wasn't his fault that he looked so similar to the pale folk. He was descended from them, after all.

Corrie shook her head in exasperation, but the moment of attraction had subsided. She released his arm.

"I hope you're right," Zeb said, clearly oblivious to Corrie's inner turmoil. "I want to believe it."

A tumult of barking from the closed front door made Corrie jump sideways. She banged into a side door of the garage, and the latch clicked open. She stumbled to her feet and looked around the dim space.

Squeaking and rustling filled her ears. Cages lined one wall of the garage, which was decidedly not filled with a car nor skiing equipment and gardening tools. Beady black eyes in faces of white fur peered at Corrie, and long rat tails whipped around as the animals explored their cages. A sophisticated laboratory bench lined with bottles of reagents and a microscope covered the back wall. Scalpels and picks covered a drying rack next to a sink in the corner. Small, furry bodies covered in blood filled a black garbage bag next to Corrie.

Corrie gasped and backed away. She quickly shut the garage door and turned to Zeb.

"Keep walking," she hissed.

Zeb frowned but followed her direction. When they reached the road and walked in the direction of his car, he glanced at her.

"What was all that?"

"Penelope brings her work home with her." Corrie took a deep breath to calm herself. It didn't work. "That lab was not to code. Biohazardous material in a regular garbage bag? Sharp syringes left out on the counter? There's no way she has clearance to be performing experiments on live animals in her garage. I can't see how the university knows about that. What is she studying? She works on rats for her research. Why would she have a set-up at home?"

"She doesn't want to commute on the weekends?"

"That's way too much money and effort for that. The microscope alone costs tens of thousands. No, she's doing experiments that she wants to keep a secret. But why? Maybe she's worried about being scooped." Corrie nodded in relief. "That must be it. Medical research is such a cut-throat world. Multiple labs working on the same thing, and it's a race sometimes. The first one to publish gets the funding and the accolades, and the others get nothing. This must be a super-secret project she's working on."

"I guess." Zeb didn't look convinced. "Can't she do it at the university and just not tell others exactly what she's doing?"

"Maybe it would be easy to guess." Corrie shrugged, now doubting her theory. "I don't know. I wonder if this project has passed the ethics board. They're strict about experimentation on animals. I could see Penelope barging ahead with an idea and ignoring the consequences." She shook her head to get the doubts out. "I suppose it's not our concern, not right now. Let's focus on finding you a cure, then we can confront her about her questionable research choices."

ZEBALLOS

After the short drive from Penelope's home, Zeb pulled up in front of Corrie's house that she shared with her roommates. She'd been talking at length, most recently about some racing sailboat show that she'd been watching, and he'd been happily letting her words wash over him like a warm shower.

"Do you want to come in for a drink?" she said suddenly. "We could refine our clues. I could print off a higher resolution map of the area and we could mark down any seamounts. The topographical info is online, we could transfer it."

What had he done to get so lucky to have Corrie in his court? Without her help, he would still be floundering in Campbell River, jobless and growing weaker by the day. He was still without work and his body was failing him, but Corrie had injected hope into his seemingly fruitless quest to find his mother's people and some answers to the burning question of his health. He needed her fire, her pluck and courage, her inability to accept "no" as an answer.

"Yeah," he said. "Sounds good."

He followed her peppy steps into the house and up the stairs to the living area. His skin tingled and itched, but he ignored it from long practice. He would swim when he arrived at the marina. His body would simply have to wait until then.

Corrie's former roommate Adrianna, the one who had introduced Corrie to Penelope, stood reading a magazine in the kitchen. A can of beer dangled in one hand. She looked up at Corrie and Zeb.

"Good, you're here." She pointed at the fridge. "Don't make me drink alone. I'm waiting for Trip, but she's taking her sweet time."

Corrie chuckled and opened the fridge. She tossed a can at Zeb, who caught it with trembling fingers. A beer wouldn't soothe his troubled body, but it might take the edge off his amped-up mind. He couldn't stop thinking about the clues they'd assembled so far. Was Krista working on another section of the notebook? He would text her tonight to hurry her up.

Corrie leaned against the counter, took a swig from her beer, then crossed her arms with a sigh. Zeb tore his eyes away from her pushed-up chest and focused on her face.

"We're getting somewhere with our search for Zeb's cure," Corrie said to Adrianna. "We've got it narrowed down to a two-thousand square kilometer area in the North Pacific. We need more clues, though." She took another drink from her can, and Zeb followed suit. "I have to get up early tomorrow if I want to get my lab work done before teaching. My day is jam-packed tomorrow, when all I really want to do is hunt down these pale folk."

She threw an apologetic glance Zeb's way. He frowned as her words sunk in.

"I don't have plans tomorrow yet," he said. "But I need to find a job. I don't have enough money to pay for moorage fees past this month. Any ideas where to look? I'm not picky."

Corrie shook her head, but Adrianna brightened.

"The wildlife center I volunteer at is looking for a part-time employee. A lackey, essentially. You'd need to be okay with scrubbing soiled kennels, shifting bales of hay, whatever needs doing, really. It'll only pay minimum wage, but you could start right away. We're desperate."

"I can do that," he said. "What do I need to apply?"

"It's not that formal." Adrianna waved her hand in dismissal. "I'll put in a good word for you, and as long as you work hard and don't turn your nose up at shoveling feces of whatever animals we've rescued that month, they'll keep you around. Come in tomorrow morning, I'll be there for a morning shift and I'll introduce you. Come ready to work—they'll want you to start right away if you can."

Gratitude swelled in his chest at the generosity of Corrie's friends. He had no qualms mucking in with the animals. It meant he wouldn't be falling off any roofs. Besides, animals didn't require much in the way of conversation, which he appreciated.

"I'll be there," he said. "Thanks."

"Good, that's sorted." Corrie graced him with her brilliant smile that bathed him in warmth. "Give me a sec, and I'll print off that map. I will have to kick you out soon because of that early morning, but we might as well plot the seamounts while you're here."

Adrianna told him more about the wildlife center while Corrie was gone. Zeb tried his hardest to pay attention and ask appropriate questions. Without Corrie's distracting presence, the need for a swim roared loudly in his ears. The skin all over his body itched and tingled, and his stomach cramped. He tried to hide his grimace by taking another sip of his beer, but the flavor wasn't what he wanted at all. With dismay, he recalled he'd left his bag of dried jellyfish in his truck.

Adrianna said goodnight before Corrie returned and left Zeb alone to scratch in the darkening kitchen. He tried to ignore the sensation, but without even the diversion of conversation, his need grew too powerful. He thrust his hand in his pocket and withdrew the small tub of cream. He didn't like using it, mainly because he owned only one jar of the product, and he didn't know what was in it. Once it was gone, it was gone, and Zeb shivered at not having the cream to fall back to. What would he do without its calming effect in his life? He had to use the cream when his need grew too strong for him to control.

With trembling fingers, he unscrewed the lid and dipped his index finger in the green-tinged goo. He rubbed the tiny portion onto his inner wrist, wanting instead to slather the entire contents all over his itching body. He dropped the tub on the counter behind him and waited with held breath for the cream to take effect.

Within a minute, the tingling faded then disappeared. His stomach cramps relaxed, and the thought of a swim sounded pleasant, not necessary. Zeb smiled widely.

He had just finished the last of his beer when Corrie returned.

"Sorry I took so long," she said. "I couldn't find the site, then it was buggy and didn't let me zoom in properly until I refreshed the page."

"It's all good. I'm fine. I talked to Adrianna for a while, then I finished this excellent beer." He held up the empty can then tossed it across the room with a basketball toss into a waiting recycling bin. He chuckled when it hit its mark. "Ta da."

Corrie frowned at him.

"Are you okay?"

"Totally fine. Hey, I should let you get to bed. Your early morning and all that." He was torn between taking her in his arms and making her forget about her responsibilities in the morning, and the thrill of going for a midnight swim. His body swayed with his indecision. Her lips did look so soft, and he wanted to feel them on his neck. He wanted to taste her again. That brief moment in his apartment had been far too short and too long ago now.

"You don't seem okay. Is it your illness? Do you need to lie down?"

I'll lie down with you, Zeb thought. He chuckled aloud which only made Corrie frown harder. At this rate, he would have more success swimming than advancing with Corrie. The ocean never frowned at him.

"Totally fine. I'll get out of your hair. Talk to you tomorrow."

The cream's blissful effects had worn off by the time Zeb

pulled into the marina's parking lot. His skin itched with fierce intensity, and the salty scent of exposed seaweed nearly drove him to wade in from the shore. He managed to drop off his clothes at the *Clicker*, but it was a near thing.

His body sliced through the water which instantly soothed his enflamed skin. The water in the marina was stale with oil from the boats, so he struck out for deeper waters. If only he could stay under here all night. The temptation to draw water into his lungs was almost irresistible, but he clamped his mouth shut tightly. If he were to try that particular experiment, it would be somewhere he could touch bottom, and preferably with Corrie watching over him. He might be dying, but he had no intention of speeding the process along.

Zeb knocked on the front door of the wildlife center the next morning. After a minute, a harried-looking young woman wearing hospital scrubs pushed the door open.

"You must be Zeballos Artino," she said. "I'm Kyrie. Adrianna told me to expect you. Come in and I'll give you the tour. She's helping with an urgent surgery—a racoon hit by a car, poor thing—but she'll be out soon."

Zeb followed Kyrie into the front room. A small desk for receiving hurt animals squeezed into the tiny space, and doorways filled the other three walls.

Kyrie led him through one doorway, and they peeked into a room with a table and a counter with drawers underneath.

"One of our surgery rooms," Kyrie said. "That's where everyone gets fixed up." She pointed at a closed door across the hall. "Supplies in there, as well as feed. We'll start you cleaning first, but if it goes well, you can help with feed prep. Everyone needs something different here."

Kyrie led him down another hall with three doors along it. She opened the first. The room was bare except for five kennels along the wall.

"Now that you know what's what, here are your cleaning supplies." Kyrie handed Zeb a broom, a bucket and sponge, bleach, and a pair of sturdy gloves. "Give the three empty kennels a good sweep and a sponge-over with dilute bleach. We have animals in cages outside destined for here. Thanks for joining us!"

With that, Kyrie bustled out of the room. Zeb was alone with his cleaning supplies and the inhabitants of two kennels. A fox lay sleeping in the nearest one, its leg in a plaster cast, but a pair of black eyes watched from the darkness of a hollow log. Zeb gazed at the eyes for a moment, trying to determine what type of creature it was, but gave up when the animal shuffled out of sight.

It wasn't dissimilar from scrubbing the *Clicker* after a haul of fish. It'd been years since George had retrofitted the boat from a fishboat into a diving charter vessel, but Zeb still remembered the hold full of flopping silver bodies and the smell of wet fish in the sun. Zeb got on his knees and scrubbed away the stains of whatever animals had occupied the kennels before now.

He was on the last one when the sleeping fox stirred. It blinked tired eyes at Zeb. Zeb gazed back, interested.

"Hi, there," he murmured.

To his surprise, the animal leaped up and screamed, its hackles raised. Then, it jumped toward Zeb, claws extended and a manic look in its eyes.

Adrianna chose that moment to enter the room, stripping off latex gloves as she walked.

"Hi Zeb."

"It just started freaking out," Zeb gasped. "I swear, I didn't do anything."

"It's not you." Adrianna gazed at the creature with pity. It spat and screamed relentlessly. "He's like that unless he's sedated. We can't keep him under all the time, but we can't release him until he's fully healed. See his leg? Caught in a trap, we think. He won't survive until the cast is off. Finish up here and you can move out so he doesn't exhaust himself. The kennels are looking good, by the way."

Adrianna left, and Zeb resumed his scrubbing. It was difficult to ignore the berserk fox beside him, but he tried his best. Finally, after the final swipe of his sponge, Zeb sat back on his heels.

"You're okay," he said softly. The fox swiped through the bars and screamed. Zeb's brow creased. His instinct was to hum reassurances to the animal as he would with a panicked fish. Would it work above water? The properties of air were so different from water, but it was worth a try. Corrie had measured his airborne vibrations in the past.

Zeb hummed deep in his chest, as loud as he could. He didn't want to take any chances that the fox wouldn't hear him. It wasn't quite the right pitch. He adjusted it until the correct tone vibrated through his chest.

The animal watched him unceasingly, although the hissing soon faded. The fox's frantic movements slowed until he stood motionless, his beady eyes on Zeb's. Zeb kept humming, pouring soothing vibrations through the room that only he and the fox could hear.

The animal circled his sleeping blanket and tucked his nose into his tail before Adrianna returned with Kyrie.

"All done?" Kyrie said brightly. Her eyes rested on the fox. "Wait a minute, I thought you said he was going mental again."

"He was," Adrianna said. Her eyes flicked between the animal and Zeb, then they widened. She raised an eyebrow at Zeb, and Zeb looked sheepish.

"I'll show Zeb his next task, if you like, Kyrie," Adrianna said aloud.

"Sure." Kyrie peered into the fox's kennel with an expression of bewilderment. Adrianna gestured for Zeb to follow her. Zeb picked up his bucket and broom and joined

Adrianna in the next room.

"Did you calm the fox?" Adrianna whispered. "With your fish-talk?"

Zeb gave a half-hearted shrug.

"I didn't know if it would work on land, but I guess it does."

Adrianna whistled.

"Our very own Dr. Doolittle. Glad to have you on board, Zeb. There are plenty of animals in the same state. You have free rein to charm any of them."

By the end of Zeb's shift, he was a mix of contentment at being gainfully employed, pleased at his ability to calm the rescue animals, and almost painfully anticipating his swim. Inside, he felt as frantic as the fox from earlier. The walls of the wildlife center felt as constraining as the bars of a cage, and his skin itched without cease.

Kyrie collected his cleaning materials, and he fled the building with a distracted wave. His hands shook so much that he could hardly fit keys in the ignition. He wasn't going to make it to the ocean without going insane. He needed a hit of the cream.

His hands patted his pockets, looking for his small tub of cream that he always carried with him. Too late, he remembered placing it on Corrie's counter. He didn't have cream, and the ocean was long minutes away. His whole body shuddered, and he closed his eyes and rested his head against the headrest. What could he do?

Corrie's house was the closest destination. He would stop there, get his tub of cream, and patch himself up enough to make it to the ocean. Yes, he could make it that far. He would have to.

CORRIE

The doorbell rang. Corrie cursed and set aside the assignment she was marking. The list of things she had to do was a mile long—mark assignments for her teaching lab, write a flow chart for tomorrow's lab work, ponder the clues she and Zeb had unearthed—and she didn't have time for a random visitor. Unfortunately, she was the only one home to answer the door.

Corrie clomped down the stairs with ill grace and swung the door open. Her heart flopped in her chest at the sight of Zeb on the doorstep.

"Zeb, hi. What's up? How was your first day of work?"

"Fine," he rasped out. His face was pale, and his forehead beaded with sweat. "Good. Thanks. I left something here last night. Can I come in and get it?"

Corrie stepped aside, and Zeb bounded up the stairs as if he were being chased. Corrie stared after him. Zeb looked terrible. Was his first day on the job that bad? Adrianna hadn't texted her with any news.

She followed Zeb up the stairs more slowly. Rummaging noises drifted out of the kitchen, and she peeked her head in.

Zeb stood at the kitchen counter, his eyes desperate. His hands shook as he unscrewed his small tub of cream. Corrie's mouth tightened. Was that what all the fuss was about? She glanced at Zeb more critically. Shaking limbs, sweating, desperation… her mouth dried with recognition and distaste. This scene was all too familiar. She'd seen it reenacted with her ex-boyfriend Dylan too many times.

What was in that cream? Was it an opioid of some sort? How could she find out what it was? Zeb didn't know—he'd found it in his father's old gear—so it could be anything.

Zeb had finally removed the tub's lid, and he dipped a shaking finger gingerly into the greenish cream. His finger rubbed the product into the skin of his inner arm. Nothing happened, and Zeb's face squeezed with pain. Blindly, he shoved three fingers into the little tub and drew out a gob of cream which he smeared onto his skin with a frenzied motion.

Corrie opened her mouth to protest, but it was too late. The cream absorbed into Zeb's skin with his frantic rubbing. Zeb dropped the cream on the counter then rested his hands on his thighs, breathing heavily.

"Zeb?" Corrie said with hesitation. "Are you okay?"

He didn't answer for a long moment. Then, the tense lines of his shoulders relaxed. He raised his head and gave her an open smile with half-lidded eyes.

"Never better." He dropped to his knees and sat on his bottom against a kitchen cupboard. His head lolled back, and his eyes closed.

Corrie's heart raced. This was too similar to Dylan. Memories of those days flooded back, the terror, the panic, the anger. Sirens wailing, vomit on the floor. She shook her head violently to rid it of the visions and dropped to her knees beside Zeb.

"Zeb." She patted his cheek. "Zeb, look at me. Stay with me, okay?"

Zeb's eyelids cracked open, and he gazed at her with dreamy unconcern.

"So tense." He chuckled and raised his hand to cup her cheek. "Everything's fine. So good. I want you to feel this way, too."

Before Corrie could react, he drew her head down to his. His lips pressed against hers in a languid kiss that deepened into slow passion. Corrie's resistance held for a full half-second, then she melted into the kiss that she'd been longing for since that day at Zeb's apartment.

Realization doused her like cold water sluiced down her back. Zeb wasn't in full control of himself. Whatever he was on, he was under its influence. She couldn't take advantage of him in this state. Even if he had started it…

Corrie pulled away. Zeb let his hand fall to the ground.

"Don't say I didn't try to make you feel better," he slurred.

Corrie stood, angry at Zeb, at the memory of Dylan, at herself for getting wrapped up in this.

"You look fine," she said in a clipped tone. "I have things to do. You can let yourself out when you're ready."

She stalked to the door and down the hall to her room. Anger pulsed through her system long after her door closed, and it took full minutes before she was composed enough to focus on the assignments before her.

After a half hour, groaning emerged from down the hall. Corrie gritted her teeth and continued to draw checkmarks with her green marking pen. Zeb was coming down from his high. The last time she'd seen this, he'd suffered from stomach cramps for a few minutes afterward, but then had been fine. He could deal with it himself this time.

Water ran in the sink, then footsteps padded down the hall. Corrie's fingers clenched on her pen, and she stared unseeing at the assignment. A soft knock tapped on her door.

"Come in," she said, her voice coming out harsher than she'd expected.

Zeb pushed the door open. He looked sheepish, but Corrie hardened her heart. She'd seen all this before.

"Sorry about that." He scratched the back of his neck. "I put on too much. I haven't swum since this morning, and it was too long for me."

Corrie nodded tightly, not trusting herself to speak. Her mind was already whirling with ways to help Zeb, but she didn't want to rush anything. The problem was, she cared about him. If she didn't, she would leave him to work out his own problems. Zeb was proving that he couldn't handle himself, so maybe it was her job to step up to the plate before she had another Dylan on her hands.

"Anyway," Zeb said with a worried glance at her face. "Did

you want to go on the boat this weekend to follow the clues? That eelgrass bed one, we really need to be on location to make sense of it. We can get to Tofino in half a day, no problem."

Despite her concerns, Zeb's proposal sparked her interest. A weekend on the *Clicker* sounded divine. She missed her time on it, the waves and the salty smell and Zeb's presence. Too bad they wouldn't have Jules cooking for them, but perfection would be too much to ask for.

Figuring out these clues was their top priority. Corrie had to make sure Zeb wasn't dying, otherwise solving his addiction problem wouldn't matter.

"Yeah," she said. "I'm game."

PENELOPE

Penelope whistled tunelessly, and her foot tapped arrhythmically to the lack of beat. An Irish setter's tail thumped on the floor where it lay, watching her. Penelope bent over her workstation, poked at the innards of a box full of wires, then grabbed a coffee mug to take a long swig.

"We're getting there, Otis," she told her dog. He looked up at his name. "George left us with a right tangle. He had good ideas but not the finesse to pull them off." She sighed. "If only I'd known about his son. I wouldn't have put aside this project when George died. Oh, well. No use crying over spilled milk. I have an opportunity, and I won't squander it."

Penelope bent over the device again. She picked up a soldering iron and attached two wires together, then she pulled a laptop closer. Her nimble fingers pulled up a video of a man soldering, and she watched intently. Otis whined when music blasted at the end of the video.

"Hush, Otis." Penelope closed the computer. "I needed to watch that. Anything is doable with brains, the right equipment, and the Internet."

She tinkered with the device a little longer, then sighed and pushed it aside. Pages of handwritten text lay on the counter beside her, and she pulled them closer.

"George was a complicated man," she said to Otis, her eyes scanning her notes. "He designed this device, but his notes clearly say that it's dangerous. He built a small version for his own protection, then he abandoned this larger prototype, half-built. Protection isn't something to sneeze at. If we're going to encounter a whole city of pale folk, I want to be prepared." She leaned back and stared at Otis, who now examined the cages of sleeping rats next to him with a longing eye. "He was a surprisingly clever man, but I can take his design to a whole new level."

JULES

Jules' long legs stretched in a fast walk past dawdling foot passengers at the ferry terminal's exit. He sidestepped a pile of luggage, leaped over a child's scooter, and dodged around a loudly gesticulating woman at the sliding doors. The evening air fell on him like a warm embrace. The humidity was slightly cloying, but an ocean breeze pulsed enough to refresh the air.

It was good to be back on the island for a visit. Vancouver was wonderful and was starting to feel like home among his new apartment and new friends, but he had people to see here. Zeb, for one. Trip, for an important second. Jules shifted a box under his arm. He hoped she was hungry.

Trip's familiar form lounged against a lamppost in the parking lot. Jules' heart leaped, and a grin spread across his face like softened butter. Too many weeks had passed since that idyllic camping trip. He couldn't wait to take Trip in his arms again.

"Hey, you," she said when he approached. Her mouth was solemn, but her eyes laughed. "I thought I'd see if there were any cute guys to pick up at the ferry tonight. You'll do."

Jules leaned over his box and kissed her long and deep. She was breathless when he let her go.

"You'll do very nicely," she said. "Come on, the car's this way."

Trip drove them to her house—she'd borrowed Adrianna's car for the occasion—and Jules couldn't keep his hands away from her shoulder, her neck, her thigh. She turned her laughing eyes toward him as he described his new life in Vancouver and his classes.

"Aren't you glad I gave you a push?" she said. "I'm taking partial credit for this."

"You can have it. I got a job, too, at a Japanese restaurant. My teaching assistant Byssa recommended me. I don't know why, but I'm grateful. She's great."

Trip eyed him, but said only, "She saw that you were worth recommending. Don't sell yourself short."

Jules didn't know what to say to that, so he focused on another issue.

"The money isn't bad, but it's not enough to live on, not really. I'll have to find something else on the side. I don't know how, though. Who would hire me?"

Trip reached out a hand. Jules expected a sympathetic stroke, but Trip pinched him instead. He pulled his hand back with a wince.

"What was that for?"

"To break you of your default defeatist attitude. I was going to slap you, but it seemed too intense for my message. I don't want to mar that pretty face."

"So how should I pay for school, then?" Jules rubbed his hand.

Trip grinned. "Welcome to the terrifying world of student loans." She patted his arm. "Don't worry, I'll sort you out. You could say I'm somewhat of an expert." Trip glanced at Jules' lap. "What's in the box?"

"Devil's food cake," Jules said. "I hope you like chocolate. It's pretty loaded with it."

"Best boyfriend ever," Trip said with a laugh. Jules' whole body warmed at the label, emitted so freely. "Feed me, will you?"

Jules happily obliged, and the rest of the drive was filled with laughter and chocolate icing.

No one was at home when they arrived, so Jules pressed Trip against the wall as soon as they entered the front door. They spent a glorious five minutes reacquainting themselves with each other's mouths and hands, then a key rattled in the lock.

Trip cursed and straightened. Jules turned away and tried to control his breathing. His body raged at the interruption, but he told it firmly that there would be plenty of time tonight for further exploration.

"Jules!" Corrie's delighted voice filled his ears. "You made it. So great to see you!"

Corrie gave him a swift hug which he returned.

"You too," he said. His eyes fell on Zeb's face, and his stomach lurched. Zeb looked even worse than he had a few weeks ago. He'd lost weight, and the dark circles under his eyes were even more pronounced. He looked genuinely happy to see Jules, though.

"Good to see you, man," he said and slapped him on the shoulder.

Jules grinned at him.

"Thought you'd gotten rid of me, but I'm like a boomerang."

"You can fly back and visit anytime," Trip purred into his ear.

Corrie rolled her eyes.

"Smoochy smoochy. Before you two get lost in your party of two, we wanted to ask if you're up for a boat trip. Zeb and I are taking the *Clicker* out for the weekend to hunt for clues, and you're welcome to come."

"I'm game," Trip said. She looked at Jules and slipped her hand in his. "As long as I have enough seasickness medication. What do you think?"

Jules wavered. He had hoped for some long-awaited alone time with Trip this weekend. But Zeb's gaunt face had smacked him with the realization of how little he was doing to help his oldest friend. Zeb was dying, and what had Jules done to help? Nothing, not even been there for support. If he could keep the boat steady this weekend while Zeb and Corrie looked for clues, then he couldn't say no. He'd just have to take advantage of every minute that Zeb and Corrie were underwater.

"Definitely," he said. "I missed the old clunker."

Zeb said goodbye and disappeared out the door, and Corrie wandered to her bedroom. Jules turned to Trip.

"Where am I sleeping tonight?" He reached for Trip's waist and pulled her closer. He was pretty sure of the answer, but it never hurt to pretend to be a gentleman.

Trip wrapped her arms around his neck. "What are you suggesting?" she said with mock-indignation. "I'm a classy lady." She waited a beat, just long enough for Jules' doubt to grow. Then she grinned. "That's why I cleaned my room before bringing you to bed."

CORRIE

Corrie flew on her bike down a steep hill that led to the marina where the *Clicker* was berthed. They had been lucky so far this year with the weather. It was late September, and still the sun shone with a warmth that took the bite off a cool autumn breeze that snuck in the cracks of Corrie's jacket.

Traffic was nonexistent this Saturday morning. It was far too early for most people, and Corrie had the road to herself. She whistled as she pushed her feet against her pedals and raced to the marina. Her angst over Zeb's strange cream, her fear of his impending fate, and her overwhelm at the amount of work she needed to accomplish at the university, it all faded into the background. She was going on the *Clicker* again. Maybe she would see some of their special sea creatures. She couldn't wait.

Trip and Jules would arrive later—Jules had groceries to buy, and Corrie wasn't about to dissuade him from cooking— so she'd told Zeb she would arrive early to help get the boat prepared to leave dock. She pulled into the marina's parking lot and locked up her bike. Then, still whistling, she adjusted her backpack and walked with a bounce in her step toward the gangplank.

The only sounds that broke the early morning silence were the clanking of rigging against sailboat masts and the occasional croaking of a crow that had found some rubbish to poke at. The scent of low tide was overpowering, and Corrie wrinkled her nose. Fresh sea air was one thing, but rotting seaweed could only be pleasant to Zeb.

She turned left at an intersection of docks and strode forward, enjoying the sway under her feet. A gasp whipped her head around.

Down the nearest aisle, a familiar figure with shockingly white hair crouched over a man lying in a puddle of blood. Zeb looked up at Corrie, his eyes wild and his hands dripping with red.

Corrie's stomach lurched, and she nearly lost her breakfast into the heaving green water underfoot. Her breath came in short, sharp bursts. The blood, the white hair, the smell of seaweed, it was all too similar to Alistair Brown's murder by the pale woman. Her lungs couldn't get enough air to satisfy her pounding heart. Dimly, the sound of wheezing reached her ears, but it took a moment to realize it was her own labored breathing. Her vision tunneled, and the only images that were painfully, vividly clear were memories of the pale woman's knife stabbing Alistair with molasses-like slowness. The blood spurting out of his wound. His look of surprise before he fell to the ground. The woman's disinterested expression, like she'd murdered before and likely would again.

"Corrie!" Zeb's voice filtered through her memories like an echo from a great distance. "Corrie, just breathe, okay? Listen to me." His voice took on a calm, commanding tone. "Everything is fine. You're safe. Breathe in, breathe out. Follow my voice. Breathe in, breathe out."

His soothing voice was like a balm on her emotions. Without effort, she followed his instructions, and soon her lungs expanded and contracted at his words. Her vision cleared, and she blinked at Zeb's red hands that covered the man's bleeding torso.

"What happened?" she said quietly.

Zeb looked relieved that she spoke normally.

"I found him like this." Zeb jerked his chin toward the groaning man. "I think he tripped on a gutting knife. I called emergency services. Listen, I think they're coming now."

Sirens wailed in the distance. Corrie's unease was returning, now that Zeb's voice didn't carry that calming cadence. She believed Zeb, she really did. But the combination of blood and white hair had triggered visions of that other pale person who committed murder without a second thought. Zeb was related to people like her. What if a part of him was like that, through no fault of his own? What had really happened to this bleeding man on the dock?

The man in question blinked rapidly, and his mouth twisted in pain.

"You're okay," Zeb said as if soothing a frightened animal. "I called an ambulance. It's on its way."

"Thank you," the man rasped. "I tripped on a loose rope and fell on my knife. So clumsy. I don't know where I'd be without you."

Corrie wrung her hands together. Zeb had been telling the truth. Of course he had. How could she doubt him? This was Zeb, who had trusted her with his secrets. Zeb, who had introduced her to the legendary sea creatures that had vindicated her life's longing for answers. Zeb, whose rare smile made her stomach twist with pleasure.

Zeb, who had hidden those same secrets for so long. Zeb, through whose veins flowed the same blood as the murdering pale woman. Zeb, who relied on a cream to make it through his days.

She didn't want to think these thoughts. She wanted to trust him entirely, but a tiny part of her wondered and questioned. So much was outside her control—murderous pale folk, Zeb's illness, her attraction to Zeb—but she could fix Zeb's addiction issues. She'd failed with Dylan, but she could fix Zeb. Drugs changed people. If she'd showed some tough love on Dylan, maybe things would have been different. She could show Zeb some tough love.

Paramedics arrived and took over Zeb's role. He backed away and leaned over the dock to rinse his hands in the water then stood silently next to Corrie. They watched the paramedics bandage the man and lift him onto a stretcher. The man waved weakly at them when he passed on his way to the waiting ambulance.

Maybe the pale folk used the cream—Zeb's mother Clicker

got it from somewhere—and that explained the pale woman's expressionless face during such a violent act. Corrie's mind rejected the notion that Zeb was following in their footsteps. She would figure out a way to get that cream away from Zeb. The aftermath would be difficult but worth it. Maybe she would bide her time and sneak the cream away when Zeb wasn't looking. Until then, she needed to push aside these conflicting feelings. She and Zeb had a mission to find clues to the Seamount this weekend. After that, she would roll up her sleeves and do what needed to be done for Zeb's own good.

"Are you okay?" Zeb said with a worried glance down at her. "Was the blood too much?"

"Yeah." Corrie shook her head then pasted on a smile for his benefit. "I'm fine now, though. Good work, hero. Now, let's get the *Clicker* ready to find some clues."

It didn't take much to get the *Clicker* ready to go, and even with the delay of the injured man, they were still finished preparations when Trip and Jules arrived with full bags of groceries.

"I told him it's only a weekend," Trip said to Corrie with a laugh. "But I'm willing to carry even more bags than these if it means Jules' cooking."

Corrie wasn't sure what to do with herself while they were underway. Normally, she would have lab work to prepare, bottles to label, or samples to add reagents to, but this wasn't a work voyage. Trip and Jules were busy in the kitchen, and she didn't want to interrupt their alone time. With Jules in Vancouver, they didn't get much of it.

Zeb was in the wheelhouse, of course, and Corrie dithered over joining him there. It seemed churlish to not keep him company, but echoes of this morning's bloody event still ricocheted through her body, and she had difficulty separating

Zeb from his red hands over the motionless injured man.

She didn't want to be weird about it, though, so after slowly unpacking her backpack into the drawers of one of the cabins, she made her way past the galley toward the wheelhouse. Trip's laughter drifted into the hallway, but Corrie kept her eyes forward, even as a smile crossed her face. It was good to see the two of them happy.

Zeb looked at ease in the captain's chair, one hand loose on the wheel and the other relaxed on the armrest. He glanced over when she entered and shuffled to a more upright position.

"I'm all settled in," she said brightly. "Jules and Trip are cooking already. Well, I don't know how much cooking is actually getting done, so I thought I'd leave them to it. They seemed pretty giggly when I passed by."

Zeb snorted and a grin crossed his face.

"I'm trying to imagine Jules giggling."

"Maybe not quite the right word," Corrie allowed. "What's the male equivalent? Chortling?"

"That's a bit better, but now I'm imagining Santa Claus."

Corrie lifted her hands in defeat then pulled out the folding chair that rested against the wall. She sank onto it.

"Ho ho ho. About our mission today. What's the plan when we get to the location? We'll just jump in and check out eelgrass beds in the area? Look for strange stones?"

"We?" Zeb glanced at her in confusion. "We didn't bring your scuba gear. I thought you were staying on deck."

"Hell, no. I'm not leaving you to have all the fun. We'll call a unicorn fish—a strolia—and I'll give it a lick." Corrie shuddered at the thought. "It's gross, but does it ever work. I'll collect some for later, too. It's good stuff to have on hand."

Zeb smiled shyly. "I like having you along."

"Besides, someone has to keep an eye on you," Corrie said. "What if you pass out underwater?"

"I swim every day, by myself." Zeb raised an eyebrow at her. "And the water makes it better, anyway."

Corrie crossed her arms.

"It's still good to swim with a buddy. Do you think a strolia will turn up? They seem pretty common these days. I keep waiting for news of one in the press, but nothing so far."

"I have a theory about that," Zeb said. He drummed his fingers on the wheel. "I can communicate with them better than with other fish. Maybe they're more crafty and know how to avoid nets and hooks."

"That would explain it." Corrie nodded with decision, even as she wanted to bounce with excitement. Today, this afternoon, she would experience that glorious feeling of immersion in a different world. Taking the strolia slime allowed her to be part of the sea in a way she'd never experienced before. The cool water caressed her skin instead of poking at it with needle pricks of freezing pain, and her limbs held a power she'd never known in water. She desperately wanted to feel that way again. She glanced at Zeb, who looked perkier than before. He must be looking forward to their swim, too. "We'll be on location soon. I'll get my swimsuit on."

"It'll be a while yet." Zeb's mouth twitched.

Corrie put her hands on her hips. "But I'll be ready for it."

JULES

Jules dusted a pinch of salt into his sauce and gave it a stir.

"And then Triston switched Isaac's sugar and salt," he said with a chuckle. "You should have seen Isaac's face during his taste-test."

Trip laughed and ran her hand down his shoulder blade.

"They sound like fun," she said.

"More than fun. They really get me, you know? I feel like I've found my people. Who knew they existed?" Jules held out his spoon for Trip to take a taste of the sauce. "I've landed on my feet, that's for sure. What do you think? Does it need more salt?"

Trip licked the spoon with gusto.

"Mmm," she said. "So good. I don't know, you're the expert. What do you think?"

Jules felt a thrill at Trip's use of the word "expert". He'd never expected that word to apply to anything he did. Experts were people like Trip who dealt with complicated wires and mathematics. Now that he was finally in the place he should be, the word didn't feel quite as absurd. Even if he were years away from qualifying for the label—Briscoe would be a better candidate—he was still on the right track.

He licked a dab of sauce that Trip had missed.

"Just a pinch," he decided. "Then we can add the mussels."

"Moules marinieres. I can't believe you remembered my last meal request." Trip grabbed his hand and played with the fingers. "We were plastered, and yet you still remember, months later."

Jules shrugged and squeezed her hand.

"I don't take food lightly." He grinned. "Besides, it was a new food to try cooking. I'm only sorry you're eating it on this old bathtub instead of in Paris."

"But the company is so much better." Trip leaned forward

and nibbled his ear. Jules shivered. She whispered, "You deserve the best, Jules Elliot."

He turned his head to kiss her lips. After a minute, they disentangled themselves, and Jules added the mussels to the sauce.

"Tell me more about your friends at culinary school," Trip said. She looked at him with a strange, keen expression that Jules couldn't translate. "What about the one who got you a job. What was her name, again?"

"Byssa, my teaching assistant. She's great. Such a good teacher, too. The instructor can be strict, but she always has a way of explaining things if you don't get it the first time. Apparently, she's also a swim teacher—in her spare time, I don't know when she fits it all in—and I bet she's great with the kids. So patient."

Jules stirred his sauce.

"I'm glad things are working out for you there," Trip said softly. "You're building your new life. I'm glad you could slot me in for a weekend of fun."

Jules put down his spoon and grabbed Trip around the waist. He twirled her around the tiny galley, and she shrieked with surprise.

"You're more than a weekend of fun," he said into her hair. "I couldn't stop thinking of you. The last few weeks were too long."

"Don't give me that." Trip slapped his chest lightly. "You were having a great time with Triston and the others."

"But you're something special."

Trip's mouth tightened, then she smiled. Her eyes still held something that Jules couldn't identify.

"You're the special one." She wrapped her arms around his neck, and Jules basked in the sensation of being held by a beautiful woman that he adored. "Don't ever forget it."

ZEBALLOS

Their first location he and Corrie had decided upon, given their clues, was less than twenty minutes away. Zeb didn't know if he could wait. His skin crawled with unbearable itching, and his stomach cramped every minute. He breathed deeply, trying to gain control over his unruly body, but it was no use. Even a piece of dried jellyfish barely eased the pain in his stomach.

He reached behind him and drew out the jar of cream. When he unscrewed the lid, his heart sank as it always did. The jar was half empty, and he had no way of refilling it. He didn't even know what it was, and the two people who might have told him were dead. He squeezed his eyes shut at the pain that thought caused him. His mother's passing was so distant, now, and anger swirled around his father's death, masking any hurt that Zeb might feel over his absence.

But he was alone to deal with the illness that ate him up inside. They could have given him answers.

But they hadn't known any answers, or else his mother wouldn't have died. What had George really been searching for with Penelope? Zeb didn't believe for a minute that it was to tell Clicker's family of her death. The George he knew wouldn't have cared about people who had never reached out to his beloved wife. But why else?

As the truth hit Zeb, he bowed his head. George had been trying to save his only son from suffering the same fate as his beloved wife. He had been following the clues to find the Seamount in the hope that he could find answers to save Zeb.

Zeb's anger with his father evaporated in an instant, to be replaced by bewildered resentment. Why hadn't George told him about his search? Had he been trying to shield Zeb from the uncomfortable truth? Zeb wasn't a child, not by the time George started searching, according to Penelope. Zeb had deserved to know.

Itching aggravated his already fraught nerves. With a curse, Zeb dipped a finger into the cream and rubbed a small dab on his skin. He didn't dare use more than that. Not only was this cream a scarce resource, but he'd made a fool of himself at Corrie's the other day. He flushed at the memory of kissing her while acting like a drunken idiot. She hadn't taken it well, but he was too chicken to bring the incident up. Luckily, Corrie seemed willing to forget it.

The cream worked within a minute, and it was with pleasing calm that Zeb greeted Corrie when she entered the wheelhouse wrapped in a towel.

"I hope we find a strolia right away," she said. "It's not summer anymore. That breeze is chilly. Not that you'd notice."

They shared a grin, then Zeb pointed at a headland.

"We'll stop the boat there. Jules can hold it steady or anchor it, whatever he wants. Send him up here, will you?"

Corrie disappeared, and when Jules traded places with Zeb, Zeb followed Corrie to the aft deck. He was wearing his swimsuit under his clothes, as always, and he grabbed his short flippers from behind the life ring. Corrie waved a pair of bright green flippers at him.

"I bought my own," she said with eager eyes. "I want to keep up with you."

"Good." He pulled off his shirt, as excited as Corrie to dive in. Sharing his underwater world was such a thrill.

"One thing." Corrie walked up to him until the warmth of her body radiated onto the sensitive skin of his chest. She held up a finger. "You need to stick right beside me. All the time. No scooting off to check something out. Last time you did that, I nearly died."

Zeb stopped breathing at the memory. Corrie in the galley, wrapped in a blanket with eyes huge in her pale face, telling him that the effects of strolia slime had run out underwater. He'd never felt so distraught, so ill-equipped to be responsible for someone else's life.

"All the time," he whispered. "That will never happen again."

"Good. Then let's jump in."

The sea enclosed Zeb's body like sheets of silk. Not that he'd ever lain in silk sheets, but he could imagine. Cool and smooth, surrounding his skin with relief and a gentle caress.

He flipped upside-down and watched Corrie's body cannonball into the water. Her flippers were bright at the surface, and they paddled in place. Zeb shot upward and surfaced next to Corrie, who shrieked in surprise.

"Oh, you." She splashed Zeb, and he ducked with a grin. "Find us a strolia, will you? The boat's attraction signal is on, but I need speed. This water is frigid."

Zeb sank below the chop and sent out a welcoming hum deep in his chest. He didn't wait long. Within a minute, three familiar shapes swam toward him with friendly flicks of their fins. Their silvery bodies glinted with hints of rainbow colors, and a translucent horn spiraled out of each forehead.

Zeb held out a piece of dried jellyfish, and the boldest fish swam closer. Zeb trailed the jellyfish toward Corrie, who watched from the surface with her eyes wide behind her mask. At his gesture, she dived down to join them. The strolia shied away at her jerky movements, but once Zeb grabbed her arm and she stopped struggling to stay under, the strolia approached once more.

Mindful of the poison that would exude from the horn's tip if provoked, Zeb let go of Corrie and ran his hand along the strolia's side. Its scales were slick with a light layer of mucus. When frightened, the strolia would produce vast quantities of the muck. Zeb hoped that the little that slid over its scales currently would be enough. He had no desire to hurt the strolia just for Corrie's companionship underwater, as sweet as it was. Besides, excess slime might summon a brigar, and Zeb definitely did not want to grapple with a giant octopus today.

Corrie took three vials from a small bag she gripped in her hand. She unstopped each and drew it along the strolia's side. Once all three vials contained slime, she bent forward. With an expression of distaste visible even through her mask, she placed her lips on the strolia's flank. She opened her mouth against the strolia but avoided letting seawater in. The process looked bizarre on the side of a fish, and Zeb wanted to replace his own lips with the creature.

Corrie pulled back from the strolia, and Zeb released the patient animal. It slunk into the murk, and Zeb followed Corrie to the surface.

"Ready?" he said once he recovered from the loud shock of surface life. His eyes changed their focus until Corrie's head turned from blurry to clear. When she turned to him after tossing her bag onto the *Clicker*'s deck, her eyes were bright.

"It's so amazing. The water is the perfect temperature, and my legs feel so powerful. Where are we going? I'll race you!"

Zeb's face cracked into a smile. Without a word, he pointed north. Corrie laughed and dived under the water. Zeb followed, his heart the lightest it had been for weeks.

They followed the curve of the shore, popping to the surface every couple of minutes for Corrie to breathe. Swarms of jellyfish bounced into them on occasion, and Zeb reminded himself to collect some on their way back for dehydrating.

He swam close to Corrie, unable to help himself. She was so beautiful underwater. Her braid had lost its elastic somewhere along the way, and her hair flowed in tantalizing swirls. Her legs, strong and well-shaped, kicked with unerring strokes. The rest of her, well—Zeb lost himself in dreamy visions while they swam. His hands and legs frequently brushed against hers, and every time they did, he wanted to get closer.

To distract himself, he swam further away and twisted in barrel rolls for Corrie's amusement. True to form, they had to surface after she released a stream of bubbles.

"You're a menace," she said, her eyes creasing at the corners. "Come on, I think we're almost there."

CORRIE

Corrie never ceased to be surprised at taciturn Zeb becoming carefree underwater. He flipped and turned for her amusement, attracted strolias to swim with, and pretended to be a breeching whale at the surface. She'd nearly choked on seawater at that one.

He even—it sounded strange to say it, even to herself— turned *flirty*. When Corrie returned from a breath of air, he swam directly underneath her, facing upward. Their eyes met, and Zeb reached out to touch her waist. He traced circles on her stomach, and her skin tingled with goosebumps that weren't caused by the cool water.

He flipped to swim beside her after that little tease, but she had difficulty forcing her head back in the game. Part of the problem was that her mind traveled to the pale woman, and how at home she had been in the water. The similarities cooled Corrie's fire. Luckily, a patch of eelgrass caught her attention.

She pointed with an eager finger. Zeb nodded and streaked down to the bed of vegetation with Corrie close behind. Was this the right eelgrass bed? Corrie was doubtful that vegetation like this stayed in the same location year after year, but if the conditions were perfect, maybe it wasn't such a stretch.

They searched until cold snuck into Corrie's limbs and made them shake. With disappointment, she gestured toward the surface. Zeb immediately drew them both upward.

"It's not here," she said. "And the slime's wearing off. Should we try the next likely location?"

Zeb nodded quickly, but Corrie could sense his disappointment.

"Hold onto my neck," he said. "I'll tow you back to the *Clicker*."

The next patch of eelgrass turned up nothing, and Corrie rubbed her shivering arms with a towel while Zeb drove with grim-faced determination to the next location. When Corrie wandered into the galley, Jules passed her a cup of hot chocolate.

"I'm so glad you came along," she said after a gulp of the steaming elixir.

Jules chuckled. "Zeb has his moments, but he doesn't understand being cold."

"How long do you think we'll search for?" Trip asked from the table. "Not that I'm rushing you, but we want to put the anchor down before dark, I'm guessing."

"Probably one more," Corrie said. Her heart sank at the thought of not finding the rock. "I have a good feeling about this next one."

Jules shot her an understanding look—he clearly didn't believe her "feeling" any more than she did—but she gulped the rest of her drink and wandered back to the wheelhouse.

"We're here," Zeb said when she stood at his side, bending her legs to absorb the boat's motion. "Are you sure you're up for another dive?"

"I have enough slime for another dive." She held up her vial. "Then we should probably call it a day."

"Yeah." Zeb looked downcast, but he nodded. "Let's try one more time."

Corrie wasn't hopeful that this dive would result in anything different than the previous two, but as soon as they descended to the seafloor, she saw it. Smack in the middle of waving brown fronds of eelgrass, a pinnacle of rock rose. In its center was a keyhole big enough for Corrie to swim through.

Zeb rose to the surface, and Corrie followed. With a gasp, she sucked in lungfuls of air. Zeb searched the shore until her breathing quieted.

"This is the location," he said. "There's no doubt. I'll mark it on our map when we get back to the *Clicker*." The tentative hope in his smile nearly undid Corrie.

"We can do this," she whispered. "One step at a time."

It was too late to return to Victoria after their swim, but Corrie had expected that. Jules' dinner of moules marinieres was exquisite. Corrie had been hesitant about eating mussels, but she should have known that Jules would turn the mollusks into something delicious.

Drinks flowed freely, and Corrie tucked away her fears, apprehensions, and suspicions to enjoy the evening. Occasionally, Zeb's gaze landed on her, and the heat of it flushed her skin with pleasant warmth. She didn't give him anything in return, unwilling to act on his invitation.

Cold chills followed the heat caused by his eyes when the unbidden memory of the blood-splattered pale woman popped into her mind. How was she going to release this association? It wasn't fair to Zeb, but she couldn't shake the connection, either. Not for the first time, Corrie thought of therapy, but dismissed it as quickly as the other times. No good would come of including another person in their secrets.

Corrie eventually propelled a giggling Trip into their shared cabin, where she passed out with a smile on her face. Corrie took longer to sleep, haunted by the sensation of Zeb's finger on her bare stomach.

The *Clicker* putted into the marina at midday. Corrie hopped in place.

"Let's stop at Penelope's house to tell her what we found," she said to Zeb once he climbed aboard after tying the boat to the dock. "This is big. And we still aren't sure how the next clue fits."

Zeb ran his fingers through his short white hair, still wet from his quick dip near Sooke while the others waited, and took a deep breath of sea air.

"Yeah," he said. "She might have an idea."

Trip and Jules departed in Trip's borrowed car, and Zeb drove Corrie up the hill. Penelope's house wasn't far, and they pulled up to the curb in front of her bungalow mere minutes later.

Barking announced their presence as before, and Penelope answered the door a moment later.

"Zeb, Corrie." Penelope's eyes flicked between them. "This is a welcome surprise. Come in, come in. Otis is shut in my bedroom, no worries there. Coffee?"

"Coffee would be great," Corrie said with a grateful nod. She followed Penelope into her kitchen and hopped into the same bar stool she'd occupied on her previous visit. Penelope bustled around the room, scarves flying and wrist bangles clacking.

"We found the holed stone," Zeb blurted out.

Penelope whipped around to stare at him. "Really? That's astounding. George and I never had a chance, if all the landmarks were underwater. This is tremendous news."

"We're not sure where to go from here, though." Corrie spread her hands helplessly. "Clicker's next instructions mention swimming over a shipwreck between two narrow rises, but I don't even know where to begin looking for that. Especially since she says she swam north for a long time to get to the eelgrass bed. How far is a long time? And the underwater topography map I have isn't nearly detailed enough to give us any clues."

"I might be able to help there." Penelope thumbed through papers in a pile on her counter island. She thrust aside pages until her eyes lit up, then she spread out a printed map. "Here. I called a colleague who owed me beers. He printed this map off for me instead. It's behind a paywall, but his lab has access."

She scrambled in a drawer while Corrie and Zeb bent over

the map. Vancouver Island was clearly demarcated in black, as was the Olympic Peninsula of the United States. In dark gray, various dots and ridges peppered the lighter shade of ocean.

Penelope held up a highlighter in triumph, then she bent her own head in with the others'.

"Look for ridges close together," she instructed. She circled one such ridge with her green highlighter. "Like this. Find any directly south of the holed stone." Another green dot of color jabbed onto the map where Zeb's finger indicated. "And we'll have something to go on."

"Here." Zeb pointed at a narrow gap between two points of raised seafloor, and Penelope jabbed her pen at the spot with a flourish.

They found six candidates in total. Corrie sat back, both elated and discouraged.

"How do we narrow it down?" she asked. "Six is a lot."

"What's the next clue after that?" Penelope looked expectantly at Zeb, who cleared his throat.

"Something about passing over a region where sulfur coated her tongue." Zeb's mouth twisted. "We thought maybe that referred to underwater vents, but I have no idea how to use that information."

"I do," Corrie said. "Where's the Juan de Fuca Ridge on this map? Doesn't it run along here?" She drew a line with her pencil.

"Yes," Penelope said with glee. "It's perfect. Wherever the Seamount is, it's past the ridge. And that cuts out these four rises." She drew X's in the paper so hard that it flew off the counter. Zeb caught it before it fluttered to the floor. Penelope continued, "That helps, but we still need to know where to go after the shipwreck. What's our next clue?"

"I don't have any more," Zeb said. He smoothed the map on the counter with careful motions. "I need another translation."

"Better put pressure on your translator. Time is ticking, my boy." Penelope glanced at Zeb with a critical eye. "You're looking too peaky to waste time."

Zeb's eyes dropped to the map, and he swallowed. Corrie took his hand and squeezed it tightly.

"We'll call Krista right away. We're so close, I can feel it."

Zeb returned her squeeze without looking at her. Penelope clapped her hands so suddenly that Corrie jumped.

"I have something for you. It's a wearable, waterproof GPS. You can download your path to your computer or phone, and it will tell you exactly where you went. So, if you find a location and forget to make note, the wristband will tell you."

Corrie reached out and took the wristband. It was sleek and streamlined, and the numbers glowed with a cool blue.

"This looks really expensive," she said. "I hope you didn't spend too much on it."

Penelope waved her concern away.

"Let me give gifts if I want." She gave them a crooked smile. "I don't have much to spend things on, and I'm still trying to assuage my guilt over Clicker. Don't argue with me on this one. A proper thank-you would be to wear it."

Zeb took the band from Corrie and strapped it on his wrist.

"Thank you," he said quietly. "This will come in handy when we search for our next clue."

"Speaking of which," Penelope said with a gleam in her eye. "When will that be? I'd love to tag along. I have a device that I've been tinkering with. George developed it, but it never worked properly. I've been playing around, and I think it might work. Open ocean would be best for testing, though."

"This weekend," Corrie said firmly. She hadn't missed the trembling of Zeb's hands when he fastened the band onto his wrist. She might have far too much work at the university to take two weekends off in a row, but Zeb's life was at stake. Time was ticking, as Penelope had said. She glanced at Zeb, who nodded, then she said, "And you're welcome to come, of course."

ZEBALLOS

A week had never passed so slowly. Zeb was tempted to take the *Clicker* out on his own countless times, but he resisted with difficulty. It wasn't a voyage he could undertake on his own. Chances were good that the seafloor would be too deep for his short anchor, and someone would have to stay with the boat while he swam.

He passed his days in the ocean and working at his new job. He'd become invested in the fox's recovery, and the creature always calmed when he saw Zeb approach. Adrianna said that he would be released in a few days once his leg came out of its cast. Zeb looked forward to that day.

Corrie was frantically busy all week after her trip on the *Clicker*, so Zeb mainly left her alone, although every day apart from her made the September sun shine a little less bright. Krista came through with more translations, although these were unhelpful reminiscences of fish his mother had seen and a pod of dolphins she'd swum with for a time. Interesting, but not useful clues in finding the Seamount.

His cream was now two-thirds gone, although he jumped in the ocean every chance he got. He simply couldn't make it through a whole shift at the wildlife center without relief. He pushed the fear out of his head. Panic wouldn't fill the cream jar nor find the Seamount. He captured countless jellyfish during his frequent swims and dehydrated them on board so he would never be without one of the few things that made his illness bearable.

Finally, Saturday dawned bright and clear. Zeb fueled the boat and was waiting on the bow when Corrie, Penelope, and Adrianna arrived with backpacks on the dock. He leaped overboard and grabbed their luggage.

"In a hurry?" Corrie teased. "Don't worry, we're ready to go. Why don't you get the boat turned on while I untie us?"

Zeb didn't need another invitation. While the others climbed aboard, he swung into the wheelhouse and turned the key. The *Clicker* roared to life, its engine noise disruptive in the quiet weekend marina. Zeb wrinkled his nose in amusement when the curtains of a nearby sailboat twitched. Nobody would sleep in when this old clunker started up.

When Corrie waved at him from outside the wheelhouse, Zeb smoothly drifted away from the dock and puttered through the alleys of the marina. Soon enough, they motored past the breakwater, and Zeb took a deep breath of contentment. Finally, they were on their way. By this time tomorrow, they should have more answers. Maybe even enough to find the Seamount and a cure for his illness.

Adrianna popped her head into the wheelhouse.

"Hi, Zeb. I hope you don't mind me tagging along. My boyfriend was busy this weekend, and I was at loose ends. Penelope's a good acquaintance of mine, too." Adrianna grinned. "I'm no Jules, but I don't mind cooking lunch today. My specialty is mac and cheese."

"No complaints here. Anything I don't have to cook works for me. Hey, while I have you here, do you want to learn how to drive the *Clicker*? If you can hold the boat steady at our location, Corrie can dive with me." At Adrianna's look of panic, Zeb chuckled. "It's not hard, I swear. Especially when we're in the open. There's nothing to hit. Your main job will be to keep the bow pointing into oncoming waves. Here, try it now."

Adrianna sat gingerly in the chair Zeb vacated for her and held the wheel with a white-knuckled grip.

"That's not so bad," she said after a while. "It's not very responsive, is it?"

"You'll be fine," he assured her. "And Corrie needs to breathe every two minutes, so we'll pop up to check on you."

Adrianna drove for another few minutes until her knuckles turned into a more natural flesh color and she even released one hand from the wheel in her ease.

"I got this," she said with confidence. She traded places with Zeb and gave him a salute. "Aye aye, captain."

He waved her away, and she exited toward the galley with a laugh.

Hours passed. Corrie entered the wheelhouse and chatted with him for a while about everything: her lab work, her family, her progress in analyzing the creatures' samples, her love of terriers. She carefully stayed away from mentioning Zeb's illness, which Zeb appreciated. It dogged every other waking moment and too many of his sleeping ones. He didn't need a reminder of his grim reality in Corrie's enchanting company. Her words washed over him in a steady, pleasing rhythm.

Halfway through the morning, he reluctantly interrupted Corrie's stream of words.

"Can you or Adrianna take over for a minute? I need a quick swim."

He avoided Corrie's concerned gaze and kept his eyes on the horizon.

"Of course. Should I hold this spot?"

Jules had taught Corrie on their last voyage, and she knew enough for that.

Zeb shook his head. "Just keep going really slowly, under a knot." He pointed at the speedometer. "Then I can get back on the boat easily. Hey, if you get Adrianna to take the wheel, look down from the bow."

He suppressed a grin at Corrie's questioning look and ducked out of the wheelhouse. When he heard the engine throttle down, he slipped out of his clothes, strapped on his fins, and dived overboard.

The cool water instantly soothed Zeb's tingling skin and grumbling stomach. He kicked underneath the boat, careful to stay far away from the propeller, and gave Corrie a minute to arrange for Adrianna to take the wheel. When he swam to the bow and flipped to look up, her wavering head peered over the railing. He grinned and accelerated. When the bow wave caught him and thrust him forward, he used the momentum to burst above the surface like a porpoise riding the waves. Corrie's surprised shriek of laughter was the only fuel he needed to repeat the motion again and again.

He could have stayed underwater forever, as always, but he only allowed himself a few minutes before he regretfully surfaced near the bow and gestured. Corrie ran to the aft deck and threw the ladder overboard. Zeb swam to the side of the *Clicker* and grabbed a rung as the boat whipped past. His body dragged through the water, but he used his muscles to haul himself into dry air. Water clung to him like it didn't want him to leave its embrace, and he nearly let go of the ladder with a similar emotion. Only Corrie's bright eyes at the top of the ladder made his hands cling to the rung tightly.

"Come on up, dolphin man," she said. "I think it's almost lunchtime. When will we arrive at our location, anyway?"

Zeb climbed over the gunwale and dried himself off with the towel Corrie offered him.

"Another hour should do it. We're facing the open ocean now—you can feel the rollers—and we're aiming for the tip of the Olympic Peninsula."

"Aren't we in U.S. waters?" Corrie's forehead creased. Zeb suppressed an urge to erase her concerned lines with a gentle caress. "Will their coast guard get after us?"

"Shouldn't be a problem." Zeb wasn't concerned. They weren't landing, after all. "As long as we don't anchor, it's fine. We won't be there long enough for anyone to bother us, anyway."

Corrie nodded without conviction.

"Better get dressed," she said, keeping her eyes on his face. A shiver of disappointment traveled down Zeb's spine. "And relieve Adrianna. We'll bring you some lunch in a bit."

When Zeb arrived, dripping, in the wheelhouse, Adrianna

passed him the wheel and disappeared into the galley. A few minutes later, Penelope entered with a sandwich.

"Hello, Zeb." She handed Zeb the sandwich and opened the folding chair without waiting for an invitation. "May I? Now, I noticed your impromptu dip. How often do you feel the urge to swim?"

Zeb barked out a laugh.

"Every single moment of every single day. If you mean how often I can't resist it, I can last about four hours between swims. More, if I use that cream I found in my mother's old things."

"Interesting." Penelope nodded quickly, her forehead wrinkled in thought. "Your mother was the same. Her swims increased in frequency. By the end, she was dipping in every hour, as I recall."

Zeb swallowed past his dry throat. Did he want to know the answer to his next question?

"How long do I have?" he whispered, his eyes on the horizon ahead.

Penelope tilted her head.

"Clicker had maybe a few weeks between the point you're at now and the end. You're different people, of course, so I can't conclude anything concrete. But not long, in my estimation."

Zeb's teeth ground together. Weeks? That was worse than his deepest fears. He suddenly had an urge to throw caution to the wind. What was he doing wasting his time working, sleeping, lounging around the boat? He needed to spend every last minute doing what he wanted to do. He could be diving to the sponge reefs in the Strait, playing his calla whistle, kissing Corrie with all the suppressed passion in his heart.

"And that's why we're out here." Penelope's pat on his shoulder made Zeb jump. He'd forgotten where he was in the damning revelations of the previous moment. "To make sure you count your days in decades, not weeks." Her gaze fell on the communication device that Corrie used a few months ago to attract sea creatures. "What's this?"

Zeb glanced behind him, his mind still distracted.

"Communication device for contacting sea creatures."

"I thought it looked familiar. But George couldn't get it to work."

"It's because we had to add an amplifier. See that bit, there?" Zeb pointed at their modification. "It wasn't loud enough before."

"Ah." Penelope nodded sagely, then she tore her gaze away from the device and focused on Zeb. "I'd like to collect some of my own strolia slime to test while we're out here, but I need to get closer to the water. Can I borrow this communication device and use your dinghy while you and Corrie look for the gap?"

"Yes, sure," Zeb said. He knew he sounded distant, but he was too caught up in gloomy thoughts to modulate his tone.

Penelope stood. "Good. Eat your sandwich. You need your strength."

Corrie jiggled on the aft deck in anticipation of their swim. Zeb looked away from her enticing bikini top and mastered himself.

"Do you think there are strolias out here?" she said. "I hope so. I wonder if they're everywhere, or if they follow your boat even when the signal isn't on. If they're everywhere, they are officially the cleverest fish in the sea for avoiding capture. Ooo, I wonder if those sea serpents—ligans—are everywhere, too?" Her eyes darted to the dark sea rolling beneath their boat. Her knees absorbed the movement without visible effort. "Stick close to me, Zeb."

"Always," Zeb assured her. He would never repeat his mistake from before. If Corrie got in trouble, it wouldn't be because he had abandoned her to freeze in the autumnal ocean.

Corrie strapped a dive knife sheath to her calf, then bent and grabbed a rope lying on the deck and tied it around her waist. When it was secured, she tucked a tall inflatable float under her arm.

"That's a good idea," Zeb said. Corrie had pulled out the float earlier in the day with pride. "Adrianna will be able to keep us in sight, even with the sea the way it is."

"Is it always this rolling out here? I'm used to waters in the Strait."

"There's nothing between us and Hawaii." Zeb spread his arm out to encompass the endless horizon, puffy clouds piled up along the edge. "And autumn storms will start brewing. These waves are nothing."

Corrie shivered.

"Let's get going," she said. "I don't like the look of those clouds."

Zeb unhooked the dinghy and winched it out for Penelope. After a minute's instruction, she flapped her hand at him.

"I've driven a little cork like this before. I won't stray far from the *Clicker*, in any event. Go on, find your answers. I'll see you shortly."

Penelope climbed over the side to reach the dinghy. After Zeb unhooked her and she puttered around the aft deck, he turned to Corrie.

"I'll jump in first," he said. "Find a strolia. Then I'll wave, okay?"

Corrie nodded, her eyes dancing with excitement, and Zeb dived overboard. It occurred to him to question Corrie's eagerness to lick a slimy fish to follow him under the waves, but to him, the answer was obvious. Surely, anyone who experienced the thrill of freediving would adore it the way he did? Jules had never taken to it, but maybe he was an oddball. Corrie's interest seemed entirely natural to Zeb.

With Zeb's hum joining the noise of the boat's intermittent

signal, only two minutes elapsed before a lone strolia swam up from the darkness below. Zeb coaxed it into his arms then kicked to the surface, humming calming vibrations the whole way.

Corrie leaped in as soon as Zeb's head breached the surface. She kicked steadily over the rolling waves, her head down with her concentration. The inflatable float streamed behind her, its long rope dragging through the peaks of waves as Corrie doggedly swam to him.

They needed to get below the commotion of the wave action. Zeb dived underneath and gestured to Corrie to do the same. She flipped upside-down and followed him until the rollers only shifted them gently.

Corrie kicked closer and rested her lips on the fish without hesitation. The strolia squirmed, but Zeb hushed it with a stronger hum until it stilled. When Corrie removed her mouth from the fish's flank, Zeb released the animal. It swam downward with unhurried flicks of its fin.

Zeb slipped his hand into Corrie's and drew her along beside him. She squeezed his fingers, and when he glanced into her eyes, they were wide with excitement.

They kicked their fins in a westerly direction—Zeb's sense of direction had never failed him, and he maintained a straight course—to intersect the ridge they wanted. The depth sounder had indicated the two ridges were directly ahead. Would they be lucky enough to discover the shipwreck between them? Zeb's entire body longed for their success, and his eyes strained uselessly through the endless green around them for sight of the wreck. He gave up using his visual sense and opened his mind to other senses.

Corrie's body pushing through the water was the loudest signal, but Zeb ignored that and focused on fainter signals. The seafloor wasn't far away here—it must be rising toward the ridge—and a single shark floated far below. Nothing else swam in front of them.

The ridge suddenly loomed into range in his senses. Zeb gripped Corrie's hand more tightly and pulled her forward. She jerked it up, and he belatedly remembered her need for oxygen. At the surface, Corrie gasped a few deep breaths amid the tall waves.

"Okay," she said when her breathing had calmed. "Let's go."

They descended, and Zeb pulled Corrie toward the empty space on the other side of the ridge. Complicated signals bounced through Zeb's mind, and he frowned, trying to make sense of the noise. Finally, his face cleared. He turned to Corrie and pointed with eagerness. She squeezed his fingers.

At another visit to the surface, Zeb chafed while Corrie caught her breath. He was almost certain that this was the place. They just needed to take a quick look, then they could head back to the *Clicker* and their maps of the region. He was torn between wanting Corrie with him and wanting to plunge to the depths quickly, on his own.

But he'd promised not to leave Corrie. Nothing would convince him to repeat that failure again.

"I'm sure it's the wreck," Zeb said when Corrie's breathing slowed. "Let's quickly check, then we can head back."

"Could we be so lucky?" Corrie's face was full of fervent hope.

"I hope so."

They flipped upside-down and kicked, hand in hand, toward the wreck. Zeb's eyes couldn't see much yet, but his other senses were firing steadily. The wreck was terribly disintegrated, but it was clearly an old two-masted wooden sailing ship. Zeb's heart squeezed with triumph at the same time as Corrie clenched his fingers. The wreck loomed out of the darkness, visible in the gloom. It was eerie in the quiet dimness. A few fish drifted around anemones that clung to rotten beams of old floorboards.

Corrie jerked. When he turned to her in concern, she

pointed at the anemones. Zeb released a bubble of laughter. Of course Corrie wanted to sample. He held up a finger for her to wait, then he slid her diving knife out of the sheath on her leg and dived closer to the anemones. A slice from one cluster, another, and a third—Corrie always took three samples per dive—and he returned with his treasure. Corrie looked confused, then she pulled out a tiny plastic bag from underneath her bikini top chest strap.

They'd been under for long enough. Corrie must be feeling the strain on her lungs. With a warm feeling of success, Zeb pulled her hand toward the surface.

Halfway up, Zeb heard the most delectable sound. He paused a few kicks away from the surface and let Corrie continue upward. What was that? Every muscle in his body wanted to investigate the source of that sound. It pulled at him with the same attraction as a cool dive in the ocean, the irresistible lure of his cream, Corrie's lips on his…

He shook his head. He had promised not to leave Corrie alone, and he would not renege on that promise, no matter how tantalizing the sound was. His body undulated until his head burst from the water.

"We found it!" Corrie threw her arms around his neck, and they both descended under the water. With a swift kick, Zeb propelled them to the surface again. Corrie spluttered and laughed. "Sorry. But we found it! This is the place. And I even got anemone samples out of it. What a great day!"

Zeb's face cracked open in a smile, and he hugged Corrie's warm body closer to his. He was acutely aware of her soft curves against his front, and he didn't want to waste a moment.

The attraction he felt reminded him of the strange noise, and his smile dropped away.

"Something's happening down there," he said. "A strange sound. Can we go check it out?"

Corrie stared at him, then the side of her mouth quirked upward.

"Absolutely." She rubbed the back of his neck with her thumb. "Thanks for asking."

Prompted by Corrie's closeness, her smile, and his ease at being in his element, Zeb leaned forward and gave her a short, deep kiss. He wanted more, but vibrations from the strange noise distracted him.

Corrie's eyes slowly opened after the kiss, and Zeb cursed the sound.

"Come on," he said. "Let's get going before that slime wears off."

The trip back was swifter because they weren't searching. Zeb's pulling at Corrie's arm might have had something to do with it, but Zeb was intent on reaching his destination. He had never heard a sound like what emanated from the unknown source, and a tantalizing thought consumed him. What if they were close to the Seamount? What if he were hearing one of the pale folk?

The *Clicker* loomed ahead, but Zeb rose only to make a "one more minute" sign to Adrianna at the helm. When she nodded, they continued past the boat toward the sound.

His senses picked up a new signal, one of thrashing limbs and frantic movements. He sped up, Corrie streaming along behind him. Her hand squeezed with her signal for air, and Zeb reluctantly rose to the surface. While Corrie gasped beside him, he scanned the waves. When they rose on a crest, his dinghy appeared on a nearby peak.

Penelope's back was turned, but even across the distance, her strident voice carried.

"Get back, you murderous bastard! May you and your worthless kind rot in the depths for what you've done. I'm coming for you!"

Zeb stared at Corrie, his horrified expression reflected in her eyes.

"Who is she yelling at?" Corrie said.

Zeb sank beneath the waves, and Corrie followed him.

They swam with unceasing kicks until the dinghy floated above them. The communication device hung from the side of the little vessel, and Zeb knew that it created the tantalizing sound. He and Corrie had never made it emit that noise. How had Penelope known? Pale limbs thrashed in the water, and rivulets of blood floated in the wash.

One of the pale folk was here. She must have been attracted to the sound, just like him. His eyes widened at the long slice on her abdomen that she held shut with one hand. Her face dipped below the water, and her face was twisted with wild-eyed rage. Zeb shrunk away at the bloodthirsty violence that the look promised. Was this what he searched for? How would someone like that ever speak to him, let alone help him find a cure?

But Penelope had clearly done something terrible to the pale woman. The slice on her abdomen was too clean and deep to be anything other than a sharp metal blade. It had a surgical precision that spoke of a scalpel. Zeb shuddered. What had Penelope done? The doubt and skepticism that he'd tried to suppress at Penelope's involvement reared its head, and for once, Zeb realized how much of him had been shaped by his father's upbringing. George hadn't trusted Penelope with Zeb's secret, and Zeb should have followed his instincts, laid down by his father. He might have pale folk blood running in his veins, but his upbringing had as large a role to play in shaping who he was as his heritage did, maybe larger.

Corrie tugged him away, clearly frightened by the rage-fueled pale woman. He let her pull him, but his eyes didn't leave the other woman. She sank suddenly, as if remembering her wounds, and dived deeper, still holding her stomach. Zeb watched her go. Was he letting his answers swim away?

He couldn't leave Corrie. He'd promised, and that meant something. His father had never promised much, but when he had, he'd meant it. Zeb would do the same.

CORRIE

Corrie's lungs wanted to hyperventilate, which was extremely awkward underwater. She tugged Zeb's hand with all her strength to get him away from the bloody scene underneath the dinghy. He followed slowly, too slowly for her liking. She could see, even if he couldn't, that they wouldn't get answers from the wounded, terrified, murderous pale woman. They had to stick to the plan of finding the Seamount, which had just been tossed a monkey wrench.

Corrie escaped to the surface when she was sure they were far enough away that Penelope wouldn't see them through the rolling waves. A few heaving breaths later, she rejoined Zeb underwater and continued toward the *Clicker*. He led them this time, his unerring navigation taking them in a direct line.

What was Penelope's game? Corrie's bewilderment was matched only by her fear. Penelope had clearly sliced open the stomach of that pale woman—she'd clutched an overlarge, blood-tinged scalpel in her hand when Corrie had glimpsed the dinghy—but for what purpose?

And the wild rage on Penelope's face as she screamed at the strange woman—Corrie shuddered. Penelope was hiding secrets from them, and Corrie couldn't trust her anymore. If she felt that way toward the pale woman, what hidden resentment did she harbor toward Zeb?

They reached the ladder at last, and Corrie climbed the rungs, cooling rapidly as the incredible effects of strolia slime left her system. She turned to meet Zeb's gaze as he hauled himself over the gunwale, his face pale and drawn.

"We have to pretend everything is normal," she hissed at him. "With Penelope. At least until we can talk. Okay?"

Zeb nodded, his jaw tight. A motor roared, and Penelope drove the dinghy close to the *Clicker*. No sign of blood marred the dinghy's bottom, but a layer of water sloshed in it.

Penelope must have sluiced it out with seawater before returning.

No sign remained of the rage that had crossed her face previously. She waved cheerily up at them.

"I'm all done," she said. "Any luck with you?"

Zeb turned away, his face contorted with anger, before he mastered his expression. Corrie was a better actor.

"We found it!" she shouted back. "All good. We can head back to Victoria now."

Zeb walked with stiff legs to the winch and operated it with automatic efficiency. Corrie despaired of keeping their deception alive and determined to uphold her end. When Penelope rose over the gunwale and climbed out of the dinghy onto the aft deck, Corrie beamed at her brightly.

"We saw the shipwreck, clear as day. Well, it was dark and murky, but still, it was there. What a great day! So exciting. Was your test successful?"

Corrie flung this last check at Penelope with the same bubbly cheer that the rest of her words had been delivered with. Penelope's mouth twisted then smiled.

"It sure was. A success all around."

A thump of something hitting the aft deck made Corrie whirl around. Zeb lay on the metal deck, his eyes rolling in his head and his limbs twitching.

Corrie's heart dropped. What was wrong with him? She skidded to her knees next to him and held his head steady.

"Take over from Adrianna at the wheel," she shouted at Penelope. "She can help. Go!"

Penelope turned in a swish of scarves and hustled up the side of the *Clicker*. Corrie held Zeb's head steady as he twitched.

"Stay with me, Zeb," she whispered. "Please. We're so close."

By the time Adrianna burst out of the back door where Corrie had her lab on past cruises, Zeb had stopped twitching and lay calm with his eyes half-closed.

"He had a seizure of some kind," Corrie forced out through her dry throat. "It's stopped now, but I don't know if he's awake."

"Jellyfish," Zeb moaned. Corrie leaped up.

"I got it. Watch him, will you?"

Corrie left Zeb in the care of a bewildered but assessing Adrianna and ran to the galley. In the usual cupboard, a bag of dried jellyfish rested beside two tins of canned spaghetti.

She raced back to the aft deck. Zeb was breathing normally and blinking his eyes while Adrianna examined inside his mouth. She picked up Zeb's left hand and scrutinized it.

Corrie fed Zeb a piece of dried jellyfish with shaking fingers. Now that Zeb seemed out of danger, the adrenaline rushing out of her body left it weak and trembling, although part of her shakes could be from cold.

"I think he's fine now," Adrianna said with a hint of doubt in her voice. "We won't know for sure until we know what sort of illness he has. But Corrie, have you considered a vitamin deficiency?" Adrianna held up the hand she still clutched. "His fingernails are pale and cracking. He gets stomach cramps. The faintness, the itching, the hunger. It's odd for a disease, but not that strange if he's missing something vital from his diet. It might explain his fondness for jellyfish. Maybe they taste like whatever he's missing, but they don't actually contain levels that reduce his symptoms."

Corrie stared at Adrianna, her mind churning with this new perspective. Was the cause of all this suffering the fact that Zeb wasn't eating properly? Latent maternal instinct in Corrie reared its head and made her want to march Zeb into the galley and eat three platefuls of dinner. With all the broccoli.

She whirled toward Zeb.

"What's your diet like?" she demanded. "Do you eat enough fruit and vegetables? What about meat and fish? Oh, do you need more fish than other people? That would make sense. We can figure this out, Zeb. I'll buy you multivitamins, we'll cook all the vegetables. This is something we can get a handle on. Too bad Jules isn't here to make them appetizing, but you'll have to make do with me."

Corrie reined in her babbling mouth with difficulty. Zeb gazed at her with tired eyes, their pale gray irises so strange yet so familiar and comforting. Zeb wasn't one of the pale folk. He was himself and no other. His pale folk side needed compassion, not fear.

Corrie needed to get a grip on herself and shake her misgivings. They would find the Seamount—because that's what Zeb wanted, and if they couldn't find the right vitamin, also what he needed—but that didn't mean that he would become one of them. He was fading fast, so she could shoulder the responsibility and take care of him. A proper dinner would be a good start.

A hint of a smile played at the corners of Zeb's mouth at Corrie's words.

"I'll make do," he whispered.

Zeb insisted on taking the wheel after he wobbled to his feet and climbed into his clothes. Corrie dressed in double-time and followed him to the wheelhouse, disliking how he held his stomach as though it pained him.

"I can drive," she said. "Why don't you just sit there and prepare to leap to my rescue if I get it wrong?" Adrianna trailed behind her, and Corrie whirled around to speak to her friend. "Adrianna, can you bring Zeb some dried jellyfish and something to eat? Lots of variety. I know we don't have much on board, but whatever you can find."

Adrianna nodded and disappeared into a side door. Zeb slipped into the wheelhouse from the outer door and Corrie followed him. Penelope glanced at the two as they entered, her

114

fingers tight on the wheel.

"Thanks for taking over," Zeb said. "I've got it now."

"Are you sure?" Penelope squeezed past Zeb, who settled in the captain's chair with a sigh. "You still look peaky."

"Thanks, Penelope," Corrie said firmly. "I'll watch him."

Penelope nodded and disappeared into the hallway. Corrie tugged at Zeb's arm.

"Come on, Zeb. Be reasonable. You should rest."

Zeb set his jaw in a stubborn line and sped the boat up with a roar of its engine.

"Stop fussing, Corrie. I'm fine. Driving the boat isn't a big deal. I'd rather do it than you, in this swell."

"You had a seizure." Corrie crossed her arms. Why wasn't Zeb taking this seriously? "Doesn't that mean anything to you?"

"It means I'm getting worse. It means I don't have time to laze around and 'recover'. There is no recovering from this, not without answers." He glanced at her, and Corrie's heart squeezed at the grief and anger in his eyes. "Thanks for trying to help, but the best way to do that is to solve this riddle."

"We can do both," Corrie said. "But fine, you can drive. I'm not going anywhere, though. Someone needs to watch your back and jump in if you keel over."

Zeb's mouth twitched, then he glanced at the open doorway behind them.

"What about Penelope?" he whispered.

"Don't talk now," Corrie whispered back with her own nervous glance at the hallway. "Pretend we didn't see anything. We'll talk later."

Zeb nodded and returned his gaze to the horizon. Corrie settled herself in the fold-out chair and prepared for the long trip back.

Adrianna stayed when she brought Zeb's food—a peanut butter and jam sandwich with a side helping of carrots and dried jellyfish—and they passed the time in idle chatter. Zeb picked at his sandwich but shoved more in his mouth when Corrie glared pointedly at the plate.

"Penelope's in the galley, working on her laptop," Adrianna told Corrie. "What time do you think we'll be back? I'm loving the sea air, but it really takes it out of you. I'm beat."

"We should arrive about seven," Zeb said. He rubbed his eyes, and Corrie swallowed her demand to take over driving. "Hopefully before nightfall."

"We were lucky that the shipwreck was at the first gap we checked," Corrie said. This day could have crumbled around them if they hadn't seen the shipwreck and Zeb had still collapsed when he had. It still felt like it was crumbling around them—what was Penelope up to?—but at least one good thing had come out of it.

Penelope waved with good humor but clear distraction when she left the dock at the marina. Adrianna quirked an eyebrow suggestively at Corrie's desire to stay behind, but she drove herself home. Once they were alone, Corrie stared at Zeb across the galley table.

"What the hell was all that about?" Corrie said. She'd had hours to think it through, and her desire to discuss Penelope's troubling behavior threatened to burst out of her all at once. "Did you see the look on Penelope's face? She was *livid*. And what the hell was she doing cutting a hole in that pale woman? How did Penelope capture her? What was she trying to achieve?"

"It was the song." Zeb rested his head in one hand, looking drained. "Penelope borrowed the communication device that you use. She set it to a call that I've never heard before, but it made me want to swim right to it. It hit right here." He thumped a fist on his chest.

Corrie frowned. "How did Penelope know that call? Did

your mother teach her? Why would she do that?"

"Penelope worked with her a lot. Maybe they were friends." Zeb traced his finger along a crack on the tabletop. "Mum could be quite trusting. Dad used to shake his head at her inviting passing strangers into the garden to say hello. He was the total opposite."

"Okay, so let's assume your mother taught Penelope a pale folk-attracting song. What was Penelope hoping to gain?" Corrie sat up straight, her heart hammering. "And why didn't she tell us about it? We could use it to call the pale folk for help. That's what we're trying to do with all this. Your problems could be over tomorrow if we had that song. Do you remember it well enough to replicate it?"

"I don't think so." Zeb's face twisted with frustration. "I could try, but I wasn't really paying attention. Not well enough to remember."

Corrie slumped her shoulders then rallied.

"We still need to figure out what Penelope wants. She attracted a pale woman, subdued her enough to slice open her stomach, then kicked her out of the boat. That slice wasn't in self-defense. You only bring a scalpel on a cruise if you're planning to use it. What did she want? Did she take a deep tissue sample of a pale folk? If so, why didn't she tell us about it?"

"We wouldn't have let her," Zeb said. "Cutting someone open against their will? That's beyond cruel."

"Penelope has a song that attracts pale folk, and she used it to get a sample from something in the abdomen. Bizarre, but I don't know what to conclude from that." Corrie leaned forward and stared at Zeb. "But her reaction to the attacking pale woman. That anger went deeper than the battle on the dinghy. Something's up. What's Penelope's history with the pale folk?"

Zeb lifted his shoulders in helpless confusion. Corrie tapped her fingers on the table.

"We should stop talking with Penelope," she said finally. Her shoulders drooped again with the weight of guilt. "Without knowing her goals, she's too dangerous. I'm sorry I introduced you to her, Zeb. You were right to be suspicious."

"No," Zeb said quickly. "It was my decision. And without talking to Penelope, we never would have pieced together some of the clues. And I still need her for medical testing. Maybe let's not report to her as often."

"Yeah," Corrie said. "I see what you're getting at. I'll pretend I'm super busy at work—ha, I won't have to pretend hard—and you can say you're recovering from this weekend. We'll do our own looking for clues. We need to keep one step ahead of her. Whatever she wants at the Seamount, I have a feeling that it's not good. She doesn't need to be involved in clue-finding. Deal?"

"Deal." Zeb yawned hugely, and Corrie jumped up.

"Go to bed," she ordered. "I'll bring groceries in the morning. We'll figure out this vitamin deficiency. That's something we can get Penelope to run bloodwork for. I guess you'll have to follow up with her tomorrow. Just look really feeble or something."

Privately, Corrie thought that it wouldn't take much acting skill on Zeb's part, and her stomach squeezed. She would do everything in her power to fix Zeb.

ZEBALLOS

Zeb dutifully presented himself at Penelope's office early Monday morning before his shift at the wildlife center, doing his best to appear drained from his seizure on Saturday. It didn't take much to play up the trembling in his hands that wouldn't go away.

"How are you feeling, Zeb?" Penelope asked once he'd seated himself. "Any improvement? Not that we can expect it, I suppose."

"Not really." He hated pretending that everything was okay between them. After the rage in her face at the pale woman's mere existence, he mistrusted Penelope more than ever. His face twisted in a frown of distaste, and he forced it into a grimace of pain to conceal his true feelings.

"I'm sorry to hear that." Penelope grabbed a basket filled with vials and tubing, and she pulled out a syringe. "Let's do some more bloodwork. That was an inspired idea of Adrianna's, the vitamin deficiency brainwave. It's certainly worth ruling out, although I imagine that your normal levels could be far different than someone with a different heritage. I wish we had a baseline for you, a sample pre-illness. Never mind. Let's run the bloodwork and go from there."

Zeb submitted to her poking and prodding with resignation. His blood boiled at the brisk efficiency masking such a vehement heart, and he wondered idly if the vials would bubble like champagne.

"Let me know what you find," he said after she declared him done. He pushed himself to his feet, pretending it took far more effort than it did. "I'm taking it easy for the next few days, trying to recover."

"Don't wait too long," she warned. "Don't forget what I told you about your timeline."

Zeb swallowed his fear. How could he forget that he only

had weeks to live? He resolved to work on the clues all night, by himself if Corrie weren't around.

Corrie was free that night, as it happened. Zeb gathered that she had pushed things aside to make room for him in her busy schedule. He felt both guilty and relieved. He hated being an inconvenience to her—to anyone, really—but he didn't have time for niceties.

He'd needed to drive like a maniac to the beach for a quick dip during his lunch break. The swim hadn't been nearly long enough, but it had taken the edge off so he could survive the rest of the afternoon. He grabbed a drive-through burger for dinner on his way back to the beach after work, trying not to imagine Corrie shaking her head in disapproval. Whatever vitamin he wasn't getting, Zeb was certain this burger didn't contain it.

Finally, wet and full, Zeb drove to Corrie's house, munching idly on dried jellyfish as he followed a meandering minivan until turning into Corrie's driveway. Trip, licking a spoon, let him in and waved him toward a rec room downstairs. Zeb entered the snug room lit with a standing lamp that looked like it had been salvaged from the roadside. Corrie kneeled over a low table in the middle of the room, but she looked up when he cleared his throat. Her eyes crinkled with a smile of greeting, and Zeb sighed happily.

"Zeb, come look at this. I've mapped out all the vents in the region on the same map as our shipwreck. We're really narrowing down our options. Your mother's stories say she rode a yatull when she came here, right? One of those seal-like creatures. Why don't you calculate how far a yatull can swim in a day while I confirm northern shoveler migration paths?"

Zeb held up a piece of paper with his handwriting on it. He'd been sitting on this news all day, and he was gratified by

Corrie sitting up like she'd been poked.

"Is that another translation?" Corrie wiggled her fingers at him. Grinning, Zeb handed over the paper. Corrie skimmed the text. "Amazing. I'll read it aloud.

My yatull and I followed the directions at the crosscurrent sign. Written in our script, it describes how to leave the Seamount and how to return. After we swam past the sign, my yatull left me for a while and returned with a clearwater squid in her mouth. She enjoyed the delicious and rare treat.

"Crosscurrent sign?" Corrie's eyes were wide. "That sounds like our final signpost. If we can get there, it will tell us how to find the Seamount. Do we know how to read their script?"

"There are odd scratchings in the back of my dad's notebook. I bet we can use them to translate. I'll get Krista to send the notebook back so we can focus on that section."

"Okay, okay, okay." Corrie looked like she could hardly contain herself, and Zeb tightened his lips to avoid laughing out loud. "A clearwater squid, that's obviously a squid from the tropics. The only one that tends to come up this far is the Humboldt squid. That means I need to look up how far north Humboldt squid come. Or, how far they came thirtyish years ago when your mother made the journey. Those squid have been moving northward due to increased ocean temperatures in the past few decades. Perfect. Work out those yatull numbers, will you?"

Zeb opened his mouth to respond—he had no idea how fast a yatull swam, having seen one in passing for the first time last month—but Corrie was already deep in her computer research, the tip of her tongue sticking out with concentration. He swallowed his words and considered the yatull. It was shaped similarly to a seal, although it was much longer. With a rider on the back creating drag… Zeb grabbed a piece of paper and pencil and got to work. Math wasn't his strong suit, but dealing with sea creature speeds made it easier. If only his high school teachers had used examples that he'd cared about. He wondered suddenly how perennial slacker Jules was faring in his classes. He must feel the same way about food that Zeb did about his yatull math. Smiling, Zeb bent his head over his calculations.

He got Corrie to check his math once she emerged from her research, then she set him to work measuring out his calculations on the map. Zeb was happy enough to let her take the lead on research. She was good at it, after all, and she seemed to need a mission to tackle. It prevented her looking at him with that frightened expression he was getting resigned to seeing ever since he'd told her about his illness.

Zeb's phone rang, and he tore his eyes away from the map to check the caller ID.

"It's Penelope," he said.

Corrie glanced up and bit her lip. "Don't answer," she said.

"What if it's about the bloodwork?"

"She'll leave a message. It's late, she won't think it's weird."

Zeb lay the phone on the table and watched it until it stopped ringing. Sure enough, a voicemail notification appeared a minute later. He dialed in, itching his arm as he did so.

"Zeb, it's Penelope. I got the results back on your bloodwork, and nothing is out of normal range except for your sodium levels as we saw before. I'd hoped some of the more specialized tests might come back with something. I'll keep thinking about the vitamin deficiency angle but let me know if anything else crops up."

Zeb itched again. He needed a swim soon, but they were on a roll with the clues. He could tough it out for a little longer. The longer he could handle between swims, the longer he could convince himself that he wasn't near the end. His mother had resorted to hourly swims before she succumbed. He wasn't there yet.

CORRIE

Zeb itched his arm again, and Corrie steeled her nerves to broach a subject she'd been wrestling with for the past few days.

"Zeb?"

"Hmm?"

"I'm worried about the cream you use."

"Me, too." He pulled out the small tub, now refilled. "There's hardly any left. I don't know what I'm going to do when it's gone."

He swallowed, and fear flashed in his eyes. Corrie hardened her heart. She didn't want to see him travel the same path Dylan had. He needed her help, and he needed it now.

"Do you know what's in the cream?"

Zeb shook his head.

"Have you considered," Corrie continued in a delicate tone. "That you have a dependency on it? That it might be a recreational drug that affects pale folk?"

Zeb stared at her. It was clear that he'd never considered the notion. Corrie took a deep breath. This was good. Maybe he would make the right choices on his own.

"Maybe," he conceded. "I don't know how I'd get along without it, though."

"And that's what worries me." Corrie smoothed her sweaty hands over her jeaned thighs. "That you might need it, that it has addictive properties. I think you should stop using it."

Zeb gaped at her, but Corrie kept her expression a mask of calm concern. Zeb needed to hear this.

"You think so?" Zeb stared at the cream in his hands, then pushed it away. "Maybe. Okay. If you think so. I should go for a swim soon, though." He looked longingly at the papers. "Maybe we can finish our map first."

"Absolutely," Corrie said. She was relieved beyond

measure that he'd taken her advice so well, and she was willing to agree to anything else. "Let's finish the map, then you can go for a swim."

They worked for another half hour, but Zeb's itching grew more frequent until his fingers clenched and unclenched with his restraint. Corrie glanced at him. His breathing was short and sharp, and he closed his eyes as if in pain.

"Are you okay?" Corrie placed her pencil on the table. "We worked too long, didn't we? Just breathe, it will be okay."

"I can't make it to the ocean in time," Zeb panted. "I can't, I can't…" His eyes opened and lit on the tub. "Just a dab of cream, that will help me last."

Corrie's stomach muscles clenched. This was too familiar. Softly, while moving her hand slowly toward the tub, she said, "That's not the answer, Zeb. You can do this. I know it's hard. Look, why don't you stand up and I'll drive you to the ocean."

Sweat beaded on Zeb's forehead as he watched Corrie's fist enclose the tub. He gripped the edge of the table.

"I don't think I can," he whispered. "Just a bit. I need it."

He doubled over in pain. Corrie bit her lip so hard she feared she'd drawn blood. This was for Zeb's own good. She had to remember that. Her shaking legs lifted her upright, and she took a step backward.

"You're doing great," she cooed. What was she going to do with the cream? Maybe she could toss it out the window for now. Out of sight, out of mind? She was highly skeptical of that expression, but removing the tub from the room would at least buy her time.

She opened the window without looking at the latch. Zeb stared at her with haunted eyes, and she kept eye contact while she tossed the cream out the opening.

Zeb surged to his feet, his eyes hard but his knees shaking.

"What did you do?" he said. He stared into her eyes, and his voice took on a strange cadence. "You need to get the cream back. You know it's the only thing that will help. You want to help me, right? This is the way. This is the only way.”

Corrie was lost in his voice. A dreamy, hypnotic quality pulled at her like gently lapping waves over the shore. She succumbed to it, drifting in Zeb’s suggestion. Of course she could get the cream back. Just a little wouldn’t harm him. Going cold turkey was too harsh, anyway. She could figure out a weaning-off regime. She turned and lifted her leg to climb out the window to retrieve the tub.

“That’s right,” Zeb purred. He coughed, and the drifting quality of his voice grew harsh, like static on the radio. “Get the cream for me.”

Corrie froze, her mind clear once again. Then a tsunami of rage welled up in her, and she whirled around.

“You bastard!” she screamed. She shoved at Zeb’s chest, and he stumbled backward on his weakened legs. “That was pale folk compulsion at work. Singing me happy. How dare you! After everything I’ve done for you, you force me to do what you want?” She marched forward and shoved him again, hard. He fell on top of the table, and papers scattered everywhere. “What the hell, Zeb. How could you?”

She was panting. Irritated tears welled in her eyes, and she dashed them away with an angry swipe of the back of her hand. She didn’t want Zeb to get the idea that she was weeping. Those were tears of pure rage at him forcing her to do his bidding.

Zeb’s jaw dropped. His eyes darted back and forth between hers, searching for answers. She glared at him, wanting answers of her own.

“I—” he stuttered. “You think I compelled you? I didn’t mean to do anything, I swear. Corrie, you have to believe me.” Panic danced in his face, and he ran his hands through his hair and gripped it tightly. “I would never—I had no idea. I’m so sorry. I don’t know anything about anything, I swear. The first hints I heard of that ability was in that translation we read. My mum never told me about that.”

Corrie breathed heavily. Zeb's apology seemed sincere, but she wasn't calm enough to accept it and move on, not yet.

"Fine," she said at last. "We're done for tonight. We can talk tomorrow."

Zeb stared at her for another moment, but she kept her face studiously on a brightly colored wall painting by her artist roommate across the room. Finally, he stood and walked with slow steps to the doorway. Corrie didn't move when the front door closed, but she squeezed her eyes shut at the sound of rustling bushes outside the open window as Zeb retrieved his cream.

Corrie's mind whirled far too quickly to even consider sleep. Her heart pounded with anger and fear. For what? She didn't know if her fear was for herself being manipulated, for Zeb and his apparent addiction, or for Zeb's rapid descent into illness.

Her back straightened. Zeb's illness was the only thing on that list she could do something about. Among other data, Penelope had given her a strange protein profile that she'd isolated from the gut of a strolia. Corrie nodded to herself and marched to the front door. A little late-night lab work would distract her from the turmoil in her head. She might as well be productive if she wasn't going to sleep.

Music blared in the empty lab, and Corrie turned up the volume to drown out her thoughts. She focused instead on loading the mass spectrometer correctly. This wouldn't give her a sequence, but it would tell her if the proteins in her anemone samples contained the same peptides as Zeb's cream. The match between the cream and the anemone sample in the database was intriguing, and Corrie wanted to see if she could replicate it. For good measure, she added in the strolia gut sample. As untrustworthy as Penelope had proven herself, she was still providing them with data and samples. Whatever her opinion of the other pale folk was, she was still trying to help Zeb.

When the data from her three anemone samples and the strolia gut sample came back, Corrie stared at the peaks in the readout. She compared them to Zeb's cream. They weren't identical, but close. Corrie's brain fizzed with an idea, and she rearranged the readouts in order of proximity to the Seamount. Sure enough, the anemone sample from the shipwreck was the most similar to Zeb's cream. What was more, the strolia gut sample was nearly identical to the cream.

Corrie sat back, trying to make sense of what she was seeing. Was there a substance produced at the Seamount that leaked into the surrounding water and was taken up by anemones nearby? She smothered a giggle at the thought of an underwater factory for recreational drugs frequented by blissed-out unicorn fish.

She shook her head and gathered her papers. It was late, and she was too worn out to think straight. Hopefully, the late-night lab work had tired her out enough to sleep without thinking about Zeb.

Corrie finally fell asleep sometime after two in the morning, and her alarm was an unwelcome intrusion into her fevered dreams. She rolled over with a groan and blindly groped her phone to shut it up. Her eyes gazed at the blank ceiling, September sunlight streaming in, as her mind ran through the events of last night. Her pre-sleep ruminations hadn't resulted in any helpful conclusions, but the morning light illuminated harsher truths.

She had been too hard on Zeb. Maybe the cream was some kind of addictive substance of the pale folk, maybe it wasn't. But what of it? Zeb was dying, and although they were uncovering clues to discover the Seamount, finding a cure at the end of their path wasn't a given. Her stomach clenched at the memory of his pain-filled face. Was the cream addictive or simply soothing? Did it really matter which, if Zeb could self-medicate with something that brought relief? If—when, Corrie told herself firmly—they found a cure, or a vitamin, or whatever Zeb needed, they could deal with the cream then. She couldn't let her past color her judgment of his cream use.

His attempted manipulation was another matter. That, she was less inclined to set aside without comment. Manipulation, in whatever form, was something she could not abide. Maybe he was telling the truth about his lack of knowledge, but Corrie knew how desperate need could justify any behavior. Now that he knew, what would stop him from using this powerful, terrifying new skill when he was under duress? Corrie shivered and hugged herself.

After she was dressed and eating a piece of toast at the kitchen table, a message from Penelope appeared in her notifications.

Testing a new device at four today in Cadboro Bay. Tag along if you like.

Corrie stopped eating and stared at the message. She wanted to stay far away from Penelope, but they needed to know what she was up to. She didn't trust Zeb's acting skills to pretend that everything was okay. She drummed her fingers on the table. Maybe they could watch Penelope from afar. Her final teaching class ended at three-thirty, which would give her just enough time to bike down to Cadboro Bay.

Decided, she called Zeb.

"Corrie." Zeb sounded relieved. "I'm glad you called. I'm sorry about last night."

"Let's just forget it for now, okay?" she said stiffly. She

didn't really want to talk about it. "It wasn't cool, but we have bigger fish to fry. Penelope wants to test a device this afternoon. I don't think we should join her, but what about watching from a distance?"

"Okay." Zeb sounded like he would have agreed to anything. Corrie tried to think of a way to benefit from this, but eventually she sighed.

"Okay. See you at Cadboro Bay at four."

She hung up and took a deep breath then released it with a whoosh. She could handle this. If Zeb had been anyone else, she would have cut him off without question. She didn't have space in her life for manipulators. But extraordinary situations called for special methods. Zeb didn't know the extent of his abilities. And he was dying. And, with every day that passed, she hated the hours that they spent apart.

Corrie buried her face in her hands and groaned. Zeb was a complication she didn't need, but that she seemed to want.

Trip wandered into the kitchen in a summery tank top and shorts, her glossy brown hair pulled back in a messy bun. Corrie sighed deeply, and Trip stopped her hand on the fridge door handle.

"That was heartfelt," Trip said. "Care to elaborate?"

"Boy troubles," Corrie said. She hated secrets, and if Trip were asking, she saw no reason not to unburden herself. Trip should know better than to ask if she didn't want to get involved.

To Corrie's relief, Trip grabbed milk from the fridge, two glasses from the cupboard, and settled herself in a chair opposite from Corrie.

"This calls for a drink, but even I put my foot down at breakfast alcohol, so here's your beverage." She poured them each a glass of milk and pushed one toward Corrie. "Now, tell

Aunty Trip what's wrong."

"It's Zeb."

"Yeah, I figured you weren't hiding some new boyfriend up your sleeve. What did he do?"

"He discovered a new ability." Corrie twisted the glass around on the table. "You know, one of his pale folk ones. He can force people to do whatever he wants. A sort of compulsion thing. He tried it on me last night."

"What happened?" Trip grabbed the edges of the table and leaned forward, her eyes concerned. "Are you okay?"

Corrie waved her hand in dismissal.

"Nothing like that. I was trying to take away that cream he uses, and he tried to get me to give it back. He uses it like—" Corrie hesitated. "Like a user, you know? I was just trying to help him, take the temptation away. Then he pulled out this weird, hypnotic voice, but it stopped working after a while." Corrie sipped her milk, needing the coolness to soothe the bitter taste on her tongue. "I freaked out, of course."

"That's a biggie." Trip sat back, looking winded. "Compulsion. What did he say?"

"He swore up and down that he didn't know what he was doing." Corrie bent her head and gripped her hair in both hands. "The problem is, I believe him. Normally, I would send someone like that packing, accident or not. But he's going to die if I don't help him. I need to fix this." She looked up at Trip, her stomach twisting with her words. "And I do trust him, despite all that."

"You're sure he's not just playing you?"

Corrie probed her memories and her feelings, then she released a mirthless chuckle.

"He's not that good of an actor." She sighed and sat up. "I don't know what to do."

"I think you do, you just don't want to admit that you're willing to forgive him. Just take it day by day." Trip drummed her fingers on the table. "I have boy troubles too."

Corrie stared at Trip. Her roommate didn't normally get attached to anyone, not enough to have "troubles". Her mind jumped on the distraction from her own issues.

"Spill," she said. "What's up?"

"It's Jules." Trip huffed. "Obviously."

"You guys seem like you're hitting it off really well." Corrie tilted her head in question. "Is it the long-distance thing?"

"No. He's just—" Trip screwed up her face. "He's too great. He's head over heels for me, thinks I'm the world."

"Too cloying?" Corrie wouldn't mind that adoration, but she could see how Trip might rebel. To her surprise, Trip shook her head.

"That's not it at all. He's just—he's wasted on me. I went into it thinking he'd be a bit of summer fun, and he's in love." Trip twisted her hands together. "He's such a great guy. I want to release him so he can find someone who's much better for him, but I don't want to break up and hurt him like that." She sighed. "It's a conundrum."

Corrie rested her chin in her hand. Poor Jules. She'd seen how he looked at Trip. She was right—he was in love or falling with dangerous speed down that rabbit hole.

"He'll take a break-up pretty rough," she said. "But probably better now than later. Don't give him any more time to solidify his feelings."

"He'll be fine." Trip played with her milk glass. "He's got good friends in Vancouver already, and some interesting women in his life. Now that he's in his element, he'll be fine." She downed her milk and slammed the glass on the table. "Boys. So much trouble."

Corrie chugged back the rest of her own milk. Her mind was more settled now, thanks to her chat with Trip. She was still angry at Zeb—she wouldn't let him off the hook that easily—but he was sincere. She'd probably forgive him with time.

And if she didn't want to deal with Zeb directly right now, she could still take charge and deal with Penelope. There was no question in Corrie's mind that Penelope had to be stopped. Corrie's brain chewed at the problem as Trip picked up their milk glasses and loaded the dishwasher.

"Don't strain yourself with all that thinking," Trip said with a playful smile.

Corrie waved at her as she left the room. She had a plan, and today was a good day to carry it out.

JULES

The restaurant had finally calmed down after an insanely busy lunch rush. Jules put down his knife and leaned against a wall in the kitchen. There was plenty of prep to do for dinner, but he could spare one minute to rest, surely.

"Jules." Kanami, a server who never seemed to stop moving, flew by Jules. "I'm way overdue for my break. If you're just standing there, can you bus tables for me? Thanks, you're a doll!"

She blew him a kiss and sailed out. Jules sighed and shuffled toward the kitchen door, grabbing a bin on the way. Briscoe had been right, working under pressure was a required skillset. He was building his endurance, that was for sure.

Only half the tables were filled, most with people on their last bites. Jules placed dishes in his bin as quietly as he could, then he noticed Byssa on her lunch break at a nearby table. He glanced at her companions, curious about her friends. The man sported a head of hair striped black and white like a skunk, but his features under his surprising mane were similar to Byssa's. A brother, maybe? The other person was a beautiful woman with unremarkable brown hair.

Jules brought his gaze back to his work before Byssa caught him snooping. Their conversation filtered over to his table.

"The marina is so oily," the brown-haired woman said. "It makes my eyes sting every time. When are you going to take me to a nice beach, Hades?"

The man Hades laughed.

"Don't be such a mooch, Lune. Why don't you save up for a motorbike of your own? Even a scooter would get you from A to B."

"What happened to your black-haired wig, Lune?" Byssa asked in a teasing voice. "I liked that one. I could pretend we were sisters. You could just dye it like I do. It's a lot less maintenance, and our hair takes to dye so well."

"It's too permanent," Lune replied. "I'm not ready to cover it up for good, not yet. Maybe I'll get there, one day."

Jules recalled the blond roots along Byssa's scalp. Did Lune have similarly pale hair? Why would she cover it up?

He wiped his table slowly, but Byssa and her friends started talking about sushi, so he moved on, his mind churning. Their conversation had been odd, and Jules would have brushed it off if he hadn't had Zeb for a best friend. No one else had hair in quite the shade of white that Zeb did, but Byssa's roots might come close. And why would Lune talk about oily seawater in her eyes, if she hadn't been swimming in the marina?

Jules didn't know what to do with that information, but he tucked it away for pondering. As far as Zeb knew, he was the only person on land with his heritage. Were there others?

Surely, Clicker would have known them. But if she hadn't? Jules returned to the kitchen with a full bin and an even fuller mind. Could this information help Zeb and his illness? Jules didn't know what sort of timeline Zeb was under—Zeb hadn't shared that with him—but finding answers would improve Zeb's life now, not just extend it. Jules felt terrible that he couldn't do anything to help his oldest friend, but maybe that wasn't true.

He would have to tread carefully, though. He didn't want to scare off Byssa and her friends. Zeb's life was too important to muck up with heavy-handed blundering.

CORRIE

Corrie couldn't break away from her teaching duties until lunchtime. She finally extricated herself from a dawdling student and walked with quick steps to Penelope's building. Inside the cool glass-and-steel interior, she padded up the main stairs and swung left down the first hallway.

Penelope's office door was at the end of the hall and around a corner, so few people passed by this section. Corrie pulled out an unbent paperclip, ready to pick Penelope's lock. She'd even watched an online video between classes in preparation. She didn't know what she would find in the office, but she would hate to be foiled by something as mundane as a lock.

Corrie knocked and waited for a sound. The hallway was silent. She knocked harder to make sure Penelope wasn't in there napping or listening to music on headphones.

Confident that Penelope wasn't in there, Corrie took one last glance down the corridor to make sure she was alone. Quickly, she put her hand on the doorhandle to steady herself for her lock-picking adventure. Her hand slipped on the knob.

The door swung open. Corrie gaped at it. It hadn't even been locked.

Corrie huffed in disappointment—she'd come prepared for locks, damn it—but also in relief. She didn't know how long she'd have in here, and not fiddling around with the lock would save precious minutes from her espionage.

She slipped inside and pushed the door mostly closed then scanned the room. Nothing blinked a neon sign saying, "suspicious material here", so Corrie hopped on the desk and reached for the file that contained Penelope's results from Clicker. She rifled through the stack of papers with jittery fingers. The papers were printouts of equipment readings, mainly, which she had no way of interpreting without knowledge of the samples they had resulted from.

One paper caught her eye. It was a schematic of a device. Scrawled words at the top spelled "stun machine."

What was this? Corrie's pulse quickened. A stun machine sounded nefarious, and plans for one shouldn't be in the hands of someone like Penelope. Corrie pocketed the paper then flicked through the rest.

Footsteps in the hall nearly stopped her heart. She shoved the file back on the shelf, clambered down from the desk, and slid into a nearby chair just as the door swung open.

"Corrie." Penelope looked taken aback. She walked in and placed a coffee cup on the table. "What a pleasant surprise. What brings you here today?"

"Just—" Corrie thought quickly. "I wanted to make sure you tested for thyroid hormones when you ran bloodwork. It's such an important gland, you know? Well, of course you know, you're the medical researcher. It just occurred to me last night, and I didn't want to leave any stone unturned."

Penelope smiled and patted Corrie's shoulder. Corrie suppressed an urge to back away from the duplicitous woman.

"I'm running every test I can think of, rest assured," she said. "Oh, did you get my message about this afternoon?"

"Yes, thanks for asking me, but I don't think Zeb or I can get away from work right then," Corrie babbled. "But please let us know how it goes."

She stood up and edged toward the door. Penelope moved behind her desk.

"Of course," she said. "I'll tell you everything."

Corrie pumped the pedals of her bike for the last stretch of road. Her cheeks flamed with exertion, and her breath came in short gasps. Class had run later than expected, and a student had held her back with questions about his grades. After calming him as best as she could, Corrie had run to her bike.

Zeb stood in the shade of a scrubby cherry tree next to the wide, sandy beach. Children shouted on the playground behind him, but his eyes never strayed from the ocean. He looked tense and uncomfortable.

Corrie secretly rejoiced. He should be uncomfortable. He'd manipulated her last night, and that wasn't something to brush off lightly.

She leaped off her bike and leaned it against a bike rack then attached her lock with jerky motions.

"Is she here?" she threw over her shoulder at Zeb. She wasn't in the mood for idle chatter, not today. She almost felt her own forehead for a temperature since not talking was so uncharacteristic for her.

"Yes," he said. "She just got into a kayak. What do you want to do?"

Corrie straightened and peered out to sea. Sure enough, Penelope's frizzy hair topped a figure in a bright green kayak. Her paddle dipped on each side with a steady rhythm.

"Unless you brought a kayak with you, we're going to have to swim after her." Corrie strode to the beach with sure steps, Zeb stumbling after her in his haste. She pulled a small vial from her pocket. "Luckily I grabbed some slime the last time we saw a strolia."

Corrie's heart leaped at the thought of swallowing the disgusting slime and diving into the inviting waters of the bay. The sensation of freediving among anemones and jellyfish thrilled her from head to flippers. She wanted to take the slime right now to make sure it worked immediately upon entering the water, but she resisted. Ingesting slime above water resulted in ferocious hallucinations.

Corrie's breath hitched. She was so fixated on stopping Zeb from using his cream as a drug that she hadn't considered that she might be doing the same thing. Was her fascination with being underwater and taking the slime whenever she could a compulsion that she couldn't control?

No, she decided. She might like the effects, but she was only using it today to follow Penelope. They had a job to do, and slime was merely a tool to complete it. Still, the disquieting notion haunted her from the back of her mind where she had shoved it.

At the water's edge, Corrie pushed off her shoes and stripped off her shirt, thankful for the modest yet pretty bra she'd chosen today. She left her shorts on—they wouldn't result in enough drag to worry about—and splashed into the bay with Zeb following her. She glanced at his face once, and his eyes were fixed on the sea. He'd stripped down to his swimsuit so quickly she hadn't seen the motions.

"No flippers," she said with regret. "I didn't think I'd need them today."

"They're a bonus, but not necessary." Zeb flashed her a half-smile that she didn't return, still angry with him. His smile faded, and a part of Corrie regretted stopping that too-infrequent expression of Zeb's. He continued, "We'll swim fast enough to keep up with a kayak."

Corrie nodded and opened the vial. She swallowed the slime in one gag-worthy drink, tossed the vial back to her clothes, then walked briskly through deepening water. When she was waist deep, she knelt and pushed forward.

The water was punishingly cold for a solid minute until the slime kicked in. Zeb dived under the surface and reappeared several strokes away in deeper water. Finally, the temperature rose from iceberg-worthy to pleasant.

"Ready," she called. After a deep breath, she dived under the surface.

Murky green surrounded her, and her heart slowed with the calm that stole over her. She smiled for the first time today—fake smiles for her students not included—and ran her fingers through the water, enjoying the cool flow over her skin.

Zeb appeared in her vision, looking relaxed and happy. He waved at her to follow him. Corrie complied, content to follow

Zeb's unerring sense of direction. He had explained the sensations he felt on his skin and how it translated into a map of the underwater world that she could hardly fathom. It was endlessly fascinating, but Corrie hadn't yet had time to experiment with him. Maybe one day, when they weren't fighting for his life. And when she wasn't so mad at him.

When Zeb's movements changed from loose kicking to a sinuous full-body undulation, Corrie tried to emulate his movements. It took a bit of practice, and she had to kick every so often to keep up with Zeb's effortless motion, but she started to get the hang of this mode of swimming. It was more efficient underwater.

After a few minutes of swimming punctuated by breathing visits to the surface, Zeb stopped. His body stiffened. Corrie swam closer and looked at his face, which was contorted with pleasure and a restraint so strong it looked painful. She clutched his forearm in fear. When he opened his eyes, she pointed to the surface.

On the way up, a strolia streaked by them, its translucent horn glinting in the dim light from the surface. Corrie frowned. Where was it going so quickly? Their movements were usually languid.

"What is it?" Corrie said above water. Zeb's face cleared of his previous expression which was replaced by a frown.

"She's doing the attraction call again." He squeezed his eyes shut. "It's so hard to resist. Every creature in the region will come flocking to her."

"She's up to something. We need to get closer. Can you plug your ears?"

"That will help a bit, but some of the call is vibration-based. I can feel it now." Zeb sighed. "I can resist it, it's just hard."

"You're strong," Corrie said in the face of his discomfort. "You can do it."

Zeb's glance was so open with hope and longing that Corrie shivered. She always forgot how different he was in the water, away from his reserve on land.

"Come on," she said to break the moment. "We need to find out what she's doing."

ZEBALLOS

They plunged into the shallow waves again, and the sounds that had faded to manageable levels above water returned with overwhelming force below. Zeb screwed up his face and pushed fingers in his ears to dampen the sound, but it barely helped. The noise vibrated through his chest and head, threatening to pull him onward without his consent. It helped that they traveled in the same direction as the pull. Zeb didn't know if he could have swum in an opposite direction.

Corrie swam at his side and glanced at him in concern from time to time. He would have appreciated the warming of her cool behavior toward him if he'd been able to concentrate. As it was, all his focus was on slowing his pace to match Corrie's slower swimming, and not racing ahead to discover the unbearably attractive sound that pulsed through his body. It sang of cool waters, his mother's almost-forgotten voice, the taste of salt, Corrie's soft body, the smoothness of a shell, everything he loved most in the world wrapped up in one seductive song.

Corrie's hand tucked itself into the crook of his arm, and his eyes fluttered closed in relief. Her touch grounded him. If the flesh-and-blood Corrie wasn't beside him to turn the song into a pale imitation of the real thing, he would already be at the source.

They were close, now. Zeb sensed the kayak in the distance ahead. Three figures swam underneath, as entranced with the song as he was. Two were strolias, and one looked like an elongated seal with a squashed face. Was it a yatull? He'd only ever seen one during the battle, two months ago, when the pale woman had used one as a mount to ride.

He swam faster, clutching Corrie's hand between his arm and his side so that she trailed behind him like a streamer of kelp. He needed to see what Penelope planned. His stomach dropped at the memory of the pale woman with a wound in her abdomen, and he pulled Corrie along with greater urgency.

Something dipped into the water below the kayak. Zeb frowned, then sound hit him like the force of a whale breaching.

He let go of Corrie's arm and tumbled backward in slow-motion. His head felt like it would explode from pain and pressure, and his body vibrated with deep notes that pulsed through him with an agonizing rhythm. Blindly, he felt Corrie grasp his bicep with her small hands and tug him upward, but he was powerless to help. He kept his fingers firmly in his ears, convinced that they were the only defense between him and greater pain from the noise.

When his head burst from the water, he gasped with relief. The sound still throbbed through his torso and legs, but without pulsing through his head, it was manageable. He treaded water with legs that felt sluggish and heavy, and his bleary eyes looked around.

Corrie stared at him, her eyes wide and her face pale. They were behind an oversized crabbing buoy, and Penelope's kayak was hidden from sight. Corrie put her finger to her lips and swam closer.

"Quiet," she whispered. "Penelope isn't far away. What happened?"

"She put something in the water." Zeb tried to control his ragged breathing. "Some device. It made a horrible noise, so painful. I don't know what it would have done if I hadn't plugged my ears. All my organs feel like someone's punched me in the gut, over and over."

"Your nose is bleeding," Corrie whispered.

Zeb wiped it with the back of his wet hand, then he stiffened.

"There were two strolias and a yatull under there. What happened to them? I can't go under, not while the noise is still there." It continued to thrum through his torso, pummeling his already beleaguered abdomen.

"I'll check." Corrie took a deep breath then sank into the water.

Zeb twisted his mouth—he was supposed to be the one checking out things underwater, not Corrie—then he sighed and focused on breathing regularly. He was lucky to have Corrie here. What would he have done without her support to lead him to the surface? After what he'd done to her last night, he was surprised she was here at all. Who knew he could force people to do things with the power of his voice? In the shadow of the buoy, he considered past events. Had he controlled others?

He didn't generally speak enough to control anyone, and he couldn't think of a time when he'd forced Jules to do anything. He could have, though, at some point. If he didn't realize he was doing it, how could he tell what was Jules' own inclination and what was Zeb's influence?

Zeb shook his head violently. He could do nothing about the past. All he could do now was learn more about this new ability so that he never used it on the people he cared about.

Assuming he lived long enough to make learning worthwhile.

The terrible sound ceased for the first time in minutes, and Zeb's body relaxed. Now that the relentless onslaught had ceased, he felt the faint signal of Corrie's passage through the water grow stronger until she popped up beside him. Her face was pale with horror.

"The strolias are dead," she whispered. "Floating on the surface. I couldn't see the yatull."

Zeb's vision tunneled with his rage. The noise that had incapacitated him had killed defenseless sea creatures. Would it have killed him, too? His breath came short and sharp once more.

"What the hell is she playing at?" he growled. "I need to see."

He dipped down until only his eyes emerged from the water, then he peeked around the side of the buoy. Waves rocked him up and down, and he was confident that his white hair would blend in with the splashing froth from waves hitting the buoy. His skin told him that Corrie treaded water behind.

Penelope's back was to them, but her crimes were clear. Dark red blood dripped down the green kayak in disgusting rivulets that stained the surrounding water with spreading clouds of darkness. Penelope's gloved hand rummaged in the sliced-open gut of the yatull draped over her kayak like a disturbing parody of a blanket.

She extracted a glistening organ from the yatull's innards and shoved it inside a plastic bag with built-in twist ties. Deftly, she wrapped it up, placed it in a cooler strapped behind her, and snapped off her gloves. With a heave, she pushed the yatull off her kayak. It slid into the water with barely a ripple and bobbed in the waves.

Penelope splashed her kayak to remove bloodstains then dug her paddle into the water. With sure strokes, she turned the kayak toward shore. Zeb took a deep breath and sunk under the water, Corrie beside him. They stared at each other for two long minutes until Corrie pointed at the surface.

"What is she doing?" Corrie gasped when they emerged, Penelope's kayak long gone. "She killed that yatull. For what? What does she need the stomach for?"

"Is that what it was?" Zeb's rage had chilled into an icy numbness. Without qualms, without any visible reservation, Penelope had attracted sea creatures, killed them, and gutted one for her own hideous experiments. Zeb cursed himself for trusting her. If he weren't careful, it would be him next on her laboratory counter, his stomach sliced open and his eyes glazed with death. He might be dying, but he wasn't willing to do it on Penelope's whim.

"She must be looking for something," Corrie said. "What do we know? She has a device that kills sea creatures, or at least incapacitates them. I wonder how that works. What makes you different from me that you are so affected, and I can't even hear it? It must be the lower frequency or something. Although I did feel queasy, so maybe a part of me could sense it."

By the end of her words Corrie's teeth started to chatter. The slime must be wearing off.

"Let me take the bodies deeper," Zeb said with a worried glance at Corrie's pale face. "I'll be quick, then I'll swim us back. Okay?"

"Yes. We don't want anyone to see the creatures."

Zeb struck out for the floating yatull and collected three strolias on the way. With his arms full—and careful to avoid the sharp horns of the unicorn fish—Zeb dived deep into the bay. When he was near the bottom, he released his cargo, and the bodies drifted to the seafloor. With any luck, they would remain at the bottom until passing fish and invertebrates cleaned the flesh off their bones.

When he returned to Corrie, she was clinging to the buoy's anchor chain with a trembling hand.

"Hold onto my neck," Zeb instructed. "I'll swim us back. Tap my shoulder when you need a breath."

Corie wrapped her arms around his neck, and he dived under water. After a moment, Corrie's legs wrapped around his middle. He closed his eyes at her warmth along the length of his back. His world might be full of wrongs, but Corrie was something right.

Once Corrie was wrapped up in Zeb's shirt on the beach and her full-body shudders had reduced to shivers, her eyebrows contracted.

"We have to stop Penelope," she said. "We can't let her kill any more creatures. They don't deserve to die for her experiments with no oversight. It's an affront to humane practices and to science. There's no way she would be allowed to slice open animals for experimenting, not without jumping through massive hurdles. And she'd never get permission for a creature like the yatull. They're unknown to science, and we don't even know how many there are. What if she captured and killed the last one in existence? This isn't the eighteen hundreds. We have regulations in place for that sort of nonsense. Not to mention the pale woman she gutted. That's assault and possible manslaughter if she didn't survive. It's wrong on so many levels, I can't keep count."

"How do we stop her?" Zeb threw a piece of driftwood into the water with a vehement motion. It cut through a wave with a satisfying splash.

"Getting that device away from her would be a start." Corrie pulled out some folded papers from her backpack and shoved them at Zeb. He took them and glanced over the contents.

"What's this?" he asked.

"Blueprints for making something called a 'stun gun'." Corrie huffed. "Clearly, whatever device Penelope was using today. But instead of stunning, it kills. She must have dialed the device up to eleven. She clearly can't be trusted with a stun gun, so we need to get it away from her. She probably keeps it at her house. By the looks of her garage, she takes her work home with her. And then she wouldn't have to explain the stun gun to any of her students or colleagues."

"Then we steal it." Zeb glanced at Corrie and saw the same determination in her eyes. She nodded slowly.

"Let's stake out her house."

A car sat ticking in Penelope's driveway when they drove past. Zeb parked a block away. He reached into the backseat and pulled out a black toque. At Corrie's questioning glance, he pointed at his white hair.

"It stands out."

She nodded and pulled the zipper of Zeb's coat tighter around her neck. Her lips were still pale from too long in cold ocean water without strolia slime, and Zeb silently cursed. Why did he keep leading Corrie into dangerous situations? To be fair, he never "led" her anywhere, and he was pretty sure that any attempt to convince her to stay behind would meet with the same anger as last night's fiasco. But still, being near him always seemed to bring her closer to danger, and he didn't know how to fix that.

They walked past Corrie's bike in the bed of Zeb's pickup and sauntered with forced casualness down the quiet road. Near Penelope's house, Corrie pulled out her phone and pretended to look at a map while Zeb glanced toward the house.

"She's unloading her trunk," he said quietly. "Good. I bet the device is in there." He watched Penelope bustle between house and vehicle, then his heart leaped. "She's getting in the car. Yes, she's leaving."

"That was almost too easy," Corrie said. "Quick, tie your shoelace or something. We want to look unnoticeable."

Zeb dutifully bent to his shoe and pretended to fiddle with the lace. Corrie busied herself with her phone, although she was so bundled up in his coat that she was almost unrecognizable. Penelope's car roared by, and Zeb sighed in relief then stood.

"Okay," Corrie said in her normal voice. "Let's get this device out of Penelope's hands. It'll be a start, anyway."

They strolled with measured strides to Penelope's front door. Zeb tried to make his steps look natural, but it was difficult to avoid jerky motions when he was this incensed. Corrie felt under the doormat, above the door lintel, then she pointed at a fake-looking rock in the garden. She swooped down and emerged triumphant with a key.

"People are so predictable," she said. "Come on, let's get this device."

She unlocked the door and slipped inside. Zeb followed with a last glance backward, but the street was deserted. He softly closed the door.

An explosion of sound nearly stopped his heart. Corrie jumped so high that she could have looked him straight in the eye. Her focus, however, was on the barking, thigh-high mop that stood in their way.

Penelope's dog growled, and his long, soft fur did nothing to soften the vision of menace. He barked again, clearly warning them to leave or suffer the consequences. Corrie flattened herself against Zeb's front.

"We should leave," she said in a high-pitched voice. The dog growled again, his low rumble filling Zeb's ears. "He doesn't like us here."

Zeb recalled the fox from work. No one had been able to settle it until he'd tried his calming hum. Was that the same thing as compulsion? He wasn't sure if there were a difference, and right now, he didn't care.

His chest vibrated with a low rumble. Corrie stiffened but didn't shift from her position against his front, her eyes glued to the dog. Zeb continued to build strength on his hum, and gradually, the dog's growls grew quiet. He sniffed the air with interest and chuffed.

Zeb's hum faltered when his knees grew weak. Damn it. Now was not the time for one of his episodes. He clenched his fists and willed the tunneling darkness away.

The dog's hackles rose again, and Corrie gasped.

Zeb took a deep breath, then another. Slowly, the hum in his chest grew louder again, and the dog's growls quieted.

Corrie melted in front of him, and Zeb wasn't far behind.

"Come on," he whispered past his humming. "The dog will let us look now."

"Wait," she hissed and twisted her head around his body. "Do you hear a car?"

A roaring noise cut off suddenly as the engine died. Zeb grabbed Corrie's forearms and steered her past the dog. He reached out and gave the animal a swift pat on the head.

"Good dog," he whispered. The dog thumped his tail on the floor in response.

They fled through the kitchen and out a door that led to a wooden patio. They crouched down under the windows and edged along the side. The dog barked again, but this time, its noises were happy. Penelope was home.

Zeb followed Corrie around the house with a sinking heart. What would they do now? How could they stop Penelope from terrorizing the creatures of his mother's world?

At his car, Corrie whirled around.

"This isn't over," she growled. "We can't go to the police without telling them about the creatures, which is a whole can of worms I assume we don't want to get into." At Zeb's fervent headshake, she continued. "We can try to get the device again when Penelope's gone, but what's stopping her from building another one?" Corrie paced on the sidewalk with her fist pounding her palm. "No, we need to take her down, hit her where it hurts."

"What are you saying?" Zeb hadn't thought Corrie was so bloodthirsty. That he felt horrified at the suggestion of harming Penelope reassured him, oddly. It meant that he wasn't as similar to the pale folk as he had been fearing.

"Don't look at me like that. I don't want to kill her!" Corrie crossed her arms. "No, there are other ways. We can ruin her career. To someone like Penelope, that would be the ultimate blow. She wouldn't have funding to siphon to her side projects, she wouldn't have access to lab equipment—it's a perfect solution, really."

"How would we sabotage her career?"

Corrie tapped her foot and stared into the distance.

"The ethics board," she said finally. "Penelope is doing really fishy things in her garage. I'm certain they aren't approved. If she's investigated, she won't come off well. That might be our key." She nodded with decision. "I'll go to the office first thing tomorrow with my findings."

Zeb wasn't convinced that stopping Penelope's career would halt her designs on the creatures, but he didn't have another option to offer. He spread his hands helplessly.

"Okay, let's take her down with paperwork."

CORRIE

Corrie straightened her blouse and pressed sweating palms against her skirt. She wanted to look as respectable as possible, so she'd gone business casual. Hopefully, that would help her be taken seriously in the ethics board office.

She pushed the frosted glass door open and walked with a straight back to the counter. A woman in a swiveling office chair glanced at her.

"Good morning," Corrie said brightly. "I'd like to register a breach of ethics by a member of the university. How can I do that anonymously?"

The woman nodded with sympathy. "We take all complaints under the strictest confidence. Is it a professor, and you're worried about getting a bad mark?"

"Something like that," Corrie hedged. "But I can't stand by and let these animals get hurt."

"I understand." The woman pulled out a form from a stack beside her desk and clicked her pen expectantly. "Your name?"

Corrie answered the woman's questions, detailing Penelope's name, address, and the cages she'd found in her garage. The woman made tsking noises but refrained from comment until she'd finished filling out the form.

"We'll take this seriously, I promise you," the woman finally said. "If your allegations are true, this is a serious breach of ethics. I have no paperwork allowing Penelope Stroud to perform experiments on animals at her residence, and ethics tend to be flouted with no oversight."

Corrie heaved a sigh of relief. There was more than one way to skin a cat—or gut a fish—and hopefully this would put a monkey wrench in Penelope's plans. If nothing else, it would keep her busy until she and Zeb figured out another plan of attack.

"It's too bad," the woman mused while she fastened

together the papers of the form with a yellow paperclip. "Penelope's had it rough. I wonder if she finally snapped, and now she can't see right from wrong."

"What do you mean?"

"It was years ago, now," the woman whispered. Corrie guessed that she didn't receive many visitors in her office. "According to the grapevine, Penelope's husband and daughter were murdered."

Corrie pulled in a sharp breath. The anger and fear that she'd been harboring for Penelope were still finely honed in her mind, but now a layer of horrified sympathy draped over top.

"Yes, it was terrible," the woman said in a hushed tone. "Penelope was found raving about white sea devils, blaming them for the murders, promising to kill them all. The shock unhinged her, as it would anyone, I'm sure. After a time, she recovered, and she's been a wonderful faculty member ever since." The woman shook her head and tapped the form on the desk. "Maybe she finally snapped. It's understandable, but no matter the reason, we can't have faculty running amok with regulations. Someone must ensure that experiments are run ethically."

Corrie nodded and thanked the woman in a daze. Her head whirled with this new information. Penelope's husband and daughter had been murdered by pale folk. The rage in her face after slicing the pale woman's stomach finally made sense. No wonder she was so keen to join Zeb on his quest to find the Seamount. She wanted revenge for the murder of her family.

Corrie shivered. Penelope wanted to hurt the pale folk, but did she even know which ones had killed her loved ones? How indiscriminate would she be in her pursuit of vengeance? And, most importantly of all, what were her feelings toward Zeb?

The next few days were a whirlwind of work for Corrie. The classes she was teaching were in full swing, the marking was piling up, she had obligations to show a new student how a piece of lab equipment worked, and she needed to complete experiments on her own project so that her supervisor wouldn't get after her. She cycled to the university early every morning and came home in the dark each night, too tired to do more than eat and sleep. Guilt gnawed at her in her spare moments, and her stomach tied itself in knots when she thought about Zeb alone in the *Clicker*, counting his days. She had called him with her news about Penelope's family, and although they had discussed it at length, it didn't give them anything definitive except another reason to stay away from her.

At last, she made it home on Thursday evening at dinnertime. After a quick gulp of tinned beans on dry toast, she threw her leg over her bike seat and pedaled toward the marina. She stopped at a grocery store on the way and loaded up with supplies then turned her wheels toward the water.

The *Clicker* was where it always was, and her insides flopped a little at the sight. She'd missed Zeb the past few days. As much as her brain told her she should still be furious with his mental manipulation, the rest of her told it to take a hike.

Corrie rapped on the *Clicker*'s rusty blue hull to announce her presence. She pushed her bags of groceries onto the deck. As she hauled herself up through the opening in the bulwark, Zeb popped his head out of the door. He gave her a shy smile, which on Zeb was tantamount to open arms. She grinned back, despite her brain's misgivings.

"Hi," he said, as eloquent as ever.

"Hi to you, too." Should she get the elephant out of the room first? It was probably smart. "Look, about the other night, when you used your new power on me."

Zeb twisted his face, but whether out of guilt or a dislike of his new "power", Corrie wasn't sure.

"I never knew I could do that," he said. "I didn't mean to.

I'm sorry. I've been trying to learn more about it, so that I know when I do it and when I don't. That way, I'll never use it on you again."

The last of Corrie's reservations melted away. She wasn't very good at holding grudges, anyway.

"Good, because it was a crappy thing to do. You might have noticed, I'm not a big fan of manipulation. Too much of that in my past. The second that sort of thing comes out again, I'm gone, sickness or no. Got it?"

Zeb nodded until she was afraid he would put a crick in his neck.

"Good," she said. "Then let's move on." She nudged the bags of groceries with her foot. "I brought food from every food group I could think of, plus a bunch of different multivitamins. Let's figure out what you're lacking."

Zeb's jaw tightened as he gazed at the groceries.

"Thank you," he said finally. "You're good to me."

Corrie shrugged, suddenly uncomfortable. It wasn't like Zeb to get emotional, especially on land. She wanted to throw her arms around him and give him a big hug, but she didn't feel ready for that. It was one thing to put the manipulation episode in the past, but another thing entirely to immediately jump into something with Zeb.

"Come on," she said. "Let's eat."

They squeezed around the galley table and Corrie spread out her purchases. Vegetables and fruit of every description, cans of artichokes, tins of oysters, marmite, cheeses with unusual mold blooms—Corrie had bought it all. Most of her month's food budget had been spent on the splurge, but she didn't mind. Whatever Zeb didn't want, she would take home and figure out how to eat. As for the rest of the month, well, she'd survived on ramen before.

Taste-testing the food was the most fun they'd had in a while, and Corrie was sad to reach the end of the choices.

"If I taste something, my body will know what to crave,

right?" Zeb said dubiously. He slowly chewed a chanterelle mushroom. "Like dried jellyfish."

"Probably." Corrie shrugged. "I'm not a nutritionist, but that makes sense. Nothing worked?"

"No. But I do have some more translations, if you want to hear them."

"Why didn't you say so before?" Corrie sat up straight, their food experiment forgotten. "Bring them out!"

"It's not a story, this time, and not more of my mother's journey." Zeb pulled out a battered notebook. "I got Krista to translate the back stuff with the scratchings. There's a translation of the script into Greek. Now, we can piece together some of their words. Hopefully, it will be enough to figure out whatever the crosscurrent sign says. We have everything else translated from the notebook, so I got Krista to send it back so we can look at the scratchings for ourselves."

Zeb spread out the notebook, and Corrie leaned over it. She traced her finger across the rough lines of indecipherable script.

"Well?" she said with an expectant look at Zeb. "What does it say?"

"It's—" Zeb swallowed. His voice was husky when he spoke next. "It's a letter to me."

Corrie held her breath as Zeb spoke words from his mother.

To my slippery minnow, Zeballos, I hope that one day you will read this and know more of yourself. I know you think my tales are only stories, but one day you will learn the truth. As much as that world is a part of you, you are yourself, the beautiful boy I am so proud to call my own. Know your history, but make your future. I love you from the surface to the depths of the sea.

Corrie fell into a dreamy trance listening to Zeb's smooth voice. It wasn't a compulsion this time—or at least, she didn't think so—but she rarely heard Zeb talk uninterrupted. He was easy to listen to.

Zeb blinked a few times and cleared his throat. Corrie jerked upright, her face flushed from realizing how zoned out she'd become while listening to Zeb.

"I've been thinking a lot about the clues over the past few days," Zeb continued after he'd finished reading. Corrie followed his lead and ignored the brightness in his eyes. "And I think we should take our next trip to one of the rises where the crosscurrent sign might be. I know there are a bunch of them, but without more information, we have to search each one."

"Would it be crazy to go out overnight?" Even as Corrie said it, she doubted herself. To travel all that way in the dark? Surely that wasn't wise.

To her surprise, Zeb looked thoughtful.

"Not really. I know these waters well. As long as we follow main shipping channels, it should be fine." He stared at her. "Do you really mean it? You want to check it out tonight?"

"Yeah," she breathed. "It's not like I have time during the day, these days. And we need to get moving on these clues. We don't have forever." When Zeb's face tightened, Corrie inwardly cursed her loose tongue. "I'm sorry, Zeb, I didn't mean—"

"No, you're right." He sighed and looked at a clock on the wall. "If we leave now, we can make it to the first rise by midnight. You can hold the boat steady, and I'll quickly taste for sulfur."

Corrie nodded, looking surer than she felt. It seemed crazy to go out at night, but also a thrilling adventure. Would they find the answers they sought under cover of darkness? Zeb didn't need light to find his way underwater.

Zeb started the engine, and Corrie unhitched the boat then hopped aboard. They puttered out of the marina, their engine noise loud in the stillness of the evening. The sun was setting, casting orange rays across a molten sea of rolling waves, and Corrie's heart leaped with pleasure. When Corrie looked back to enjoy the sight of their gleaming wake, a small motorboat leaving another marina nearby caught her eye.

Zeb turned the engine to full throttle, and they roared west. After ten minutes, Corrie glanced behind them again. The motorboat was still there, no closer and no further away. Her forehead creased.

"Zeb, did you notice that motorboat behind us?" she asked. Zeb pointed at the wheel, and Corrie held it steady while he stepped outside and looked back. When he returned, she said, "A motorboat can go a lot faster than us, can't it?"

"Yeah, way faster. Maybe they're crabbing." Zeb didn't look like he believed his own words, but he took the wheel again without further comment.

Corrie checked behind them five minutes later. Sure enough, the motorboat continued to follow them.

"I'm probably being silly," she said. "But I think they're following us. Am I just being paranoid from our previous encounters? Who would care enough about our movements to follow us?"

"Penelope," Zeb said. "She might care."

"And we already know that her scruples are questionable at best, and murderous at worst." Corrie bit her lip. "Maybe she's onto us. We haven't talked to her for a week, whereas before we kept coming with translations. Maybe she suspects."

"That's why we're going around this island." Zeb pointed at a forested island large enough to cover them from the other side. When they were almost past it, Zeb made a hard left and aimed for the western end of the island.

"How did she find us?" Corrie mused aloud. She snapped her fingers. "The GPS wristband. Do you think she can track us with that, or have I been watching too many spy thrillers?"

Zeb glanced at her with concern. He unstrapped the band from his arm and held it out to her.

"I don't know. Maybe. How can we check it?"

"We can't." Corrie held the wristband up gingerly. "But

what do you bet she has the GPS data uploading to her own computer?" She sighed. "Now, what do we do with it?"

"Throw it overboard," Zeb said. "Then we're heading back to the marina. We'll have to try the next clue another day."

Corrie sighed in disappointment and walked to the bulwark to toss the wristband into the sea. Every day that passed was another day Zeb wouldn't get back. It hadn't escaped her notice that his hands trembled on the wheel, and that his hair had been wet when she'd arrived.

"Okay," she said when she returned, defeated. "But we'll have to go out on Saturday for sure."

ZEBALLOS

Corrie disappeared from the wheelhouse and returned with the loose papers of translations and clues that they'd amassed. She pulled out a chart from the pile and spread it on the dashboard.

Zeb glanced at it but brought his eyes back to the windshield. Driving in the dark was risky. He much preferred swimming in the dark, where his skin sense told him exactly what was around him. In the boat, he felt almost blind.

Corrie hummed absently as she worked, occasionally chattering her observations out loud. Zeb smiled as he drove. It was comfortable having Corrie up here. He'd missed her this week.

"We've almost got it." She put her pen down and stared at him. "We didn't need to check out a random rise tonight, after all. I applied a little logic and figured it out. Here." Corrie pointed at an empty blue spot on the chart. "There are five small rises in this area. The rise we're looking for could be any of them, right? But if we remember that we want to stay south of hydrothermal vent activity." Corrie circled a few points on her map. "That rules out these two. And Clicker mentioned that she watched the bottom of the northern shoveler ducks' migration, and according to my online sources, they rarely come lower than the forty-eighth parallel, which leaves this rise here." She jabbed her finger in triumph on a marking on her map. "If we go here, and dive down to read the pale folk script etched on Clicker's rock, it should tell us where the Seamount is."

Zeb stared at Corrie, his concerns about driving in the dark forgotten. His normally slow heartbeat picked up pace.

"We almost know where the Seamount is?" He breathed heavily, then huffed in disbelief. Should they turn around right now and figure this out tonight?

The darkness, his bone-weariness, and their tail convinced him to wait until morning. A few hours wouldn't make or break him, he hoped. And he needed his strength, because once they found the Seamount, he still had to convince the pale folk to talk to him and help him.

But still, finding the Seamount was beyond his wildest dreams. He wondered suddenly what his mother would have said if she were still alive. Why had she left in the first place? Would she be happy that Zeb was finding his roots, or would she be appalled that he was returning to somewhere she had fled? For the thousandth time, Zeb wished he had asked more questions before she passed.

Corrie laughed with delight and grabbed a fresh sheet of loose paper.

"This is it. This is really it. I can't believe it. I'm going to write down all the clues and locations in a row, so we have a record of your mother's journey. And when we find the final location, we'll write it after the last clue." Corrie scribbled furiously, then she put her hand on her heart. "I don't know, Zeb. I might explode from excitement."

Zeb surprised himself by laughing out loud.

"The source of our mythical creatures," he said, still chuckling. "You've been waiting for this day for months. Try to avoid getting my wheelhouse covered in Corrie bits."

Corrie grinned with that bright happiness that Zeb loved.

"I'll do my best, but no promises. Okay, here's the plan. We go back to the marina, get some sleep—I'll bunk here tonight, if that's all right—then at first light we'll head out. Let's get this solved. Maybe by this time tomorrow we'll have the answers we need."

"If we do," Zeb said, his eyes on the dark water ahead but his attention fully on Corrie's infectious happiness beside him. "Then drinks are on me tomorrow."

The motorboat that had been tailing them veered off once Zeb turned the bow toward the marina. Zeb nodded in grim satisfaction. Tomorrow, they would leave so early that he couldn't imagine Penelope would be watching them, and since they didn't have the tracker anymore, she would have a hard time finding them in the vastness of the ocean.

Corrie completed her master list of clues and locations with a flourish and held it up to admire it.

"Wow," she said. "I can't believe we did it."

"Me neither. We're almost here, could you tie us up?"

"Sure thing." Corrie disappeared into the darkness outside the wheelhouse as Zeb eased into their berth. She was almost as comfortable on the *Clicker* now as Jules was, and he liked how well she had adapted to being on the water. This was his element, and sharing it with her was an exquisite pleasure.

Zeb turned off the engine, and Corrie hopped on board once more. They met in the galley, and Zeb's brain stalled. It was late, but not that late. Corrie was staying the night on the boat. What should they do now? What would she expect?

"Beer?" he said, feeling lame, but what else should he have said? To his relief, Corrie nodded with a relaxed expression.

"Perfect. We should get to sleep soon since we're leaving early tomorrow, but I'm too jazzed to go to bed yet. Maybe a beer will calm me down."

Zeb opened the tiny fridge and removed two cans from the interior. It was far emptier than when Jules was on board, despite the groceries that Corrie had brought. He took the cans to the galley table where Corrie lounged.

"Food?" he offered. "We have vegetables of all kinds, canned clams, dried shitakes…"

Corrie laughed and waved her hand. "I'm good, thanks. Do you find yourself craving any of them?"

"No." Zeb cracked his can open and took a sip. The cool beer slid down his throat pleasantly, but not as well as dried jellyfish did. "Unfortunately. But I'm taking multivitamins, just in case."

"Good." Corrie stared at her can for a moment, then she glanced at Zeb. "Have you been practicing your manipulation trick?"

Zeb winced at Corrie's words. "Do we have to call it that?"

"Sorry." Corrie fidgeted with her fingers. "Forcing voice? Compulsion tone?"

"Sure, compulsion tone. And yes, I've tried. It's hard without testing it on someone else, though."

Corrie worried her bottom lip with her teeth. Zeb wanted to lean over and release the lip with a kiss.

"You can try it on me," she said finally.

Zeb's eyes widened. Was she serious? He'd never seen her so mad as the other night, when he'd tried to make her give him the cream.

"You need to practice," she said firmly. "So you know when you're doing it and when you're not." She took a deep breath and released it with a sigh. "I trust you, Zeb. Just don't abuse that trust, okay?"

Zeb shook his head violently.

"Never," he whispered then cleared his throat. "Okay, what should I make you do?"

"Something boring, but that I wouldn't likely do on my own. Surprise me so I don't subconsciously do it myself."

Zeb's palms were sweating. He had to get this right to prove to Corrie—and himself—that he could use this new ability with finesse and in full knowledge of his actions. He needed the control so he wouldn't force anyone without meaning to.

His breathing slowed, and he centered himself to prepare. When he spoke, it was accompanied by a deep hum that vibrated through his chest, too low for Corrie to hear. His words, layered on top of the hum, took on a smooth, weighted cadence.

"You want a chart, Corrie. A chart of Northern Vancouver

Island. They're right behind you. Grab one and spread it out on the table. Pick up your hands and twist your body to find the charts."

Corrie's eyes grew glazed as he spoke, and Zeb's stomach shriveled with disgust at his power over her. She turned and shuffled through charts in a pouch on the wall until she found the right one, then she unfolded it and ran her hands over the creases until the chart covered the little table. When her hands were in her lap once more, Zeb ceased humming. Corrie blinked and frowned at the chart, then she stared at Zeb.

"I guess it worked," she said hoarsely.

Zeb couldn't meet her eyes. His fingers clenched and unclenched. Now that he had shown her how easily he could control her, what would she feel? Their relationship was already filled with barriers, but this one might prove to be the deepest trench between them. He wished he hadn't given in to her suggestion. He could have practiced his ability on anyone else except Corrie.

She shuffled closer and laid a hand on his forearm.

"It's okay," she whispered. "I'm okay. From the way your face is all twisted up, you're feeling guilty and weird about using your compulsion tone on me. And, you know what? That expression is the best evidence I have that you'll never use it on me without my permission."

Zeb tore his eyes away from the chart and risked looking into Corrie's eyes. She was close now, close enough that the warmth of her body radiated to his. Her golden-brown eyes were so warm and full of life, and Zeb's vision narrowed until they were all he could see. He glanced down at her lips, plump and soft-looking, and his breath quickened.

Swiftly, like a darting minnow, Corrie leaned into him. Their lips met, and nothing was more right than her warm softness against his mouth, her roving hands, her chest as he pressed her into the bench. She leaned backward with a gasp of pleasure, and he covered her body with his despite the small space between table and bench back. Her leg wrapped around his, and he groaned at the exquisite torture of her closeness.

His breathing grew shallow. At first, it was merely a side effect of Corrie's body pressed against his, but when his chest squeezed with uncomfortable tightness, his eyes popped open. He sat back and wheezed, fighting to pull enough air into his lungs.

Corrie wriggled upright and placed a hand on his shoulder.

"What's going on?" she said, her expression of frustration morphing into one of worry. "Hey, stay calm. You're okay. Steady breaths. In and out, in and out."

Zeb sucked in air with frantic heaving. His stomach cramped painfully, and he pushed his fist into the cramp. Corrie's eyes flicked down, then she slid off the bench and ran to the galley. Zeb tried to breathe regularly, although the pain in his stomach made it hard to concentrate, and panic licked at his mind. He clutched the edge of the table with both hands.

Corrie raced back with something clenched in her fist. She leaned over and held up a piece of dried jellyfish.

"Can I tuck this in your cheek?" she said. "Just so your body knows it's coming? I don't want to get in the way of your breathing."

Zeb nodded quickly, his mouth salivating despite his ragged breaths. He opened his lips and Corrie carefully placed the piece between his teeth and cheek. The flavor seeped onto his tongue even without chewing, and he closed his eyes to better appreciate it.

Zeb's next few breaths managed to pull in more air than before, and each breath was a little longer. His pounding heart was suddenly louder than his gasps. When he finally felt he wasn't fighting for every molecule of oxygen, he cautiously chewed the piece of jellyfish, even as his body rebelled with cramping. When he swallowed the piece, his mouth opened involuntarily, and Corrie placed another piece on his tongue.

The cramps slowly faded, and Zeb was able to release his

death-grip on the table's edge. Corrie stared at him with a pale face. The bag of his dried jellyfish sat on the table. Zeb looked at it with longing and loathing in equal parts.

"Thanks for helping," he muttered. "Having a hard time breathing was new. I'm sorry for interrupting things."

Corrie darted her hand out and squeezed his quickly. "Tomorrow we'll figure this out. Everything changes tomorrow."

Zeb nodded. His body was a mess—leftover pain from his episode, the weariness that constantly plagued him, heat that still throbbed from his previous proximity to Corrie—and he knew the moment between them had passed.

"We should get some rest before our early morning." Corrie pulled her phone out from her pocket and checked her email. Her eyes widened. "I got an email earlier from the ethics board, but we were so busy that I hadn't checked. They said that proceedings have started to investigate Penelope's unethical conduct. Depending on what they find, it might be grounds for dismissal." Corrie looked at Zeb with shining eyes. "That would take away Penelope's funding, her access to equipment, everything. She would be hamstrung in her search for the Seamount, in studying you, all of that. It's not perfect, but it's an important step toward stopping her for good."

A burning glow of purpose filled Zeb's chest. Whatever Penelope had planned for the Seamount, it wasn't good. If Zeb could help his mother's people, then he would in any way he could.

"Good," he said. "And when we get back tomorrow, I'll find a way to steal the device from her. We might not stop her for good, but if we put up enough barriers, maybe she'll give up."

Corrie graced him with her brilliant smile, and his stomach flopped over.

"We've got this," she said. "Tomorrow, you'll be cured and Penelope stopped. The future is bright, Zeb."

She reached out her hand again to clasp his, and Zeb felt the truth of her words resonate deep within him. Tomorrow, his life would start again.

Zeb dived into the oily waters of the marina for a quick swim before bed. The episode had robbed him of any shred of composure he'd had, and he needed to rest for their mission tomorrow. When he returned, Corrie was in the other cabin with her door closed. Zeb entered his own cabin, but sleep eluded him for a long while. Imagining Corrie on the other side of the thin wall was distracting.

His dreams were of wild waves and crashing water against rocks. Throughout, his mother hummed, out of sight but as familiar as the sea.

JULES

Jules had woken in a sweat from a dream of Zeb's gaunt face being nibbled by piranhas until only his reproachful eyes remained. He'd stayed awake until the autumnal skies brightened, desperately thinking of ways to help Zeb. Jules had been too immersed in his new life to bother with his old friend, and his subconscious had reminded him of how wrong that was.

What could he do? He wasn't a veterinarian like Adrianna, or a scientist like Corrie, or even clever like Trip. He could make food taste good, but that was about it.

But he couldn't sit around while Zeb withered away to nothing. Byssa Sweetcurrent crossed his mind, her blond roots bright in his memory. Or were they white roots?

Too many signs pointed to Byssa and her friends being whatever Zeb was. If they knew what was wrong with Zeb… Jules' heart thumped faster. Could Byssa have a solution to Zeb's illness? Could Jules be sitting on answers?

He needed to find out if Byssa really was someone like Zeb. If she was half as secretive as his friend was, she wouldn't take a direct confrontation well, and Jules couldn't afford to mess up this chance.

Jules twisted his face in thought. Maybe if he followed her after work today. That was weird and creepy, he knew, but Zeb's life was at stake. He would have to be careful to stay out of sight, that was all.

Jules went through the motions of his morning classes in a daze, his mind whirling through his upcoming plans. During dinner rush at the Crispy Prawn, he tried his hardest to act normally around Byssa. Luckily, it was so busy that neither of them had much time for idle chatter, and Jules could pass off his nervous sweat as the byproduct of hard work.

When Byssa called out a farewell at the kitchen's door, Jules gave her a minute's head start then grabbed his coat and slunk out behind her. Byssa's red raincoat was disappearing around a corner as she trudged down the street through the dark drizzle, and Jules hurried after her with his own hood up against the rain.

"This is stupid," he muttered to himself. The swish of wet tires on pavement drowned out his words. "She'll be going home now. It's late and dark."

He'd started this crazy stalking, though, and he would carry out with his half-baked plan since he was in the thick of it. The thought of Zeb bolstered his courage, and he continued to follow Byssa's red coat toward the ocean.

At the waterfront facing English Bay, Byssa walked straight toward a tall figure with a shock of long white hair standing beside a lamppost. Jules walked past with his head down to avoid detection, then he ducked behind a large hedge nearby and strained his ears to listen.

"You're finally here," Byssa's friend Lune said. "I thought you weren't going to show."

"Work was crazy busy today." Byssa pushed back her hood and tipped her head to allow raindrops to coat her face. "I can't wait to get wet."

"My colleague at work tried to give me her old flip flops because I said I didn't have any." Lune's voice dripped with amusement. "Could you imagine more uncomfortable footwear? My toes wouldn't stand for it."

Byssa chuckled. "Your feet aren't made for those, that's for sure. Mine would be okay, but they're still not great."

"Do you ever think about what you'd do if someone found out about you?" Lune's voice was contemplative. Jules sneaked a glance through the branches at the pair. Byssa faced the water, and her expression was thoughtful.

"I don't know," she said. "Probably move to a new town."

"What?" Lune sounded scandalized. "You'd uproot your whole life? Why wouldn't you use your song? It's the simplest solution. That's what I'd do."

"You know I'm not very good at it. Besides, I don't like using it on people. It feels underhanded. Sneaky."

"But if someone found out…" Lune let the sentence trail off.

Byssa sighed. "I don't know. Cross that bridge if I get to it, I guess. Now, are we going to jabber all night, or are we going for a swim?"

The two women walked toward the beach. Jules remained behind his hedge, his heart pounding with the revelations of the past few minutes. Byssa and Lune were definitely something, and he'd bet everything in his meager bank account that they were just like Zeb.

But Byssa was skittish beyond reason about anyone knowing what she was. How could Jules approach Byssa without forcing her to run for the hills or using her 'song' on him? Jules didn't know what that meant, but it didn't sound good.

This mission would take greater delicacy than he'd banked on. He would have to think carefully about his plan of attack. Thinking and planning weren't his best skills, but for Zeb, he would make this work. He had to.

CORRIE

Corrie's phone alarm jangled near her ear when the sky was still a deep blue with the coming dawn. She yawned hugely, then her brain caught up with the events of yesterday. She leaped out of bed and pulled her discarded jeans on as fast as she could manage. Today they would find the Seamount. She didn't know whether to be excited or terrified, so she settled for both at once. Her heart could hardly keep up.

She sent a few emails to the university, pleading a sick day. Then she splashed her face with cold water, pulled her hair into a ponytail, and threw open the cabin door. Zeb's door was still closed, so she hammered on it.

"Wake up, Zeb," she called. "Let's get cracking. Answers await."

She bounced into the galley and rummaged in the cupboard for food. Her searching hands uncovered bread and peanut butter, so she toasted two slices while she waited for Zeb. When he emerged, yawning and rubbing tired eyes in his too-thin face, Corrie's heart clenched. She reminded herself that today they would fix him. What the multivitamins couldn't do, the Seamount hopefully would. She would get them there, even if it took some pressure on her part. Zeb needed steering, sometimes, for his own good.

"Toast," she said brightly. "Eat up, then we'll go. It's a long trip out there. I've already called in sick to the university and texted Adrianna about your work, too. She'll make your excuses." When Zeb simply blinked at her barrage of words, she clapped her hands. "Chop, chop!"

He shook his head as if to clear it and accepted the plate of toast. Corrie grabbed her own and munched it as she walked to the galley table. Her eyes raked over the furniture, and her heart squeezed again, but this time with a different emotion.

"Did you move the clues somewhere?" she asked Zeb. He

followed her into the small space and looked around.

"No, we left the master list on the table last night. Why, isn't it here?"

Corrie set her plate down and picked up charts and pieces of paper, shaking each to be sure. When she had gone through the pile, her breathing was unsteady.

"I don't know where it is."

"It's not a big deal," Zeb said calmly. "It's probably under something, that's all. You can redo it while we're underway."

Corrie scanned the small room, and her eyes fell on the doorway. She was probably wrong, but what if she weren't?

"You never lock the door, do you?" she said.

"No. I don't have anything worth stealing, so I don't bother." Zeb frowned at her. "What are you saying?"

Corrie raced out of the room, heart hammering.

"That list of locations was worth stealing," she called over her shoulder. "To Penelope, at least. And she knows where you're parked. What if she came here last night to investigate after we ditched the GPS? What if she took the list?"

Corrie skidded to a halt at the edge of the bulwark. Her brain took a moment to process what she saw. When the blood trail penetrated her mind, her stomach roiled.

Zeb stopped beside her. When he saw the bloody woman lying on the dock below them, ghostly pale in a flowing dress the color of kelp, he leaped over the gunwale and dropped to his knees beside her.

"She's still alive," he said hoarsely. He glanced over her body, his hands hovering as if unsure what to do. "Get the first aid kit."

Corrie shook her head, her hand over her mouth. The pale woman's gut was slashed open from ribcage to groin, and intestines spilled out onto wooden slats below. The woman's chest rose and fell with rapid movements, but there was no way she would last another minute.

"There's nothing in the first aid kit that would help. I'm

sorry."

Zeb stared at her with a wild look then jumped when the woman opened her glazed eyes and lifted a hand to Zeb's chest. With supreme effort, she drew Zeb's hand to her own chest. Zeb's eyes widened, then he closed his eyes with intense concentration.

Corrie barely breathed. Was the pale woman communicating with Zeb somehow? Whatever it was, Corrie didn't want to interrupt. The pale woman had only moments left to live.

Those moments were the longest of Corrie's life. When the woman's hand dropped from Zeb's chest and her eyes closed for the last time, Corrie released a shuddering gasp of pent-up emotion. Zeb looked up at Corrie with haunted eyes, and she climbed down to the dock to join him. Her eyes finally registered a dead strolia on the dock nearby.

"Penelope got her," he said in a dead voice. "Called her with the irresistible song. Penelope only wanted a strolia for the slime, but when the pale woman arrived, Penelope attacked her then gutted her and left her here to die." Zeb's voice shook, and his eyes squeezed shut. Corrie placed a light hand on his shoulder. "Penelope gloated for a bit, showed the woman my father's notebook with the script in the back. Penelope has everything she needs to find the Seamount: instructions to the crosscurrent sign, slime to get down there, and the notebook to translate the sign. She's going to kill everyone at the Seamount." His pain-filled eyes landed on Corrie again. "The pale woman made me vow to Ramu that I would destroy the notebook so no land-dwellers could ever find the Seamount."

Corrie's breath hitched. Did that include Zeb? Surely not, but how would they find the Seamount without the notebook?

"There must be a way to get the notebook from Penelope," Corrie said firmly. "And you're not exactly a land-dweller."

"She was clear." Zeb glanced at the woman then quickly back to Corrie. "This is a whole civilization of people that are in danger. I can't risk them for a slim chance that I might survive a little longer with their help. My mother believed with all her heart in the goddess Ramu." Zeb swallowed, his eyes pleading. "I can't go back on my word. We have to destroy the notebook."

Corrie's heart was made of brittle glass, and every word that Zeb spoke hammered another crack in its fragile surface. She needed to fix Zeb, and the only way they knew how to do that was by finding the Seamount. He needed her to push him in the right direction. She had a wild urge to stamp her foot and insist they follow Penelope, not to destroy the notebook in her possession, but to get it back. She knew Zeb well enough to know that he would eventually cave under her steamrollered insistence. It would be for his own good, something he wasn't always the best at seeing.

But forcing Zeb to choose the path she set out for him wasn't the answer. He might allow her to push him over, but he would resent her for it. She shuddered at the memory of him manipulating her, but wasn't her pressure its own form of manipulation? Maybe what Zeb needed wasn't tough love, but support for his choices, to decide for himself the direction of his life. She had said she trusted him, but trust went further than words. Allowing him to decide what was best for himself, even if it meant his death, that was the ultimate trust. She swallowed past a lump in her throat.

"Okay," she whispered. "Okay. If that's what you want, I'm with you all the way."

ZEBALLOS

Zeb was numb as they bundled the dead woman in a sheet and hauled her onboard. Corrie sluiced the dock with buckets of seawater to fade the bloodstains, and Zeb prepared the boat for departure while his mind whirled.

He'd given up his chance at finding his mother's people, his chance at answers, his chance at life, all for a promise to a dying woman that he dared not break. The memory of her passionate plea echoed with phantom vibrations in his chest. With weak movements of her free hand, the expression on her face, and the hum in her chest, she had made herself understood.

"Promise you will destroy the notebook," she had said, her pale eyes fixed on Zeb, her chest fluttering with breaths she couldn't fully take. "Keep our people safe. Destroy it before she destroys them all. Swear to me in Ramu's name."

For one brief, hanging moment, Zeb had hesitated. Did the woman know what she was asking of Zeb? She wanted to destroy the only way he had of saving his own life. Finding answers had been his goal ever since the death of his mother so many years ago, and that desire had only sharpened into need with his illness.

But if he didn't destroy the notebook and its translation of pale folk script, he would have nothing to find at the Seamount. Anyone with answers would be dead. Maybe he could comb through the wreckage of their civilization to find answers to save his own hide, but the cost would be too heavy to bear. As much as he wanted to cling to this beautiful, tumultuous, uncertain life, he couldn't risk genocide to do so.

"I swear," he'd said. "On Ramu."

The woman had breathed her last, a look of satisfaction flitting across her face before it froze in her final expression. Zeb had been left with the taste of his vow on his tongue. Ramu was the goddess of the sea people. While he'd never been particularly spiritual, his mother had taught him all the stories of Ramu. She'd been clear in her awe and reverence for the goddess and had impressed upon Zeb the sanctity of Ramu's name. His word was his bond, now.

Zeb turned on the engine, its roar loud in the silence of the sleeping marina. Once Corrie leaped aboard, he pulled away from the dock.

His mind turned over his unwillingness to save himself over a group of people he had never met, he knew little about, and who proved themselves time and again to be murderous and unsavory. Then it hit him. They might be his ancestors, at least in part, but he wasn't shaped by them, not where it counted. His compassion had been absorbed swimming at his mother's side, as she carefully unhooked caught fish and untangled fishing line from seals. His sense of justice had been honed from his father's stern but fair ruling of his crew on the *Clicker*. He was the product of his upbringing, not the result of his blood. He might have a connection to the people of the Seamount, but he was not one of them. He didn't choose to save them because they were his people, but because it was the right thing to do, because his parents had raised him better than that. He would rather have the pale folk intact and a mystery than revealed but dead.

Zeb's stomach cramped, and he bent over it, wheezing. He groped desperately for the bag of jellyfish that always sat on the counter behind him, and he shoved pieces in his mouth until his stomach calmed. It was easier to know he was making the right decision when his body didn't scream at him to change his mind.

Corrie emerged from the hallway and clutched the dashboard to brace against the growing waves. She frowned at Zeb, who had hidden his distress too late.

"Are you having another episode?" she asked. When he shook his head, not trusting himself to speak, she sighed. "I'll get the charts. We might not have your father's notebook anymore, but we can at least get to the same location as Penelope. Maybe we'll overtake her before we get there."

"And stop her," Zeb croaked. "She knows the secret of how to get to the Seamount."

"Okay," Corrie said. "I'll get the chart and clues to figure out—again—where exactly we're going."

Zeb gripped the wheel to keep himself upright. The cramping from his most recent episode was taking its sweet time to fade, and the recurring pain drained him of what little energy he had. He tried to hide his discomfort and fatigue from Corrie. She glanced at him with worry in her eyes from time to time—apparently, he wasn't hiding anything—but she kept to her task. It didn't take her long to recreate the coordinates for the final, clue-bearing rise, and she circled the spot in pencil on his chart.

"There." She laid the chart over the dashboard. "Hopefully, Penelope will stop there first. That's what your pale woman said to do. Here's hoping she's right."

"I wonder how close to the Seamount this location is." Zeb drummed his fingers on the wheel, the discomfort in his gut lessening with his distraction. "From my mother's description, it isn't far. Although it's hard to judge. Details were lacking in that section."

"She was too busy describing the interesting new creatures she saw." Corrie chuckled, although the sound was thin with strain. "Like great white sharks and transient killer whales. They were a nice switch-up from boring old ligans and brigars."

A shudder of dread rolled over Zeb's shoulders at the memory of the brigar. Its tentacles haunted his dreams some nights.

"I don't know if boring is ever how I would describe ligans and brigars." Zeb checked the chart and counted with his fingers. "We should be on location in four hours, unless we catch up with Penelope first."

Corrie sank into the folding seat and propped her feet on the dashboard to brace against the wave action. Zeb suppressed a smile at her comfort and ease on board.

"Waiting for confrontation is stressful," she said. "I hope we can calm Penelope down easily enough."

The unlikeliness of this hope made Zeb wrinkle his nose, but he didn't comment. Corrie knew well enough what they were up against.

Zeb concentrated on steering the *Clicker* through heavy seas. Dark clouds boiled on the horizon, and he swallowed past a lump of fear in his throat. His father George had always warned him about clouds like that. Sure, the *Clicker* could handle some weather, but why risk it? Plenty of nicer days existed in the future.

Ordinarily, Zeb would have turned around. But with Penelope threatening genocide of his mother's people, they didn't have a choice. The *Clicker* was a sturdy vessel, and Zeb a proficient captain. They would weather this storm.

Corrie rustled around random papers and detritus that had accumulated on the counter behind the captain's chair. Zeb wished she wouldn't. It only served to highlight his slovenly housekeeping now that the boat was his home.

"Where's my communication device?" Corrie said. She dropped a pile of papers with a huff of annoyance. "I thought I'd left it here."

"You did." Zeb glanced behind him, but the little box with dials wasn't in sight. He thought back to the last time he'd seen it, and his heart sank. "Penelope borrowed it when she was on the boat. Maybe she never gave it back."

Corrie cursed and sat back in the folding seat.

"What does she want with it? Wait, that's how she made

the irresistible song. Of course." Corrie's eyes widened, and she gripped the sides of her seat. "The amplifier. Did you tell her about that? She has the death noise, but the sound only travels so far. She wants to kill pale folk at the Seamount. How far will the amplifier allow her to send the sound?"

Zeb rarely felt changes in temperature, thanks to his mother's blood. But now, a chill ran down his back.

"Too far," he answered. "If I were writhing in pain with my ears covered from many boat lengths away, the sound traveled way farther than that. With the amplifier…" He let his words die away, too horrified to complete his sentence.

"So, if she has the location of the Seamount—and with the slime, notebook, and a good depth sounder, she should be able to float right on top of it—she can blast the death noise across the entire Seamount." Corrie sat back, looking winded by the revelation. "How many pale folk live there? What about the other creatures? How many deaths are we talking about?"

"And that's why we're following Penelope, despite this brewing storm." Zeb gripped the wheel with tighter fingers, wishing the boat weren't already moving at top speed so he could turn up the throttle. "She needs to be stopped."

Hours was too long to maintain the high level of tension that had propelled them in the early hours of their journey. Corrie eventually disappeared through the hallway and stumbled back with a cobbled-together meal of whatever she'd found in the fridge. Zeb ate it mechanically, his eyes on the water. Corrie picked at her meal with a nauseous expression, and the waves grew higher with every passing hour.

No sign of Penelope graced the horizon, no matter how intently Zeb scanned the waves. He knew the ocean was a vast place, but her coordinates were the same as his. Surely, they would overtake her at some point. The motorboat was faster, but she would have to stop to refill her motor from a spare gas can now and again.

Less than half an hour before their expected arrival, Zeb couldn't take the wait any longer. He hadn't dived this morning in his usual pre-breakfast swim, and his skin felt three sizes too small. His stomach cramped horribly and wouldn't be satisfied with the dried jellyfish he shoved into his mouth. When Corrie wandered into the wheelhouse next, Zeb stood.

"Can you take the wheel for a minute?" he gasped. "I need a swim. I can't wait."

Corrie bit her lip and stared at him with uncertain eyes, then she glanced out the windshield, where raindrops mingled with salt spray and were swept away by the boat's wipers.

"But the waves are huge," she said.

"Just keep to the course." Zeb pointed at a compass embedded in the dashboard. "I'll throttle it down for you. You'll be fine."

"I wasn't worried about me." Corrie put her hands on her hips and glared at him. "You're the one throwing yourself in the drink. It looks like a blender out there."

Zeb almost laughed aloud. Corrie was worried about him in the water? With the promise of swimming, his emotions grew expansive, and he threw an arm around her shoulder and gave her a squeeze.

"I'll be fine," he said. "I've swum in worse. Besides, once I'm deep enough, I can't feel the waves. I'll be as quick as I can, I promise."

Corrie sighed deeply but didn't protest further. She bumped his hip with hers to sneak behind the wheel. Once Zeb throttled down and was convinced that Corrie was set up, he leaned in and gave her a swift, hard kiss.

"You're captain now," he said to her pink-cheeked face. With a parting grin at her exasperated expression, he tore out of the side door into the weather.

Zeb ripped off his shirt, hopped out of his jeans, and threw them through the still-open door. He closed it to conserve Corrie's heat, then he braced himself between bulwark and cabin wall to walk down the side deck toward the life ring. Flippers in hand, he walked with bent-kneed gait to the aft deck and threw over a rope ladder he'd installed for quicker access. The red-stained bundle tucked behind the winch caught his eye, and his heart sank. He should send the pale woman into the depths, the way the last dying woman had asked him to do. He unrolled the body and heaved it overboard then dived headfirst into the rolling waves.

He'd timed it perfectly to hit the bottom of a trough, and his momentum propelled him deep into the water. The wave motion caught at his legs, but he grabbed the floating body and kicked downward with it. In his upward glance, the *Clicker* loomed large on the surface, bobbing like a bathtub toy. He shook his head and dived deeper to escape the relentless pull of wave action.

Despite the intense relief of being in seawater, Corrie's nervous face swam in his mind's eye. He wanted to swim for hours, but a minute would have to last him long enough to get to their location and deal with Penelope.

Once he was deep enough that gravity pulled him down more strongly than the air in his body tugged him up, he released the pale woman. She drifted downward, and Zeb watched her until her pale features melted into the darkness. This was another death he'd witnessed of the people he didn't know but desperately wanted to. It only solidified Zeb's desire to prevent Penelope from destroying more of them.

It was strange swimming in midocean. Floating in the ocean without seeing bottom and without any visible landmarks was an unusual situation for him. Even his skin couldn't feel any features within sensing distance.

Only one object joined him in the water. Zeb pulled up and concentrated on the approaching animal. It was shaped like a seal, but longer. His heart leaped. Was it a yatull? His chest vibrated with a welcoming hum that sprang out of him, unbidden.

A sleek shape darted through the green water, directly at him. Zeb continued his welcoming hum, but a spark of fear ignited in his gut. He didn't know much about yatulls except for the few references in his mother's stories. They were often used as mounts for the pale folk, but what of wild yatulls? Would one attack him, unprovoked?

The yatull pulled up sharply within an arm's length and gazed at him with intelligent black eyes that flicked over his body in an assessing way. Zeb continued to hum, but now in a soothing tone.

How intelligent were yatull, anyway? Zeb's mother had communicated with fish, and they had responded to her suggestions. Could he ask the yatull about Penelope's boat? He frowned and framed his question in his mind. Then he lifted his hands and changed the cadence of his humming.

He kept his question simple. *Boat ahead?*

The yatull flipped in a circle. Heartened, Zeb asked more. *Near or far?*

The creature swam only one short stroke of its flippers. Zeb grinned widely at his success.

If he could ask the yatull questions, maybe he could give it a warning. He didn't want the yatull anywhere near Penelope and her death noise.

Dangerous boat. Be careful.

The yatull stared at him for a long moment. Then, with a flick of its powerful tail and a twist of its front flippers, the animal soared away with sinuous grace.

The distraction of the yatull had clouded Zeb's senses, but now that it was gone, he felt seven large animals heading straight to him. He froze. Notched fins and streamlined bodies marked them as offshore killer whales. Their preferred food? Sharks.

Zeb didn't feel confident that the whales wouldn't see him

as an oddly shaped shark. Their movements were too purposeful for his liking. His heart beating faster, he pointed his body in the direction of the *Clicker*.

Zeb had been underwater for long enough. The *Clicker* was far ahead by now, and he propelled his body forward with powerful undulations. Once the boat was directly overhead and throwing a dim shadow over his body, Zeb angled upward.

His skin warned him of danger before teeth pressed against his leg with crushing force. Zeb kicked frantically, and the exploring mouth released his limb. He twisted and stared at the animals surrounding him.

Huge black and white bodies swirled in circles below. The one who had grabbed his leg in an inquisitive bite loomed closely. Was it wondering what Zeb was? How could he use their confusion to his advantage? His leg throbbed with bruising pain, and a trickle of blood stained the water with a cloud of darkness.

The killer whale pressed closer. Zeb backpedaled away, too panicked to move in a more controlled fashion. Without thinking, he released a hum of distress. He hadn't done that since he'd swum with his mother, years ago. Why would he bother when no one would come to save him?

The killer whales below him scattered, although Zeb was too transfixed on the whale eyeing him to pay much attention. A sleek brown torpedo emerged from the depths. Zeb tore his gaze away from the assessing whale and nearly gulped water in surprise.

The yatull rammed into the killer whale's flank with a blow of its squashed face. The killer whale spun around to see its attacker, but the yatull was too quick. It rammed into the whale from the other side and darted away again before the whale could react.

Zeb didn't wait around. With strong kicks of his battered legs, he aimed for the *Clicker*'s hull, away from the black and white menaces below.

The waves were chaotic, and he'd surfaced too far away from the boat. He gulped a breath of air and dived under once more, kicking closer. When his head breached the surface again, the rope ladder swayed sickeningly against the side of the heaving vessel.

With a kick of his powerful legs, Zeb leaped out of the water and grabbed the second rung of the rope ladder. He hauled himself up, every atom of his body screaming at him to get back in the water, and his bruised and bleeding leg aching horribly. He gritted his teeth and climbed.

Corrie let out a huge breath of air when he entered the wheelhouse, dripping despite the towel wrapped around his waist.

"You made it," she said with a huff of frenzied laughter. "I thought I'd have to drive back to Victoria all by myself in a raging storm."

"I wouldn't leave you out here." He recalled the whales and amended his statement. "If I could possibly help it. I talked to a yatull down there, and it said that Penelope was close. Let me put my clothes on, then I'll turn up the speed. Maybe we can finally overtake her."

CORRIE

Corrie flopped in the folding seat once Zeb was dressed and in the captain's chair. Adrenaline had powered her through the endless minutes of Zeb's absence, but now that helpful hormone had deserted her. She felt drained, like the only thing stopping her from sinking into the wheelhouse floor was the flimsy folding seat. The very real fear that had overwhelmed her—of Zeb never returning, of being stranded in the middle of the Pacific with only her wits and this old fishing boat between her and a watery death—well, she was glad Zeb was back. Even if they were still in a rusty old bucket of a boat in the middle of a storm, at least she wasn't alone.

Another tense twenty minutes passed, and Corrie grew sick of endlessly smacking their hull against steadily increasing waves. Zeb's normally tanned face was pale and stuck in an expression of concentration. The air temperature dropped the further they went, until it sent Corrie searching through Zeb's cabin. She reentered the wheelhouse with two toques. A blue one warmed her chilly head nicely, and she pulled a black one over Zeb's wet hair.

He glanced at her with amusement.

"I'm not cold," he said. "Those are Jules' hats that he forgot on board."

"It was making me cold just looking at you." Corrie wrapped her arms around her body. "Humor me."

Corrie scanned the horizon in futile hope. She'd been looking for Penelope's boat for hours, and nothing had ever appeared to her searching eyes.

She almost skimmed over an object in the water because she didn't expect it. When her brain caught up to her eyes, she stared intently at the spot.

There. A motorboat, too small to be out in this weather, rode waves far ahead like a car on a rolling roadway.

"There she is!" Corrie grabbed Zeb's bicep and squeezed it with her excitement and relief. "See?"

"I see her." Zeb angled the *Clicker* toward their target, and they barreled through the punishing waves.

Corrie's lip was bruised from her teeth worrying it before they finally reached Penelope's boat. The open-topped vessel rolled around like it was in a washing machine gearing up for the spin cycle. Penelope had one hand on the wheel to keep the boat facing oncoming waves, while the other fiddled with a device in her lap. She looked up when the *Clicker* approached broadside, and her face hardened.

Corrie leaped out of the wheelhouse and hung over the gunwale.

"What the hell are you doing?" she screamed over the whistling wind. "Stop trying to kill the pale folk."

"Do you have any idea what they've done, what they will do?" Penelope screamed back. "Your precious Zeb is dying because they won't reach out a hand to save him. They're ignoring his suffering just like they did Clicker's. She was my friend. She didn't deserve her fate. And they kicked her out of her home in the first place." Penelope brushed hair away from her face with an angry swipe of her fingers. "That might not be reason enough, but I have more."

"Your family," Corrie shouted. "I heard. I'm sorry."

"Me too," she yelled. 'But sorry doesn't bring them back."

"Neither does killing the pale folk."

"But it prevents someone else from suffering what I did. You're not a mother, you can't possibly understand what it means to lose a child." Penelope's face worked. "And my husband, who was my rock, my best friend. Both taken from me in the same moment by those bloodthirsty monsters you're so eager to protect." Her shoulders straightened. "My family wasn't the only one. There have been others. Someone has to wipe out these murderous bastards before another family is ripped apart."

"Genocide isn't the answer," Corrie cried. Penelope stood up, her hand still on the wheel.

"I'm doing this for Zeb, too," she screeched. "The protein he needs, it's something the pale folk eat. Those data I gave you? Don't forget, they were stomach contents of the strange creatures. They're all the same, eating something down there on the Seamount. Once they're all dead, he can dive down and find it. He can live, Corrie."

Corrie's freezing fingers clenched harder on the gunwale. The results from those samples were clear—the protein in Zeb's cream, although degraded, was clearly the same as in the stomach samples. Whatever nutrient Zeb lacked, it was likely found at the Seamount. If they had no opposition, they could get what Zeb so desperately needed. She couldn't imagine him dying, not when he was so full of life, not when she had so much to say to him, so much to do by his side.

But she could never condone murder, especially when Zeb had made his choice. He was willing to sacrifice himself to save the pale folk. It didn't matter who they were, or what they did. It was Zeb's decision, and Corrie would stand back and let him decide his own path. It nearly tore her apart to not swoop in and fix things for Zeb, but she had to let him follow his own decisions.

"Not at the cost of death," she screamed over the pounding of the *Clicker* against wave troughs. Spray drenched her with every thundering wave, but she had to make the other woman see reason.

Penelope opened her mouth to retort, then something smacked against the side of her motorboat so hard that she fell to her knees. Corrie squinted through the rain. Bodies swam through the water, surrounding the small vessel. They carried long poles wielded like spears. Although their arms and torsos looked human, the relentless waves gave glimpses of their odd legs…

"Zeb!" Corrie screamed with delight and terror over her

shoulder. "Zeb, I see mermaids!"

This moment, this one right here, was the one Corrie had been waiting for her whole life. Ever since her sighting of a mermaid as a young child, she'd been obsessed with proving to herself the reality of her mermaid. She'd devoted countless hours researching sightings of selkies and kelpies, mermaids and sirens, sea serpents and krakens, but until she'd met Zeb, she hadn't seen anything else out of the ordinary. She and Zeb had discovered many creatures unknown to science—and many bearing a striking resemblance to legends—but mermaids had still been a myth.

Until today.

Corrie's jaw dropped when a mermaid leaped out of the water and clung to the motorboat's side, a vicious-looking white spear clutched in his hand. Mer folk, she mentally corrected herself. The broad shoulders and firm pectorals of this person bore little resemblance to a picture-book. Water dripped off greenish-brown skin, and his teeth were sharp like a carnivore.

Another mer folk leaped onto the other side, this one clearly female, and Penelope screamed in horror and anger. She picked up a net that was strapped against the side of her vessel and whacked the nearest mer folk around the head. The female dropped into the sea, but the male grabbed the net as it swung through the air. He yanked it from Penelope's grip and tossed it aside. It sank instantly, swallowed by gravity and the endless heaving waves.

Penelope corrected her course with a jerk of the wheel and bent to feverishly twist the wires of her device. More mer folk leaped onto the sides of her boat.

"Let me see," shouted Zeb, the excitement in his voice palpable. Corrie grinned despite the circumstances and darted into the wheelhouse to hold the wheel steady. Zeb squeezed past her and hung over the edge.

He jumped back, and Corrie gasped. A mer folk had

somehow leaped all the way up to Zeb and now hung on the gunwale, his face contorted with fierce determination. His mission to capture Zeb was clear from his grasping hands and the writhing of his well-muscled body.

A strange whistling sound filled Corrie's ears, then a ping of metal on metal rang through the air. The mer folk's mouth opened in a round 'o' of surprise. Corrie glanced at his chest, where blood blossomed from a wound above his sternum through which emerged the barbed tip of a speargun's spear. His arms relaxed their grip, and he fell backward. His splash made a small noise in the vastness of the stormy waves.

"They don't deserve your compassion," Penelope screamed at Zeb. Corrie kept her eyes on the approaching waves, trying to keep the boat steady and level with Penelope's, but the other woman's words were hard to miss. "They're murderous devil spawn, and they need to be wiped from the face of the Earth. I'm doing this partly for you. You'll thank me one day!"

Penelope's motor suddenly roared to life, and Corrie watched it zoom away. One mer folk clung gamely to its side but fell off when Penelope zigzagged. The mer folk vanished beneath the waves.

"Damn it, there's another one," shouted Zeb.

"Why are they attacking us?"

"I don't know!" Zeb backed away from the vicious-looking female who clung to the gunwale, her sharp fingernails filed into points. He gestured at Penelope's retreating boat and shouted at the mer folk. "Get her, not me. She's the dangerous one!" He lifted his hand to his head and pulled off his toque. Did it make him too hot, even in this weather?

The female's eyes widened as she took in Zeb's white hair, then looked at his pale eyes. Her own eyes narrowed as she gazed at the motorboat growing smaller in the distance. She released her hold on the gunwale and fell backward with a splash.

Zeb raced to the edge.

"They're leaving," he shouted. He faced Corrie with a quick shrug of confusion. "One look at me, and they swam away."

"Either you're too tough-looking for them," Corrie joked, her voice high-pitched with nerves. "Or they recognized a pale folk descendant."

"Do you think that's it?" Zeb stared at Corrie. "I should go after them."

"And leave me to drive the boat?" If Corrie's voice rose any higher, only dolphins would be able to hear it. She cleared her throat. "It's awfully stormy. And shouldn't we be chasing after Penelope? What if she deploys the device?"

Zeb's brow contracted in frustration. Corrie sympathized, although she didn't budge from her stance. Those mer folk looked dangerous, and Zeb wasn't one of them. They might have recognized him for one of the pale folk, but who knew what relations between the two peoples were? Maybe they'd left to gather reinforcements.

And the waves were scarily high. Corrie gulped and kept her white-knuckled hands tight on the wheel.

"Okay," Zeb said, his jaw tight. "I'll stay. Here, let me drive. You're right, we need to catch up to Penelope."

Corrie gratefully made way for Zeb in the captain's chair, although he didn't sit. Both stood, braced against the wheel and dashboard, and peered through the wet windshield. Penelope's boat appeared and disappeared at regular intervals as troughs swallowed the small boat and then lifted it high. In the distance, a fork of lightning dazzled Corrie's eyes with a brilliant display of electricity. She gulped.

Penelope had stopped again, and the *Clicker* drew closer to her target. The small figure in the motorboat bent over something in her lap. Corrie clenched her fists.

"Should we ram her?" she said suddenly. "Stop her from finishing the device?"

"That might kill her." Zeb looked queasy, and Corrie was

fiercely glad. Bloodthirstiness wasn't in his nature, despite his heritage. Zeb was himself. He continued, "But keep your eye on her. If she looks like she's finished, I'll have to ram her boat then retrieve her afterward."

"Okay." Corrie strained to watch Penelope. They drew closer, until they were within shouting distance. Corrie had to try one more time, despite Penelope's drive to carry out her plan.

Corrie opened the door, wincing at the cold saltwater that infused the air and splashed her with every wave.

"Stop it, Penelope," she shouted. Her voice whipped away with the wind. Could Penelope even hear her? "This is crazy. You don't need to do this. Come back with us and we can talk about it."

"You'll thank me later," Penelope shouted without looking up from her task. "When Zeb is alive. And tell my dead daughter that I don't need to do this." She looked up at Corrie, and the wild light of madness filled her face. "How can you defend them after what they did to Zeb's mother, what they are doing to Zeb? No one will miss the destruction of these murderous monsters."

Corrie bit her lip and retreated into the wheelhouse. She closed the door and sighed.

"No luck?" Zeb said.

Corrie shook her head. "She's too far gone. Keep watching—we might have to ram her."

A tremendous wave, bigger than the rest, hit them sideways. Corrie staggered and smacked her head against the doorframe. She slid down to the floor, momentarily stunned.

"Corrie!" Zeb's urgent voice woke her from her trance. "Corrie, are you okay?"

She looked up and worked hard on focusing until only one Zeb stood at the wheel, the lines of his face etched with taut fear.

"I think so," she murmured. She touched her fingers to the

back of her head and brought them to the front. "Oh, look, blood."

PENELOPE

Penelope's jaw was tight as she gripped her motorboat's steering wheel with whitened knuckles. The next wave threatened to tug it from her hands, but she grimly held on. The bow slid down the next wave with a jarring jolt.

"Why won't you twist?" she muttered. The wires in her free hand were slick with salt spray. The device was clenched between her knees. Every time a wave rocked the little vessel, it ripped the wires out of her fingers, and she would have to start again.

Why hadn't she attached the amplifier back at the dock? She'd been in danger of Zeb seeing her, for sure, but the risk would have been better than trying to fix the device in the middle of stormy seas. And the damn boy had caught up with her anyway.

Her blood boiled at the thought of Zeb. He should want this. Why couldn't he see that she was doing all this partly for him? He clearly didn't know the extent of how the pale folk had mistreated his mother.

She recalled Clicker opening up to her, a few months after George had brought his wife to Penelope's office for testing. They'd become friends by then—Clicker's dreamy gentleness complementing Penelope's sharp inquisitiveness—and Clicker had told Penelope a little about her childhood.

"I was less than the others," she'd said, gazing down at her arm where Penelope drew blood with efficient motions. "My own mother abandoned me because I was different. There were many of us different people. We were never accepted by the others. I left to find somewhere where I could be myself without shame."

"Can your people not help you?" Penelope had asked. She'd run so many tests on Clicker, but nothing had come up that would help the rapidly fading woman, nothing but more questions. Penelope had worked night and day to solve her friend's mystery, but she'd despaired of finding a cure before Clicker succumbed to her illness.

"No," Clicker had said with finality. "They will not help. I can never go back."

Another wave hit the motorboat almost broadside, and Penelope cursed. She wrenched the wheel to turn the bow into oncoming waves. Zeb didn't know enough about his mother's past to know that the Seamount's people held no love for him. Couldn't he see that as soon as they rid the Seamount of its inhabitants, he could find his cure?

The pale folk didn't deserve to live. Penelope twisted two wires together and they miraculously stayed put, but her mind was in the past, nearly seven years ago. It had been a beautiful sunny day, and her husband Fredric had taken their daughter Charlotte to the beach. Penelope had stayed at their rented beach house to tidy up some work, but when midmorning came, she'd put down her laptop and wandered in search of her family.

The secluded cove near their rental had been deserted. With horror, Penelope—from her vantage on a cliff above the cove—had watched a tranced Fredric walk with stiff legs into the water toward a woman with long white hair and a strangely pale face. Little Charlotte had followed her father into the water, calling for him to stop.

Penelope had been too far away for them to hear her shouts. She'd scrambled down the path, heedless of slipping, but by the time she'd reached the beach, Fredric had been gone. She'd dived into the water and eventually pulled out Charlotte's limp body. No amount of frantic resuscitation had revived her beautiful child.

Fredric had been found washed onto a nearby beach the next day. After a long darkness of frozen horror, frenzied anger, and wild grief, Penelope had settled on grim purpose: if she ever had a chance to take revenge on the pale folk, she would make them pay for what the woman had done to her family. The pleasant ones—like Clicker—escaped the Seamount on their own. Anyone who was left deserved what they got.

Another wave pushed her boat aside, but she'd nearly finished the device. If only the relentless motion of the sea would stop for just a minute, she'd be done.

A thump pounded the side of her boat, and she looked up in confusion. Surely, no driftwood floated this far from land. Had the mer folk returned?

Penelope peered over the edge with one hand still firmly on the wheel. Her eyes widened in horror.

ZEBALLOS

Zeb stared at Corrie, aghast. The blow to her head had dazed her until all sense of fear or caution was gone. Would she be okay? He tried to remember the signs of concussion, but his panicking mind came up blank. Vomiting was bad, so was blacking out. When should she go to a hospital? He nearly laughed out loud at that ridiculous notion. They were in the middle of the Pacific. What hospital would he drive her to?

"Just sit and rest, Corrie," Zeb said. "I'll take care of everything."

Corrie nodded and put her head in her hands, whether out of pain or to protect it from bashing against the wall, Zeb wasn't sure. In an ideal world, he would get her to lie down in a cabin, but that wasn't possible today. As hurt as she was, he might need her.

Zeb peered out the windshield at Penelope. It was getting harder to see her through the rain and spray, and harder to stay in position. The *Clicker* groaned valiantly, but she was an old vessel and more suited to cruising the calm Strait than the open ocean.

The water around Penelope's boat boiled with slick bodies. Zeb blinked and squinted to see better. Creatures he knew and creatures he didn't, yatulls and dobars and trobas, unknown animals with scales and fur and horns, all writhed beside the motorboat. They bumped the sides until the small vessel, already pushed to the limit with the heavy seas, tipped dangerously.

Penelope shrieked and poked her empty speargun butt into the frothing mass of animals. The motorboat tipped again, and Penelope screamed. She grabbed her device—unamplified— and dropped it in the water dangling from a rope.

The animals twitched as one, then froze. Zeb's heart almost stopped when bodies rose to the surface and floated away—

sleek yatulls, shark-shaped krolls, and dozens of strolias. His heart started up again with a vengeance. Penelope's disregard for the awesome life at the Seamount was too terrible to ignore. She had to pay.

Zeb pushed the throttle to the max, and the *Clicker* roared in response. Penelope looked up in surprise. Zeb charged forward.

The engine sputtered and coughed, and Zeb's anger twisted into fright in an instant. He recognized that noise, and it wasn't good. With a lurch, he remembered he hadn't changed the air filter in months. He'd meant to—he even had a new one in the engine room—but with one thing and then another, he'd pushed the task aside. All thoughts of revenge toward Penelope floated to the background. The *Clicker* continued to move forward, but slowly enough that Penelope kicked her own engine into gear and zoomed away.

"Corrie," he said. "I need you to hold the boat steady while I fix the engine. Can you do that?"

"Oh, probably." She wobbled to her feet. "It doesn't look too hard."

"Keep the bow into the waves." He repeated his instructions from before. In her current state, he didn't trust her to remember them. He wished fervently that he could stay behind the wheel, but wishes didn't make things happen. "When I shout, turn off the engine, here. When I shout again, turn it on right away to keep the bow into the waves. You'll be fine. I'll be quick."

Before Corrie could protest, he guided her hips to sit in the captain's chair, placed her hands on the wheel, and fled into the hallway. Down he went, into the bowels of the ship, near the bow where the engine roared. He knew the air filter needed changing, and it wouldn't take much to fix. But any time not in control of the boat, any time away from his pursuit of Penelope, was too much time. If he didn't get the *Clicker* in working order soon, would Penelope deploy her device?

Zeb's face dripped with sweat from the engine's heat and his fears. He dropped to his knees for balance against the heaving floor. His fingers grabbed the filter and ripped off its packaging, then he unscrewed a cap that held the filter in place.

"Now!" he shouted.

Miraculously, Corrie must have heard him because the engine spluttered and died. Zeb only had seconds to complete his task. Already, the deck under his feet swayed with an alarming motion as waves caught the bow and pushed it around.

He pulled the filter out and threw it aside. His fingers shoved the new one in. He cursed when the filter snagged, then his heart leaped when it slotted into place under his frantic pushing.

"Turn it on!" he screamed.

A wave tossed him sideways into the wall, bruising his shoulder. He cursed again, but the too-quiet space filled with a roar. Quickly, he screwed the cap back on and climbed up to the wheelhouse, holding on while the boat tilted and shook with wave action.

Corrie was still pale, and the back of her head oozed blood, but her eyes were clear. She glanced at Zeb.

"Is the engine okay?"

"It is now. Nice work keeping us steady. Scoot over and I'll drive. We lost Penelope again, no doubt."

"She's not far." Corrie pointed at a tiny patch of white. "Fixing her device, I guess. Let's get her and end this circus."

Zeb snorted, amused by Corrie's description and relieved that she was coherent.

"Complete with circus animals and freak shows."

The engine roared with beautiful clarity, and they cut through the waves, if not with ease, then at least with precision. They were soon upon the motorboat, and Corrie gripped Zeb's arm.

"I need to get on that boat," she said. "Grab the device, talk her down, overpower her, whatever it takes."

"Why you?" Zeb rebelled at the thought of Corrie taking such a huge risk. Her head was still bleeding, and she was in no condition to swim to Penelope's boat, no matter how much slime she ingested. "I'll go."

"No, you can't. What if Penelope uses her device? Even without the amplifier, it could kill you if you're close enough. I can't even hear it. It has to be me. With strolia slime, I can make it."

Her face was so determined, so hellbent on doing whatever she could to make all this right, that Zeb couldn't contain himself. He leaned forward and planted a swift kiss on her forehead.

"Don't you dare get hurt," he warned. "And take a knife. You left your dive knife here last time—I put it in the top drawer of your lab."

Corrie nodded swiftly, then she pulled out a bottle of slime from a small drawer under the counter that Zeb never used. Her flippers were in there as well.

She caught Zeb's eye and flushed. "Be prepared, right?"

Zeb grinned. He liked how Corrie was making herself at home on his boat. His grin faded when she gave him a swift smile, tipped the slime back, then left the wheelhouse. He turned to the windshield again, hoping that he hadn't made a terrible mistake.

CORRIE

Corrie hid her shaking hands from Zeb as she walked down the tipping hallway, away from the wheelhouse. The waves were insanely large, and only the memory of her increased strength underwater after ingesting strolia slime gave her the courage to even attempt reaching Penelope's boat. She stripped off her shirt and pants, threw them in the galley, then ran to her old lab. It was mostly empty except for her knife clattering in the top drawer. Corrie grabbed the sheathed knife and strapped it to her calf, then she tipped the vial of slime down her throat. Now armed and prepared, she swung the outer door open.

Frigid air that was more than half water doused her with a cold slap to the face. She couldn't jump in the water. She would die, no two ways about it. If she didn't jump in, Penelope would carry out her diabolical scheme. That would be sad, but life would carry on.

But it wouldn't carry on, not for the creatures at the Seamount. Corrie recalled her excitement and utter awe at seeing her first strolia, and her sense of vindication when the mer folk swam around Penelope's boat. Her scientist's heart rebelled at the extermination of entire species unknown to the world, and her humanity cried out at the loss of life. She had to do something.

A pterodactyl swooped down at her, screeching like a banshee. Corrie ducked, her heart pounding even harder than before. Then she frowned. Pterodactyls were extinct, and she doubted they could have hidden from airplanes at the Seamount.

The slime's hallucinations must have kicked in. It was now or never. Corrie slipped on her flippers, took a deep breath, and threw herself overboard.

She fell for years until her shoulder smacked the water, far below. It was cool under the waves, and surprisingly quiet after the tumult above. Corrie would have sighed with relief had that been an option. Instead, she kicked furiously toward the rocking white hull next to the hulk of the *Clicker*.

Corrie frowned as she studied the situation. Getting aboard the motorboat without braining herself would be a challenge. She watched and waited, but her lungs reminded her of their need for air. She kicked hard with her now-considerable strength toward the surface.

To her surprise, she burst out of the water up to her ankles. She flailed forward and smacked over the side of the motorboat with a blow that forced a cough out of her lungs.

Penelope stared at her with wide-eyed shock, one hand clutching her device. It looked distressingly put-together.

"Where did you come from?" Penelope gasped, then she shook her head. "Never mind. Get off my boat. You can't stop me, and you shouldn't want to."

"Let's go back to land and talk about this," Corrie wheezed. She climbed over the side and edged closer to Penelope. Her hands gripped a seat back for balance in the cork-like boat. "There are other ways to protect people from the Seamount folk. Maybe we can reach out and understand them better. Maybe there was a reasonable explanation for your tragedy, and now we can learn from it and prevent it in the future."

"Stand back, girl," Penelope growled. "This is the best and safest answer. One blast of this device, and the ocean threat will be over forever."

Corrie's heart squeezed. She'd really hoped that she would be able to reason with Penelope, but she didn't have any other words to try. Penelope was beyond reason, and no negotiation would sway her firm opinion. In Penelope's mind, the Seamount's inhabitants must die today.

Not on Corrie's watch.

She lunged forward. Penelope's eyes widened with surprise. Corrie grabbed the device and yanked backward, but

Penelope's tight grip only made her fall toward Corrie. Corrie pulled harder to get Penelope off-balance, and the older woman fell hard against a seat. A wave hit them almost broadside, and Corrie let go of the device to grab a seat for stability. Penelope hauled herself to the wheel and turned the bow into oncoming waves.

Corrie needed that device. With it, Penelope was a genocidal maniac. Without it, she was just a soaking wet woman in a small motorboat. Corrie withdrew the dive knife on her leg and brandished it at Penelope. She tried her best to ignore the purple bats swarming above and a giant sombrero floating beyond the motorboat. Being out of the water with strolia slime coursing through her veins was no joke.

"Give me the device," she shouted. "I don't want to hurt you."

Penelope laughed, and Corrie's ire rose.

"Put that down, you silly girl." Penelope grabbed a long-handled hook from its clasp on the side of the motorboat and swung it at Corrie. Corrie ducked too late, and the hook tore into her arm and hooked under the elbow. She gasped with pain, but Penelope wasn't done yet. She pulled with a jerk, and Corrie's arm twisted until it popped with an agonizing lance of pain in her shoulder. Her knife clattered to the deck. She screamed, and Penelope dropped the hook.

"If you aren't with me," she said. "Then you're against me. I'm sorry it had to come to this."

Penelope turned at a dangerous angle to the waves. Corrie's heart stopped, and she watched through watering eyes as the boat tilted, more and more, until her perch on the edge grew too precarious for balance. Too late, she tried to throw herself into the boat, but her equilibrium was lost. She toppled sideways, and the water swallowed her up.

Quiet enveloped her again, but the water's coolness did nothing to soothe the fire in her shoulder. She clutched her arm to her chest to keep it steady while she kicked far enough down to escape the relentless pull of rollers.

The *Clicker* was close, but it felt way too far for Corrie's state. Every kick she pushed through the water jolted her arm with twisting knives of pain. Her tears mingled with seawater.

She surfaced beside the *Clicker*, and her heart dropped to the ocean floor. A rope ladder swung and swayed with the boat's rolling path over the waves. How would she climb up? Even with two working arms, it seemed an impossible feat.

Water sloshed over her head, and she spluttered. She couldn't stay in the water. Soon enough, the slime would wear off, then she would be dead for sure. To get on the ladder, she would have to rely on her slime-induced extra strength and hope it would be enough.

She dived underwater again then angled her body to point toward the rope ladder. A countdown ticked silently in her head. At zero, she kicked upward with all her might.

She burst out of the water, even higher than she had at Penelope's motorboat, until even her feet left the water. She held her good arm at the ready, and when a rung of the ladder met her grasp, she gripped with all her might.

Her other shoulder didn't dislocate, but from the wrenching pain, it was a close thing. She swung wildly from the flimsy ladder, whacking her bad shoulder against the hull with agonizing force before her floundering feet found their grip on the bottom rung. She used her chin as a second hand and managed to crawl up the side, mainly through sheer willpower.

Once over the bulwark, she collapsed on the aft deck, every part of her body throbbing. Saltwater fell over her in frothy sheets. If she didn't move soon, the slime would wear off and she would freeze to death on the deck.

"How ironic," she mumbled to herself. On knees and her one good hand, she crawled to the back door of the *Clicker* and let herself in. She ignored the dog-sized spiders that accompanied her—after the horror show that was Penelope, giant hallucinatory arachnids couldn't hold a candle.

Corrie crawled to her clothes on the floor of the galley, but the thought of moving her arm to put her shirt on almost made her throw up. She bit onto the shirt and pants and dragged them up the hallway to the wheelhouse.

Zeb whirled around, his face pale and his eyes haunted.

"Corrie." He reached out with his free hand and hauled her up by her good elbow. She grimaced but allowed him to pull her upright. She wobbled and leaned into him. Tears of exhaustion and pain leaked down her cheeks.

"I saw you drop off the boat, and I thought…" Zeb didn't finish his sentence. Instead, he squeezed her tightly.

Corrie squeaked with distress. "My shoulder," she gasped. "I think it's dislocated."

Zeb glanced at the offending joint and nodded.

"Looks like it. My sister Krista used to get those when we were kids. Dad learned how to pop them back in." He wrinkled his nose. "I think I remember how."

"That's not very reassuring," Corrie said. She glanced down at Penelope, who was working hard on her device in the tumult of wave action. "But if it can get me back in the game, you'd better try."

Zeb pressed his hip against the wheel to steady it while his hands reached toward Corrie's arm. She stopped him with a raised hand.

"Wait," she said. She couldn't believe what she was going to ask Zeb, but if any circumstances warranted her request, it was this one. "Could you use your voice power to reduce my pain? Is that possible?"

Zeb's eyes widened, and he stared at Corrie.

"Maybe," he said slowly. "I can try, if you're okay with that."

"Yes. Do it." A larger wave rocked the boat, and Zeb steadied the wheel with his hand. "Quickly."

"This won't hurt a bit," Zeb said in a smooth, deep voice. Instantly, Corrie's uninjured shoulder relaxed. She stepped closer so that Zeb could easily reach her arm. "I'll place one hand here. Sit up straight, arch your back, good. Breathe deeply. Straighter, even straighter. You're almost there. Arch your back, a little more…"

A sickening pop reverberated through Corrie's body, and she hissed with pain, her trance broken. She gingerly rubbed her shoulder and glared at Zeb, who looked apologetic.

"I thought you were going to take away the pain," she said.

"I guess that's not within my abilities. But I calmed you down enough to handle it, so that's something. Is it back in?"

Corrie gingerly lifted her elbow. It was sore, but not agonizing.

"I think so." Fused and elongated feet that appeared like tails danced in the nearest wave peak, and she pointed. "Look, mer folk." She squinted through the rain and spray. "I think they want to talk. We're not getting anywhere with Penelope. Maybe you should see if they can do something."

"I don't want to leave you alone again." Zeb looked distraught. Corrie didn't want him to leave again, either, but their mission was too important to waste time indulging in feelings.

"This is you." She grabbed his free hand, and he stared at it. "I accept that. A part of you will always belong to the sea. Go, talk to the inhabitants of the Seamount, get their help. This is their world we're trying to save, after all."

It pained her to encourage him to leave and solve their problems himself. She wanted to spearhead the solution because that's what she always did. But Zeb truly was the best person for this job, and saving the Seamount had been his decision, at great personal cost. If the only thing she could do was support him, then so be it.

She squeezed behind him and took the wheel.

"Go!" she said with a flap of her hand. "Before Penelope finishes her device. She must be almost done, despite the weather."

Zeb stripped off his clothes, fled out the door, and raced across the bow. He dived into the waves in a beautiful, perfect arc that Corrie admired before she turned her full attention to keeping the *Clicker* afloat.

ZEBALLOS

The instant Zeb swam below the wave action, spears surrounded him. He froze and looked wildly around. Mer folk, their greenish-brown faces flat and eerie, stared back at him with hard expressions. Kelp-brown hair floated above holes where ears would have been on a human. Their elongated fused legs, the same color as their skin, flicked with purposeful motions to keep the mer folk in place. Zeb put his hands up in surrender, then he wondered if that gesture meant the same underwater as it did on land. Hopefully, he wasn't insulting them.

"Who are you?" A female mer folk with bone beads in her hair floated to the front and spoke to Zeb with the mix of hand gestures, hums, and clicks that his mother had taught him. It had been so long since he'd spoken the undersea tongue that it took him a moment to understand. With a look of impatience, she said, "Why are you here, pale hair?"

"The Seamount is in danger," Zeb said carefully. He wanted to get his words right, and they didn't come easily after almost two decades of disuse. Luckily, he was excellent at languages. "The small boat, the woman on it has a—" Zeb faltered. He didn't know the word for "device" or "machine", and he doubted they existed. "A bad thing on board. It will kill you and all animals at the Seamount. I'm trying to stop her."

The mer folk simply stared at him with their too-large eyes unblinking. Zeb grew exasperated.

"I'm trying to save your home! Won't you help? Can't you do something? I know I'm not one of you, but help me help you."

The lead mer woman stared at him for a moment longer.

"The animals died," she said finally. "Now they float away. We will have to collect them. Will she kill us like she killed them?"

"Yes," Zeb said emphatically.

"Then we dare not approach, despite our weapons." She glanced down, and her hard face tightened. "Only one of the pale folk can call our salvation."

Then, without further word, she twisted with a sweep of her elegant tail and darted away. The rest of her people followed until Zeb couldn't see or sense them anymore.

Frustration welled in his chest, so hot he was surprised that the water surrounding him was still cool. It built and built until his chest was on fire. He couldn't contain it any longer.

He channeled his fear and rage into a vibration that shook his whole body with its power. It was a plea for help and a demand for retribution all in one. It thrummed through the water with a sharp, powerful burst.

The call left him limp and defeated. No sound echoed back in reply.

Useless, the lot of them. He was on his own, as he always was. They wouldn't help him save his life, they wouldn't help him save theirs—Zeb had done his best. The only path left to him was to ram Penelope's boat and try to save her from the wreckage. He hoped the *Clicker* was strong enough for that extreme action.

His senses picked up on motion all around him. He focused, and the shapes began to make sense. Creatures of all descriptions swam, floated, zipped, and twisted underneath him. He recognized otter-like dobars, sleek yatulls, hook-finned krolls, and many others with half-forgotten names.

His cheeks rose with his wide grin. The Seamount must be close, and the creatures that inhabited it had come out to investigate his cry for help.

A vast, serpentine shape twisted toward him. Zeb's smile slid off his face. The ligan at home was his friend, but not all sea serpents were friendly. He kicked toward the *Clicker*, but the ligan was faster than he thought. It slid around him, sinuous and deadly, its monstrous head massive. A striated yellow and green eye stared at Zeb as it passed. Zeb kicked faster, all his focus on reaching the *Clicker*. The ligan's head disappeared behind Zeb, but he didn't dare lose speed to watch it.

Pressure against his leg blossomed into pain from a ligan fang. He pulled his legs into his torso from the searing torment, then his brain took over. He didn't have time to give into his agony. If he didn't want to end up as ligan lunch, he needed to get out of the water.

With his good leg, he kicked feebly upward. The ligan circled him again, and Zeb was convinced the massive serpent was toying with him. He thought desperately of Corrie, frightened and alone at the wheel of his boat in a raging storm, and he kicked as hard as his beleaguered muscles would go.

He burst above the surface and latched onto the rope ladder just as the ligan grazed his foot with its sharp fangs. Zeb screamed aloud, able to give voice to his pain, but he didn't stop moving up the ladder, grunting with every step on his injured foot.

The *Clicker* tipped sideways, and Zeb's heart nearly stopped. Although he was already halfway up the ladder, his feet dipped again into the water. The boat tipped back again, and Zeb held on with both hands so he wouldn't fly off with the wrenching movement.

The ligan was playing with his boat. What would it do next?

Zeb scrambled up the ladder, his foot and leg almost forgotten in his panic. On deck, he held onto the gunwale and waited for the next onslaught.

Nothing happened for a full minute, and Zeb finally relaxed. Once the ligan's toy disappeared, it must have lost interest.

Zeb limped to the wheelhouse, where Corrie stood at the wheel. Tears streaked down her face, but she wiped them with the back of her hand when Zeb appeared.

"You're back," she said in a choked voice, then her eyes dipped down to his bleeding leg. Her jaw dropped. "What happened?"

"Ligan," he said shortly. His leg wept blood, so he grabbed the first aid kit and carelessly wrapped gauze around his calf. Then, he carefully wrapped a towel around his middle to avoid touching the offending wound.

"Oh, no," Corrie whispered. She pointed at the motorboat, where Penelope held up her device with triumph. "She's done."

"We'll have to ram the boat," Zeb said without enthusiasm. It was such a barbaric move, and too risky for his liking, but he didn't know how else to stop her. "The mer folk were no help. Get ready to take the wheel so I can grab Penelope in the water."

Corrie nodded and gripped the dashboard to steady herself. Zeb put the *Clicker* in reverse and backed away to give himself enough room to barge into the motorboat.

"Quick," Corrie said. "She's going to throw it over. Quick!"

Zeb reached for the throttle, but his hand never made it. His eyes widened. What was he seeing?

A huge greenish mound of roughened surface pushed upward. Water flowed off its sides in great rivers of liquid, past growths that looked like clumps of grass or bushes. The mound grew and grew, and Zeb's jaw dropped. It was larger than Penelope's motorboat, then larger than the *Clicker*, and still it grew. It towered over the boat's cabin, and Zeb clutched the wheel to ride the wave that the tremendous object pushed in its wake. Distantly, the sound of Penelope's shrieks reached his ears.

"It's a back," Corrie said in awe. "The back of an enormous sea creature."

Zeb stared at the monstrous mound, which had now settled in place. It looked just like an island, complete with vegetation. His brain shot into action, and his hand pushed the throttle. He cranked the wheel to starboard as far as it would go. The

Clicker roared away from the mound with desperate speed. Zeb was torn between an urge to dive under and see the extent of this unimaginable beast, and to drive away as fast as he could.

"It's a *dascor*," he shouted. "A gigantic fish from my mother's stories. It usually sleeps on the seafloor and only wakes up in times of great need."

Zeb paused with his mouth open. His hum of distress had been prompted by the mer folk's refusal to help. The mer woman's words about calling for salvation came back to him. Had he summoned the dascor?

Corrie rushed to the door and hung over the gunwale, heedless of salt spray.

"Penelope's shooting at it with her speargun!" she shouted. "She must have reloaded. Woah, I think it felt it. It's going down. Oh, Penelope's going to get sucked into the vortex."

Zeb needed to see what was going on. He banked sharply, and the *Clicker* groaned at the strain as a wave hit it broadside. Corrie screamed and ducked beside the bulwark as a wave splashed over her.

Zeb wrestled the boat into the waves once more and scanned the water. The motorboat was miraculously upright, and Penelope clung to its wheel with a death grip, her frizzy hair plastered to her head. In one hand, she clutched the completed device.

Corrie dragged herself back into the wheelhouse. She stared at Zeb, her clothes soaked and her eyes large in her dripping face.

"This is your chance, Zeb," she said. "Penelope will deploy the device any minute. The Seamount's creatures will be destroyed. You need to make a choice: ram the motorboat and risk the *Clicker* getting close to the dascor, swim to Penelope and get the device from her, or drive away and forget about the Seamount." She swallowed. "I will support you whichever you choose."

Zeb saw how much it cost her to say those words. Corrie wanted to fix everything, but here, she was giving him the gift of choice. Zeb dithered for a moment, but in his mind, there was no decision.

"I'll go," he said.

Corrie's lips tightened, and she nodded. He passed her the wheel, not daring to bring the *Clicker* closer to Penelope. Who knew where the behemoth swam? It was clear to Zeb, after the mer's words, that his distress call had sent it to attack Penelope. Zeb had a much better chance of survival swimming near the beast than bringing his boat to it. The massive creature wouldn't even notice something his size, and he could dive and hold his breath if its wake pulled him under.

He threw down his towel—again—and raced to the door. With a messy dive off the heaving ship, he sliced into the water and swam with desperate intent toward Penelope's boat.

He had to be quick, otherwise she would blast the water with her death noise. Not only would the Seamount's inhabitants perish, but so would he. Zeb pushed his body to move faster. Then, his senses kicked in, and he almost froze with fear.

What he had thought was ocean floor was moving. The dascor was down there, and his heart stuttered with fear. It had only showed its back before. What if it opened its giant maw and swallowed them whole? Zeb pressed on through the heaving water, filled with grim determination to reach Penelope.

The motorboat finally emerged above his head, and he directed his strokes upward. He shot out of the waves and onto the motorboat's aft deck. Penelope screamed in fear and anger.

"You're too late," she shouted. "The device is done, and it's going in the water now. Stop fighting me. You'll be thankful later, especially when you're not in the belly of the behemoth."

Penelope wound her arm back, clearly intending to fling the

device into the water, but Zeb threw himself forward. He crashed into Penelope and pushed her to the floor. She wriggled like an eel under Zeb, but he grabbed the device and held it up. A buoyant keychain dangled from a clasp on the machine.

"How do I turn it off?" he shouted.

"It's remotely detonated." She pointed at a button taped to the dashboard of the motorboat. "No matter where you put it, I can turn it on."

Zeb cursed and tossed the device to the aft deck. His target was now the button. He pushed off Penelope, intending to rip the button off the dashboard with his bare hands if he had to.

He was flattened to the deck with an invisible hand, then everything turned upside down. He plunged into the water, and his instincts turned on. His legs propelled him down, out of harm's way. When he was deep enough, he looked back.

A wave had tipped the motorboat with Penelope's grip off the wheel. Penelope's legs kicked furiously near the overturned vessel, and the device bobbed behind her. Zeb swam to the surface and grabbed the device.

"It's over, Penelope," he shouted and ripped off the buoyant keychain attached to the device. When he let it go, it started to sink. "Come with us to the *Clicker* and forget all this."

"Never," she screamed. Her eyes were wild. She bobbed at the surface in her lifejacket and kicked intently toward the motorboat. "It will still work if I press the button."

Zeb doubted that—signals were difficult through water— but he supposed it wasn't impossible. The way Penelope was swimming, though, she had no chance of reaching the motorboat.

His lower body felt the pressure of an enormous shape passing through the water. His chest squeezed with fear. The behemoth was back.

"Get to the *Clicker*," he shouted at Penelope. "The beast is coming!"

"I just need to get to the button," she shrieked. "Then it will die!"

Zeb stared at the deranged woman. The behemoth was coming for the motorboat, he had no doubt. Penelope would be caught in the crosshairs.

A part of him stared dispassionately. It would be a tidy way to end this saga. Penelope was too dangerous for the Seamount. Even if she didn't succeed today, what was stopping her from trying again in the future? Killing her today would be sensible. The behemoth would likely take care of the job for him.

The other, larger part of Zeb rebelled against this calculated bloodshed. Condemning a woman to die wasn't in his nature. He might be related to the pale folk—who didn't shy away from murder—but he was raised on land. He wasn't them, and he didn't need or want to be.

Zeb dived under the waves and sent out the loudest, most desperate hum of calming he could muster. The massive back that rose underneath the motorboat paused, and Zeb's heart leaped in his chest. Had he calmed the beast? Now, if he could get Penelope to swim toward the *Clicker* while the beast was calm, they might get away from this madness.

Zeb dived under and shot toward Penelope, ignoring his throbbing leg. He grabbed her around the waist and dragged her along the surface toward his boat. Her fists beat against his back, but he only gritted his teeth and continued to kick up and down the rolling waves. He might have white hair, but he hadn't been raised to coldly watch another's death, even if it benefited him. He was his own man, and not subject to the whims of his heritage. He could make his own choices.

The back rose again, despite Zeb's humming, and his stomach clenched. He burst forth humming about the motorboat to direct the monster's relentless progress. If he could use his pale folk abilities to focus the dascor's might on destroying the motorboat and its fateful button, their mission would be complete.

To his intense relief, the moving seafloor shifted away from them and toward the motorboat. Zeb kicked harder, away from the zone of impending destruction.

Penelope jabbed her elbow into his kidneys. Zeb doubled over with pain, and she wriggled free. With frenzied strokes, she swam back the way they had come, clearly desperate to reach the button of destruction.

"Get away from the motorboat," he screamed to Penelope. She ignored him, whether because she couldn't hear him over the storm or because she was too intent on her mission.

A mound of water grew on the other side of the motorboat from Zeb. He watched in horror as a gigantic tail, as wide as four *Clickers*, rose, dripping, from the sea. It raised higher and higher, and even Penelope stopped her frenzied swimming to gape at the spectacle.

The tail hung in midair for an eternity. Zeb held his breath despite being above water. Then, with a tremendous, ponderous descent of flesh and muscle, the tail slapped the water.

The motorboat disappeared under the unfathomable weight of tail. A wave from the descending limb swamped over Zeb, and he tumbled in the wash. A confused vision of a huge body loomed in the dimness, then it swam with languid movements into the depths.

The button and the device were gone, destroyed by the dascor that Zeb had summoned. Zeb surfaced and gasped for breath, his relief overwhelming him. The Seamount was safe. It had taken his pale folk abilities combined with his human empathy to defeat Penelope's plan, but he and Corrie had done it.

Penelope. Where was she? Now that her boat was demolished, he needed to get her on the *Clicker* if she were to survive. Zeb looked frantically for Penelope. When he crested a wave, her orange lifejacket and flailing arms showed him where to go.

Before he took one stroke toward her, a sensation of rushing movement hit his skin. It felt like the seafloor rising with impossible speed. Zeb's jaw dropped, but before he could shout to Penelope, swim away, or do anything, a great fin sliced out of the water. He shouted in panic, but the fin wasn't aiming for him. It rose, too fast for something so large, the membranes between bones at once delicate and hideously strong. Water droplets the size of Zeb's body flicked through the air with the fin's motion.

Penelope didn't stand a chance. One moment, she perched on the crest of a wave, her open-mouthed horror clear on her face. The next, the tremendous fin slapped down on her then slid under the water. With massive movement, the dascor slid away from the area and swam west until Zeb couldn't feel it anymore.

Zeb swam under the waves and came up next to Penelope's floating body. She wasn't breathing, and he couldn't sense her heartbeat. If she wasn't breathing, then he reasoned that she wouldn't mind being underwater. He dragged her below the punishing waves and swam with his inert burden until the *Clicker* loomed overhead.

A hum made him pause, and he turned his head. Mer folk were arrayed below and beside him, their bone spears pale and sharp-tipped. The leader caught his eye and nodded at him. Then, before he could call out or say anything, the entire group twisted their long bodies and disappeared into the murky storm waters.

Zeb watched the final mer swim out of sight with a lightening of his heart. He might not survive for long, but the Seamount would endure. Through his actions, he'd kept the world of his mother's people alive, and that was something.

Bringing Penelope's deadweight aboard proved difficult, especially when he put weight on his injured leg. In the water, his pain hadn't felt like much. Above the waves, it screamed with hellfire. Zeb gritted his teeth and put Penelope in a fireman's carry, then muscled his way up the rope ladder. He almost slipped twice, but luck was on his side.

On deck, he slung Penelope off his shoulders and onto the deck. He tried CPR for a solid two minutes, but without much hope. Sure enough, Penelope's body remained unmoving, and he abandoned his efforts with guilt.

He sat back and regarded the woman. Penelope was dead. Her death was of her own making, but he still mourned the loss of life. She'd been wronged by the pale folk, and even though he would never condone her plans, still, he sympathized with her grief. It wasn't easy losing one's family, no matter the cause.

She was dead, and there was nothing he could do about it now. He stumbled to the wheelhouse, suddenly alert to Corrie at the wheel. She didn't know what had happened, even whether he was dead or alive. He couldn't leave her in suspense any longer.

CORRIE

Letting Zeb go after Penelope was the hardest thing Corrie had ever done. She wanted to take control of the situation, direct Zeb where to go and what to do, and make the decisions. But she couldn't be the driver of this situation, not here. Like it or not, this was Zeb's world and his life, and if he wanted to die attempting to save the Seamount, that could only ever be his decision.

It didn't mean it was easy for Corrie. But the best thing she could do now was to keep the Clicker's bow into the waves and make sure that Zeb had a boat to come back to. She didn't want to die out here, even if he were okay with it.

Corrie fought to keep the boat steady even through the tumult of the dascor's emergence. Her grip on the wheel threatened to crush it into sawdust when the beast's massive fin rose from the sea and slapped the waves like an enormous playful whale. When it disappeared, she waited without breathing. When the dascor didn't reappear, she allowed herself to look around.

The motorboat was in pieces, and the other two were nowhere to be seen. Corrie's heart thundered painfully in her chest. Where was Zeb? Corrie had a horrible vision of driving the *Clicker* into the waves for hours, waiting for Zeb, until the gas ran out and she was stranded in the middle of the Pacific by herself. She swallowed back tears of fear and impotence.

The side door slammed open. Corrie whirled around but kept her tight grip on the wheel. Zeb stood in the open doorway, glistening with wet and his face twisted in grief.

"Penelope's dead," he said without preamble.

Corrie sat down hard on the captain's chair, then she righted the wheel to correct her course. Zeb was fine. Of course, he was. A giant fish couldn't take him down, and it was unlikely he would ever drown. She shouldn't have doubted him. Her heart pounded in her chest from adrenaline.

"I saw the tail slap down," she said. Tears pricked at the corners of her eyes, which surprised her. Penelope had been deceitful, manipulative, and genocidal. But Corrie couldn't forget the picture of a much happier woman with a little girl in her lap and a man embracing her. Corrie wouldn't have wished for this sort of ending for her.

Zeb pulled on his shirt, soaked from constantly being tugged over wet muscles, and stepped into his jeans.

"The dascor left," he said. "And the device is gone. It's time to go home."

He gently moved Corrie from her station at the wheel and took over. Corrie slumped into the folding chair and gripped the dash as Zeb turned toward home, expertly avoiding the worst of the waves threatening to tip their boat sideways.

They were silent for a long time afterward. Corrie eventually wandered to Zeb's cabin and found a few dry shirts in his drawers. She changed her own sopping shirt for his then wobbled back to the wheelhouse. Zeb nodded his thanks and exchanged his own shirt. After a few more minutes of silence, each lost in their own thoughts, Zeb spoke.

"I have her body." He swallowed. "On the aft deck. In case she has family that wants to know. Lost at sea is a difficult way to say goodbye."

Corrie nodded tightly. Penelope might have siblings, nieces and nephews, friends, all of whom would want to know what had happened. She sighed at the thought of inventing a cover story. Hopefully, they wouldn't be under fire for her death.

"I tried to save her," Zeb blurted out. "I tried to stop the dascor. I swear, I'm not like them."

His last words were said so quietly that Corrie had to strain to hear them. Her breath caught as she understood his meaning.

"You are not like the pale woman who murdered Alistair," she said, surprising herself by how firmly she believed this, right to her core. Zeb was himself and no other. "We did everything we could to stop her while trying to save her. Penelope made her own choices."

Zeb nodded, and his expression relaxed slightly. Corrie's mind wandered to the repercussions of their misadventure. They knew roughly where the Seamount was, but not close enough to pinpoint it. They knew where the final clue lay under the water, but without George's notebook—now lost in Penelope's motorboat—they had no way of translating the script etched on rocks. They couldn't reach the Seamount to find a cure for Zeb, and he didn't have long to get one.

"I'll analyze your cream some more when we get back," she promised. "To see if we can replicate it somehow, make more of it, since it's infused with the substance you need. Does that make sense to you?"

Zeb nodded, then he glanced at her. His eyes were full of gratitude.

"Yeah, it does." He swallowed and looked back out the windshield. "That will help."

A few days later, Corrie stripped off her latex gloves with a happy sigh. Three small plastic tubs of hand cream sat on the lab counter before her, each one filled with a mixture of pharmacy-bought hand lotion and distilled proteins harvested from her anemone samples. She'd chosen samples from along the west coast of the island, as their protein signatures were similar to the one from Zeb's cream. None was identical, but they were all worth trying.

If she could bring some relief to Zeb's suffering, then she would. She couldn't fix him. No matter how hard she had tried, her attempts had only backfired or driven a wedge between them. The cream brought him a measure of comfort, and it was something that Zeb chose. If she couldn't fix him, then at least she could support him.

She dropped the labeled tubs in her backpack and slung it over her back, then clattered down the stairs of her building and found her bike outside. As she meandered through clusters of students on the wide pavement, she passed Penelope's building. Her former building.

Corrie's stomach gave a twist of guilt, loathing, and sympathy. Penelope had allowed her passions to lead her into a pit of vengeance until all rational thought had been pushed out of her mind. Corrie's heart ached for Penelope's pain, but she could never have condoned her reaction.

The authorities had accepted their cover story—they'd come across Penelope's boat in the storm but hadn't been able to save her before she drowned—and Penelope's body had been whisked away from the *Clicker*.

Corrie pushed harder on her pedals. Penelope had chosen her path, and now Corrie would choose hers. For however long Zeb had left, she would try to help him, in whatever way he deemed best.

ZEBALLOS

Zeb checked the large clock on the kennel wall. Five more minutes, then he'd be done. Other than his grumbling stomach and itching skin, he didn't feel the need to rush out the door.

He scratched the chin of a racoon he'd befriended while cleaning. The animal rubbed against his finger through the bars, and Zeb smiled. This racoon had alternated between viciously angry and terrified during her first day here, and only after Zeb had hummed his calming tone had Adrianna managed to sedate her long enough to patch up the wound in her side. Now, the racoon adored Zeb. He would be sad to see her go, but she was healing nicely, and she would be happier back in her wild home.

It was nice to have a job he enjoyed. Working on the *Clicker* under his father's authoritarian rule had been bearable when fishing, and mildly interesting when George had switched to running diving charters. Roofing had been a means to an end. Now that he'd discovered that his calming power worked on land as well as in the sea, working with animals felt right.

It was better than using it on humans, that was for sure. Corrie's horrified expression was seared into his memory. Even though she had forgiven him, he didn't know if he could forget. He didn't want to. Remembering her reaction was a useful deterrent should he ever feel tempted to use his compulsion tone on someone else.

The racoon chittered, and Zeb scratched behind her ears. It felt good to sort out who he was. He could use his pale folk abilities in a way that jived with his own values. Just because he could manipulate others, didn't mean that he would. He might have the white hair and gray eyes of the pale folk—and their need for whatever substance he lacked—but he could choose his own path. Nothing was predetermined for him.

He might not have many weeks left, but he would live them as himself.

"Zeb?" Adrianna's voice broke his reverie. The racoon scuttled to the back of the kennel, and he turned around. Adrianna smiled at him. "Visitor for you. Anyway, you're done for the day."

A visitor? Zeb frowned and propped his broom against the wall. Who would know to come to the wildlife center? He hoped it wasn't anything to do with Penelope's death. As far as he knew, her case was closed.

His heart lightened when he exited the front door. Corrie stood by her bicycle with something in her hand and a grin on her face. She waved him over.

"I want to try something," she said, then she looked sheepish. "If you want to."

"That depends. What is it? I'm not interested in karaoke night, if that's what you want."

Corrie burst into laughter, and the sound was a balm to Zeb's soul.

"Nothing like that." She held up three small tubs with white cream inside. "I isolated the proteins from anemones closer to the Seamount. The protein isn't identical to your cream, but it's a lot closer than anemones from the Strait. I want to see how you react to them. Maybe we could manufacture our own cream to make you feel better."

Zeb stared at Corrie. He'd known that she'd been working night and day at her lab for the past few days, but he'd assumed she'd been catching up on her own work. Had she been making creams for him? His throat tightened, and he thrust out his arm in reply.

"Hit me up," he said. At the tightening of Corrie's face, he backtracked. "Sorry, bad choice of words. Experiment on me."

Corrie opened the first tub and smeared a dab of cream with a cool finger. They stared at the patch for a full minute.

"Nothing," Zeb finally said. He tried not to get excited.

Hope was a dangerous thing. It could lift you high then crush you in the depths.

"That was the least likely to work." Corrie opened the second tub. "This one is the most likely."

She rubbed the cream with more vigor onto Zeb's wrist. Zeb watched the spot, trying not to hold his breath with anticipation. Nothing would happen, and then he would be no worse off than before. It was fine. He knew his fate, and he'd accepted it.

A tingle traveled across his arm. His skin, itchy from his long afternoon shift, shivered then cooled slightly, bringing partial relief. He ran his hand over his forearm with wonder.

"It did something," he whispered.

Corrie's face lit like a shaft of sunlight through a wave.

"Yes!" She pumped her fist in the air. "Yes. We can go get more anemones from that patch and make as much cream as you need. Even if it's not as good as the original, it's something to keep you going. And what if you eat it? It's probably not strong enough to work like that, or else your mother would have eaten her cream ingredients, but at least you don't have to worry about running out."

Corrie threw her arms around Zeb and squeezed him tightly. Zeb embraced her back. Hope and resignation flowed through his veins in equal measure. The cream was a stopgap—it was a palliative, not a cure—but Corrie was on his side and by his side. She was fighting with him and for him, every step of the way. Even if he only had weeks left, he wouldn't want to be anywhere else than here with her.

Corrie pulled back and looked him in the eyes. She had that inquisitive look in her face that Zeb loved.

"Want to go for a swim?" She held up her last vial of strolia slime. Zeb grinned and squeezed her waist in agreement.

"Always."

JULES

Jules entered the Crispy Prawn's kitchen with a heavy heart. Zeb had called with the news of his failure to find the Seamount last night. Even through Zeb's stoicism, his pain and fear were blatant.

Jules blamed himself. He could have been there to help. Not that he was much good in that kind of situation, but he could have at least held the boat steady while Zeb and Corrie did the real heroics. Now Zeb had no ideas on how to save himself, and who knew how long he had left? Jules hadn't dared to ask that thorny question.

His eyes lit on Byssa, alone at the sushi counter. The restaurant wasn't yet open, and she and he were the only ones there to start food prep for the dinner rush. Byssa's sleek black hair was tied in a neat bun at the nape of her neck, and Jules' breath hitched. She was Zeb's last chance, and Jules steeled himself to confront her. He had an idea that hopefully wouldn't backfire on him. Zeb needed him to at least try.

Jules washed his hands and joined Byssa at the counter. She smiled at him as he grabbed a peeler and some cucumbers.

"How's it going, Jules?" she asked in her light voice. Jules let out a heartfelt sigh.

"Okay." He let the silence gather for a moment. "I'm worried about my friend. He's sick, and no one knows what the problem is."

Byssa's eyes lit on his face, and sympathy welled in them.

"I'm sorry to hear that."

"Thanks." He shot her a swift smile then returned his gaze to the cucumber in his hand. "Like, really sick. I don't know how long he has, actually."

He dropped the cucumber and shoved a hand into his pocket to extract his phone. In his photo app, he swiped until he found a selfie he'd taken. His face was pulled in a goofy grimace with crossed eyes—Jules couldn't remember, but he was pretty sure copious booze had been involved that day—and Zeb was behind him, looking both amused and resigned at Jules' antics. His white hair glinted in sunlight, and his pale gray eyes were prominent.

Byssa's eyes widened, and that was all the proof Jules needed. His heart squeezed with fear and anticipation. "This is your friend?" At Jules' nod, she huffed a laugh of disbelief. "Then I know why he's sick." She looked Jules in the eye, and he held his breath. "And if you let me talk to him, I can help."

ALSO BY EMMA SHELFORD

Depths of Magic
Sea Fire

Nautilus Legends
Free Dive
Caught
Surfacing
Hooked

Magical Morgan
Daughters of Dusk
Mothers of Mist
Elders of Ether

Immortal Merlin
Ignition
Winded
Floodgates
Buried
Possessed
Unleashed
Worshiped
Unraveled

Forest Fae
Mark of the Breenan
Garden of Last Hope
Realm of the Forgotten

ACKNOWLEDGEMENTS

Thank you to Bettina Luna, Nadene D, and Steven Shelford for helping me polish the manuscript. Thanks to Miblart for an exciting cover. Thank you to Matthew Connor and Karolynn Sackett (Fantasy Writers Critique and Support Group) for consultation on boating matters.

ABOUT THE AUTHOR

Emma Shelford feels that life is only complete with healthy doses of magic, history, and science. Since these aren't often found in the same place, she creates her own worlds where they happily coexist. If you catch her in person, she will eagerly discuss Lord of the Rings ad nauseam, why the ancient Sumerians are so cool, and the important role of phytoplankton in the ocean.

Emma is the author of multiple urban fantasy series, including Magical Morgan, Immortal Merlin, Depths of Magic, Nautilus Legends, and Forest Fae.